A Woman of Salt

A Woman of Salt

A Novel

MARY POTTER ENGEL

COUNTERPOINT
NEW YORK, N.Y.

The Library of Congress has cataloged the hardcover edition as follows:
Engel, Mary Potter.
A woman of salt : a novel by Mary Potter Engel.
p. cm.
ISBN 1-58243-156-6 (alk. paper)
1. Mothers and daughters—Fiction. 2. Terminally ill—Fiction. 3.
Women—Fiction. I. Title.
PS3605.N44 W6 2001
813.54—dc 21 20011028896
PAPERBACK ISBN 1-58243-249-X

Jacket and text design by David Bullen

COUNTERPOINT
387 Park Avenue South
New York, NY 10016-8810

Counterpoint is a member of the Perseus Books Group.

10 9 8 7 6 5 4 3 3 2 1

for Win, Sam, and Miriam
and for Laurie

יְבָרֶכְךָ יהוה וְיִשְׁמְרֶךָ.
יָאֵר יהוה פָּנָיו אֵלֶיךָ וִיחֻנֶּךָּ.
יִשָּׂא יהוה פָּנָיו אֵלֶיךָ וְיָשֵׂם לְךָ שָׁלוֹם.

Acknowledgments

For help with this book I thank Win, Sam, and Miriam; Geri Thoma, Judith Grossman, Kelly Malone, Richard Schmitt, Laurie Mills, Mary Farrell Bednarowski, David Den Boer, Carol Graf, Dianne Probst, Ellen Steinberg, Carole McCurdy, David Bullen, the women at Hedgebrook, and the Hedgebrook Foundation; Dawn Seferian and the others at Counterpoint Press: Jack Shoemaker, Trish Hoard, Keltie Hawkins, Heather McLeod, and John McLeod.

Contents

Who will flee You, over a bridge of longing,
Only to return again?

JACOB GLATSTEIN, "Without Jews"

The two angels arrived in Sodom in the evening, as Lot was sitting in the gate of Sodom. When Lot saw them, he rose to greet them and, bowing low with his face to the ground, he said, "Please, my lords, turn aside to your servant's house to spend the night, and bathe your feet; then you may be on your way early." But they said, "No, we will spend the night in the square." But he urged them strongly, so they turned his way and entered his house. He prepared a feast for them and baked unleavened bread, and they ate.

They had not yet lain down when the townspeople, the men of Sodom, young and old—all the people to the last man—gathered about the house. And they shouted to Lot and said to him, "Where are the men who came to you tonight? Bring them out to us, that we may be intimate with them." So Lot went out to them to the entrance, shut the door behind him, and said, "I beg you, my friends, do not commit such a wrong. Look, I have two daughters who have not known a man. Let me bring them out to you, and you may do to them as you please; but do not do anything to these men, since they have come under the shelter of my roof." But they said, "Stand back! The fellow," they said, "came here as an alien, and already he acts the ruler! Now we will deal worse with you than with them." And they pressed hard against the person of Lot, and moved forward to break the door. But the men stretched out their hands and pulled Lot into the house with them, and shut the door. And the people who were at the entrance of the house, young and old, were struck with blinding light, so that they were helpless to find the entrance.

Then the men said to Lot, "Whom else have you here? Sons-in-law, your sons and daughters, or anyone else that you have in the city—bring them out of the place. For we are about to destroy this place; because the outcry against them before the Lord has become so great that the Lord has sent us to destroy it." So Lot went out and spoke to his sons-in-law, who had married his daughters, and said, "Up, get out of this place, for the Lord is about to destroy the city." But he seemed to his sons-in-law as one who jests.

As dawn broke, the angels urged Lot on, saying, "Up, take your wife and your two remaining daughters, lest you be swept away because of the iniquity of the city." Still he delayed. So the men seized his hand, and the hands of his wife and his two daughters—in the Lord's mercy on him—and brought him out and left him outside the city. When they had brought him outside, one said, "Flee for your life! Do not look behind you, nor stop anywhere in the plain; flee to the hills, lest you be swept away." But Lot said to them, "Oh, no, my lord! You have been so gracious to your servant, and have already shown me so much kindness in order to save my life; but I cannot flee to the hills, lest the disaster overtake me and I die. Look, that town there is near

enough to flee to; it is such a little place! Let me flee there—it is such a little place—and let my life be saved." He replied, "Very well, I will grant you this favor, too, and I will not annihilate the town of which you have spoken. Hurry, flee there, for I cannot do anything until you arrive there." Hence the town came to be called Zoar.

As the sun rose upon the earth and Lot entered Zoar, the Lord rained upon Sodom and Gomorrah sulfurous fire from the Lord out of heaven. He annihilated those cities and the entire plain, and all the inhabitants of the cities and the vegetation of the ground. Lot's wife looked back, and she thereupon turned into a pillar of salt.

Next morning, Abraham hurried to the place where he had stood before the Lord, and, looking down toward Sodom and Gomorrah and all the land of the plain, he saw the smoke of the land rising like the smoke of a kiln.

Thus it was that, when God destroyed the cities of the plain and annihilated the cities where Lot dwelt, God was mindful of Abraham and removed Lot from the midst of the upheaval.

Genesis 19:1–29

A Woman of Salt

Joys impregnate. Sorrows bring forth.

WILLLIAM BLAKE, "Proverbs of Hell"

Trance

By the time I left home at seventeen, we had lived in eight apartments, five houses, three motels, and one freezing lake cottage we rented after all the summer vacationers had left. I don't count the times we stayed with my aunts in Michigan and my grandmother in New Jersey or the month we slept in a musty camping trailer in the dominee's backyard. As a minister, Dominee VanderTuin probably felt obligated to love his neighbor when my mother called upon him in need. Or maybe Mrs. VanderTuin felt sorry for us, the wandering mother and her brood: *her* husband, with his dignified position and guaranteed salary—brick parsonage included—wasn't always giving up on one business and starting another, dragging his family to a new city or state each time.

The place all five of us kids liked best was the Villa Serena, a beach motel north of Fort Lauderdale. Whenever two or three of us get together we end up telling stories from our days there. We still joke about Mark—the fastidious one—stepping barefoot on a glob of spit on the concrete walkway one morning and screeching hysterically until Mother tossed a pan of water at him. Though he laughs when we tell that story, he's never forgiven Mother for that.

The Villa Serena was cheap, and off-season rates made it cheaper, but it was the deal my mother worked with the manager—no air conditioning or maid service, Calvin helping in the yard, me in the office—that made it possible for us to stay there. We ended up with two rooms facing Highway A1A. My parents used the fold-out couch in the sitting area of the kitchenette. In the adjoining room, Calvin, Mark, and Paulie shared the double bed, while Debbie and I slept head to toe on a roll-away jammed against the foot of their mattress. Once I woke with Debbie's vomit wetting my legs. We cleaned ourselves up and spent the rest of the night wrapped in beach towels on the floor. The three boys had the measles together in their bed. For weeks the rest of us whispered and tiptoed around them, kept the room dark so their eyes wouldn't weaken. Paulie, the youngest, got rheumatic fever and almost died. We all agree, though: the Villa Serena was a child's paradise.

That summer we spent every minute barefoot in our bathing suits, exploring. We would swim across the intracoastal to hunt for manatees napping in the canals, beg fish from the tour boats that docked on the other side of the bridge, chase fiddler crabs into their holes, climb coconut palms. If we managed to knock down a coconut, we'd smash it on the patio to split open the husk, scrounge a hammer and screwdriver to pound holes in the three eyes of the shell, and fight for turns at draining the sweet milk into our mouths. When it rained we walked across the street to the dimestore in search of affordable wonders: floating key chains, rubber flippers, hula dolls that danced on dashboards, sets of plastic swizzle sticks chronicling the story of a woman's life— slim brown body, new breasts and bottom, pregnant stomach, shriveled breasts sagging to the knees.

Most days we packed ourselves a lunch and hiked the beach, north to the stand of rubber trees where old straw-hatted men drooled in the shade, or south to the pier where tawny fishermen cast for hammerheads. If they caught one they dragged it down the pier and hung it from a piling near shore, the eyes bulging on opposite sides of the mon-

strous head like twin horns of perception, the belly slit from throat to
tail so the insides showed—masses of glistening, translucent sacs
plump with liquid and suspended like tears. We used to stare at those
bulbed pouches shining purple and orange and yellow until we were
dizzy and all the colors ran together. Some days I couldn't speak for
hours afterward—it was so beautiful.

We were always in the ocean playing, even Mark and Paulie, who
couldn't swim. Sometimes Dad came with us on Saturdays. When he
had finished swimming to the horizon and back in his graceful crawl,
he'd let us dive off his shoulders into the breaking waves. But mostly
he was away, having "idea sessions" or finagling start-up loans from
banks. Mother was never around. She was either in bed with one of her
headaches or out combing the junk shops for bargains. Some months,
reselling her hard-won finds at a profit, she made more money than
Dad. They used to fight about it, my mother sniping, my dad kicking
holes in the mover's cartons, banging on locked doors, throwing shoes
and furniture. But she wouldn't quit. "Florida's the best place for this
business," she would tell her sisters when they called. "All those old
people moving into smaller apartments and getting rid of a lifetime of
treasures."

Once my mother came down to the beach to bring us cold bottles
of Yoo-Hoo and scream at me for not watching the little kids carefully
enough. Water scared her. She didn't know how to swim.

It was Debbie who called me with the news about Helen. My brothers would never call. They haven't contacted me in years—too loyal to
Helen, who has forbidden them to have anything to do with their
heartless sister. Debbie's call woke me out of a dead sleep. "Ruth," she
said, "it's Mom. You have to come right away." I was confused and
thought she'd said Helen had died.

Debbie couldn't stop sobbing. When she calmed down, I figured
out that Helen was still alive. Minutes before Debbie called me, the
doctor had pulled her into the hospital corridor and told her to prepare herself and the rest of the family, because Mother could go any
time.

A Woman of Salt

"She asked for you today," Debbie said.

"She wants me to come so she can gloat over disinheriting me for marrying a Jew."

"That was two years ago. She's different now."

"Sure. Have you forgotten what she said to me when I called her two months ago to tell her I was pregnant? 'If that baby is not washed in the blood of Jesus Christ, it's going straight to hell.' Fourteen years we haven't spoken and that's the first thing she says to me."

"Please come, Ruth."

I did my best to comfort my sister. I told her she had done all she could and that we were all grateful for the way she had cared for Mother the past months. I said I'd consider canceling my classes the rest of the week so I could drive down and help her and Jake with the kids, that maybe I'd leave for Boca as soon as it was light and be there by late afternoon.

Calvin won't show up. He'll call from his fancy house at Lake Tahoe or his office in San Francisco, all charm and cheer, thanking and praising Debbie until she forgets her fear and the burden of her duties. Then he'll smooth his way into apology and regret, leak out that though he has had his secretary working for hours to rearrange his schedule, he can't make it to see Mother just now. He's off to Paris or Frankfurt to close a once-in-a-lifetime deal with a difficult client he has been wooing for years. *Unfortunate timing,* he'll tell Debbie, rushing words into the silence of the sick room, *can't be helped, sure you understand, be there if I could, Mom knows that, give her a kiss and tell her I love her, I'll come as soon as I can.*

But Calvin won't come, tomorrow or next week—if it comes to that. And no one will blame *him* for not being present as his mother draws her final breaths.

I told Debbie how frantic I am, that Michael and I are moving to our new house at the end of the month, that I haven't finished the lecture on Plato's notion of eros I'm scheduled to deliver at a conference next week, that my essay for a collection of feminist biblical interpretation—a study of rabbinic and patristic exegesis of Genesis 19, bundled notes that refuse to become a whole—is overdue and absolutely has to be at the publisher's before the baby arrives, that I'll have to ask the midwife if it's okay for me to drive long distances this late in the pregnancy.

I never promised Debbie I would come. All I said was I'd think about it, for her sake.

It was during the Villa Serena days that I saw the turtle. One night in July, long after I had fallen asleep, my mother shook me awake, calling "Ruth, Ruth." She waved a flashlight across my face and in a voice lively with conspiracy told me to get up and follow her.

Peeling off the sheet, I sat up. The bedsprings creaked and I glanced at Debbie to see if the noise had disturbed her. I didn't want her or any-body else around. I thought my mother was going to tell me the "woman" things she had been hinting about lately. Whenever she saw me get out of the shower or sit on Dad's lap, she would give me a look and say, "Don't think you're so smart, young lady. You don't know everything." She didn't like it that I knew more about hormones, ovu-lation, and menstruation than she did. I'd learned all this from a film they showed us during P.E. and a booklet the nurse passed out, whose pages I studied for hours at a time. I knew about tampons, too. My cousin had shown me how to use one the summer before, advising me never to use anything else when my time came. Thrilled that Harriet, full and gorgeous and seven years older, had invited me into her pink-tiled bathroom and revealed herself to me, I promised I wouldn't. There were lots of things I didn't know, but I wasn't sure what they were; I was waiting for my mother to tell me.

I took the flashlight my mother handed me and followed her. As we crept away, her beam shone across the three boys in the big bed. Cal-vin's long bony leg, scarred by barnacles when he fell into a canal try-ing to net a flying fish, hung over one edge of the bed. On the other side Mark's head rested on his stuffed beaver, the only thing that calmed his asthma attacks and night terrors. Paulie snuggled between them, his shoulders and back covered with shiny red patches framed in stiffened curls of skin. He never took off his T-shirt during the day, even to swim, yet blisters formed continually on his freckled back, a

A Woman of Salt

fresh layer over a raw layer over a drying layer of peeling skin. Whenever Mother tried to dress them with salve and zinc oxide, he would scream and pull away from her.

Her flashlight skipped toward the door, across the boxes stacked against the far wall, each one labeled in her perfect Palmer script—Taxes, Winter Clothes, Letters, Misc., Music. Though I had never heard her play, my aunts insisted that my mother played the piano and organ better than any of them. *She has a gift,* they would say. *A pity she doesn't use it. Wasting the Lord's talents.* They couldn't understand why Helen didn't give lessons or play for church services and weddings the way they did. *It's easy money,* they would tell her.

We stooped under the clothesline strung across the room, my mother holding aside the damp clothes for me to pass through, and left the children sleeping.

In the kitchenette the fluorescent light over the sink flickered and crackled, making the cramped space shimmer as if it were about to explode. A bucket and broom stood by the stove. Every night after we were in bed, my mother swept out all the sand and scrubbed the floors, furniture legs, counters, and walls with Lysol. She did it as much to discourage bugs and mildew as to keep my dad from waking in a temper over the mess.

Across the room, on the opened sofa bed, lay my dad, the sheet bunched around his feet. He was naked. My mother repeatedly asked him to wear pajama bottoms, "for the children," but he refused. He didn't like feeling constricted, he said. Besides, if she wouldn't act such a prude, we'd get used to it soon enough. My dad's left knee was drawn up toward his chest. Curly hair covered his back down to the top of his buttocks, which shone sleek and round in the dim light leaking through the jalousies from the outside hallway, and underneath, more black hair and a mound of wrinkled rose-brown flesh disappearing into darkness.

My mother yanked the sheet over him, motioning me with her flashlight to get out. I shifted closer to the door, but stood watching as she secured the sheet under the mattress, forming neat hospital corners and pulling it tight over his arched form. He looked even larger spread out under the sheet, his broad shoulders rising like mountains and his

MARY POTTER ENGEL

athlete's arms stretching from edge to edge. Looking up, my mother waved me angrily away.

Outside, I stepped carefully around the shallow pan of water we kept beside the doormat. Before entering the room, we had to rinse the sand from our feet and inspect them for tar. If we discovered gummy blotches, we used the rag and bottle of turpentine stored on the window ledge to rub them clean.

My mother emerged from the room flat backside first, curly head last, listening once more for stirrings before she closed the door. We hurried down the walkway and across the patio. She walked fast, dodging the stacks of pool chairs and rotted cabanas like a child intent on reaching treasure. As I followed her, I imagined the two of us on the beach, nestled in the warm sand under the stars, far from others' ears, hunched eagerly toward each other and saying the things that were waiting to be said, the things that would change everything between us.

Before we reached the edge of the patio we heard voices over the plashing of the waves. A small crowd had gathered near the shore. Flashlights streamed across the water, searching. They're looking for a drowning victim, I thought, a body discolored and bloated with death. Fear and anticipation rose within me.

My mother slipped her arm around my waist and squeezed me to her. "It's sea turtles," she whispered excitedly. "They're coming to lay their eggs."

I hardly knew if I was awake or asleep. I had never seen my mother so light-hearted, expectant, lively—though a boy had written "Helen = Scintillating" across her picture in her high-school yearbook. And she had chosen *me* to share this adventure. She had never shown much interest in me before, other than to scold me—for not cleaning up the kitchen properly, for forgetting to give the little kids their bath, for my stringy hair or too-thick nose, for spending too much time with Dad.

I threaded my hand between her arm and body, inched it to the other side of her waist. The curve of her hip surprised me and I let my hand rest there on the softness, lightly so I wouldn't frighten her away. Holding each other like this, hip to hip, arms round waists, we

A Woman of Salt

joined the others watching from the shore. We stood in the moist half-darkness a long time, eyes fixed on the moving edges of the water. Behind us, the breeze through the palm fronds sounded like gentle and reassuring rain, like the mercy of God falling on the just and unjust. Ahead of us the moon, bright and full, shimmered on the waves. I watched hard, believing each moment I saw a head emerging—there, no there!—or heard a heralding splash. Every new hope turned into a trick of the waves, but I didn't mind; I could have stood there forever.

When my arms had almost fallen asleep from trying to hold still, my eyes fixed on a glistening just beyond the surf. A faint spot seemed to disappear and appear, always moving closer. It felt deep and round. At the edge of the surf, a black hump emerged and someone called out in a loud whisper, "There's one!"

I turned to my mother. I thought if I saw her face, saw her gazing back at me happy, for one moment, I would be able to bear the burden of joy pressing me from every direction. But she was staring at the ocean with the others, eager not to miss a thing.

The turtle was definitely approaching, its back gleaming dark in the moonlight and rising slowly, irrevocably, toward us.

The crowd made room for it. My mother let go of me and we moved back with the others as the turtle drew nearer. It struggled out of the water, dragging and pushing its awkward body across the wet sand. Once on dry ground it rested a moment, then heaved its bulk forward to a place it seemed to know, and stopped. With its back flippers it scooped out a shallow hole, then settled over it, enormous and silent.

I could hardly stand the long waiting. I wanted to clutch my mother round the neck and crush her to me, take both of her hands in mine and jump up and down, to keep from bursting.

The air had grown close, still. The palm trees had stopped rustling. The moon, swollen and fixed, bound up the sky, veiling everything above and below in a heavy light. The turtle's back seemed coated with it, as if that were the reason it wasn't moving, that extra burden of white.

Without making a sound, I slid my hands down my thighs and dropped one knee to the sand. Bodies near me shifted, whispering broke out. I tensed, thinking they were warning me to move back, but

MARY POTTER ENGEL

when I looked up, the others were hunching toward the turtle's hindquarters.

She had started laying.

The eggs burst from her one at a time. Transfixed, I counted each soft, rubbery globe as it fell. When I reached fifty-nine, the white-haired woman next to me sucked in her breath, as if frightened. I stood up, my heart racing and my muscles readied for escape, sure the old woman's cry meant that the laboring monster was about to open her sharp beak in a hiss and charge us. A few months before, on a school trip to the Everglades, I had seen an alligator snapping-turtle threaten a park ranger that way. He told us their jaws could snap a child's leg in two, that they disabled their prey before dragging the body into the water to drown it. Positioning my feet to run, my whole body alert, I glanced at the sea turtle's head. She was motionless—neck withdrawn, beak closed, eyes fixed on the water. She looked far away and lonely. She blinked and a drop, glittering with moonlight, ran down her smooth cheek and disappeared into the sand.

"She's crying!" the old woman whispered.

Again the turtle blinked out a tear. As she lowered her thick lids and opened them, drop after drop spilled to the sand and I forgot the eggs falling into the hole behind her. I began counting the tears.

"Animals don't cry," a man behind us said. "It's a reflex. Gets rid of extra salt."

My mother sandwiched my cheeks in her hands and turned my face to hers. She had to do it roughly because I was concentrating so hard on counting.

"Don't listen to him," she said. "He doesn't know what he's talking about."

She shook my head until my eyes focused on hers. I stared at her lashes, looking for traces of mascara. It was against our church's rules to wear makeup, but sometimes my mother brushed Maybelline Smoke on her scrawny lashes. The aunts talked about it behind her back, saying *Never content with what she has.* To her face they said, *It's whorish; a Christian woman is modest and pure, not tempted by things of the World.* My father said, "Go wash off that gook."

"Those tears are from pain," my mother said. Her hands squeezed

A Woman of Salt

my face hard, pressing into my jawbone. "It hurts. That's all you need to know: it hurts."

I slanted my eyes away from her. The turtle was still staring out to sea, crying.

"Do you understand?" my mother asked, speaking less harshly now.

I understood. I understood that having growing pains and cramps and rebellious hair, being hit by your mother with a wire brush for using the Devil's paint on your pitiful eyelashes, being shut up in the attic overnight by your father to break your spirit, feeling your exuberance and talent fester in a world of unrelenting severity, having your intelligence mocked, marrying, undergoing intercourse, douching with Lysol solution, birthing babies, raising unwanted and unruly children, selling your piano for rent money, hauling groceries for seven in a bicycle basket, watching your mother die young and hardened, having a tumor sliced out of your womb when you haven't yet given up being a girl—that all of it, all of it, hurt, and when it hurt *me* I was to keep quiet about it and go on. I understood it all and I hated my mother for that knowing, for making me know it that night by the turtle.

My sister says I couldn't have known all that then, on that beach by the Villa Serena; no twelve-year-old—no matter how many books she reads, *A*s she gets, prizes she wins—can see the past and the future crushing through each other in one moment. She says I'm exaggerating as usual, making things up, pretending they were worse than they were so I can live with myself: to justify not coming to see Mother all these years, even now at the end, when the pain has traveled to her bones and she is begging for me to come and be reconciled so she can die a perfect death, all five of her children returned home, repentant.

But Debbie's wrong. I heard what my mother was saying to me that night, everything she wanted me to know: that I was to be like her, emptied of hope, bitter. I don't need to go to a hospital in Boca Raton to hear her say it out loud. I don't want to walk in her room, have her look at my swollen belly and sneer, "A forty-year-old woman *pregnant?* Disgusting." Why should I listen to her tell me one last time that I had better stop drinking, quit my volunteer work with sexual-abuse victims, give up feminism and other anti-biblical ideas, stay married for once, come home to Jesus, convert my Jew husband, keep my hair trimmed, my pride in check, my mouth shut, and accept that no one expects to be happy, because that's what it means to grow up and I was long overdue.

That night on the shore, with Mom's hands squeezed hot and scratchy against my face, her eyes seeking mine, I nodded to show her I understood.

"You're a good girl," she said. She drew me to her, kissed me on the cheek, and released me. Immediately she was absorbed in the turtle.

"We're up to ninety-three now," the white-haired woman whispered in my ear. "Sometimes they lay over a hundred."

I stared at the turtle, barely able to see her. Though the moon was higher, it seemed darker than before.

"Ninety-eight. We're getting close, eh?" the old woman said, turning to me.

I shook my head at her in agreement, hoping she would leave me alone so I could find a path out of my heart into a clear, redeeming thought. Her face was as smooth as my youngest aunt's, and livelier, even though it wasn't moving. It was her eyes that looked old—milky and soft. They scared me.

"That was ninety-nine!" she said. "Oh, oh, here comes one hundred! She made it!"

She grinned crazily at me, grabbed my arm with both of her hands, stabbed three kisses into it just below the elbow.

The crowd shifted back and the old woman let go of me to look.

The turtle had awakened out of her trance. She was flapping sand over the mound of eggs. Almost instantly the nest vanished. Though we knew the eggs were only inches from our toes, we couldn't see any evidence of them. We backed away farther as the turtle pushed off, thrusting herself toward the ocean. In seconds she had disappeared.

The waves became deafening. They pounded against my ears with a pressure so great I was sure it would push everything inside out. I wanted it to, so all that was wavering inside me would explode and I could rest in the empty quiet left behind—yet I feared it, too.

A Woman of Salt

"Let's go home," Mom said, taking my hand.

She led me back, guiding me around the billowing Portuguese men-of-war caught in clumps of seaweed on the wet sand, through the prickly grass in the dry sand, toward the coconut palms. A few feet ahead of us, a coconut dropped. We heard it detach, whiffle down, and strike the sand with a dull blow. She stopped and shone her light on it. Green and unfrayed, it looked as if it had always been there, cradled by the sand. To our right another coconut fell, swishing through branches and thumping on the ground.

"Don't worry," Mom said to me in the heavy darkness, urging me toward the motel. "We're almost there."

On the edge of the patio I stumbled against a heap of concrete blocks, fell, and scraped my knee. Blood rose to the surface.

"Pay attention," Mom snapped as she helped me up. She was as tired as I was and as eager for sleep.

We skirted the pool. Sand drifts and brittle palm fronds dotted the lit bottom. As we passed the deep end, fiddler crabs scrambled down the cracked walls toward the drain.

We entered the walkway perpendicular to ours. As we passed Room 21, she shone the light on the concrete so we could slalom safely around the old man's spit. Turning the corner, we saw six pairs of zoris hugging the wall by our door—her large yellow ones first, then Calvin's black ones, my red ones, Debbie's pink ones, Mark's orange ones, and Paulie's small scuffed brown ones with the toe piece that kept breaking no matter how many times she fixed it. She swished her feet in the pan of water, wiped them on the mat, and went inside. I followed close behind her.

Inside, the terrazzo floor, always so smooth and cool, felt gritty, fiery. I stopped and shone the light on my feet. I had forgotten to wash them. They were covered with sand and bits of shell. It looked like I was wearing snug, glittery slippers.

Mom was watching me from the bathroom door. Already undressed, she was wearing only her underpants, her pale blue nightgown, one arm pushed through its armhole, scrunched over her chest. The white nylon stretched smoothly over her rounded belly. The elastic band cut into her just below her navel and the flesh above it was soft and dimpled, sprinkled with tiny blood blisters. On the left side, the scar from her operation, shiny gray, jagged toward her ribs.

I stared at my feet again. I had never seen her before. Even in the motel she made sure none of us caught her undressed. She always changed for the night after we were all in our beds and she had closed the door to our room. She kept her robe on the fold-out sofa and in the morning pulled herself into the faded cotton before throwing off the covers. Whenever she went to the bathroom she announced she was not to be disturbed and noisily locked the door. She washed out her bra in the bathroom sink late at night and removed it from the door hook the minute she got up, hid her sanitary pads—before the operation—with her mascara, in a cosmetic case stuffed behind the couch.

Now it seemed none of that mattered to her. She stood there without embarrassment, not displaying herself to me, but not hurrying to hide herself from me either, her skin and her secrets exposed as if they were nothing remarkable.

I couldn't stop looking at my feet. I knew there was something I should do, but I couldn't think what it was. I couldn't move or speak.

"Sit down," she said, turning slightly and raising the nightgown with both arms. As she ducked her head into the neck opening, her breasts jiggled far and long over her abdomen, their large brown eyes pointing down and away from each other, as if scared of what they might see if they turned toward each other.

"I said sit down, young lady," she said as she pulled the cotton over her breasts and let it fall around her knees. "Now. And mind your own business."

The last command was full of sharp edges and impatience, but it seemed friendlier, more forgiving than the others, as if my confusion amused her.

Trying not to move my dirty feet from their spot, I leaned toward the coffee table at the foot of her bed and lowered myself onto it.

Behind me my dad lay sleeping. He was on his side now, under the sheet, with both knees drawn up slightly, but he still took up the entire mattress. I wondered where she fit herself in when she came to bed at night, how it was possible.

In the bathroom, she searched among the litter of wet suits and

A Woman of Salt

towels. She lifted a large yellow towel off the rack, sniffed it, and threw it over her shoulder. As she walked past me, she raised her finger to her lips. Without making a creak, she opened the door, slipped out, and shut it behind her.

Outside, the water pan scraped across the concrete, and then water splashed on the ground a few feet away.

My dad stirred, pushed his head and chest up, demanding "What? What is it?"

Against that white sheet, his swarthy skin looked darker than it ever had.

I held absolutely still, outside and in. I didn't want the sheet, which had slipped to his waist, to fall away more.

"It's nothing," Mom said from the doorway. "Just me." She spoke coolly, evenly, holding the door open with one hand and the empty water pan against her waist with the other. "Go back to sleep."

"For Pete's sake," he said, throwing himself on his other side and drawing the sheet tight around his neck. He knocked his head against the pillow, then raised it and punched it into another, more comfortable spot. "Always something." He yawned, covered his head with his bent arm, and was still.

Mom waited a moment, then took the pan to the bathroom and filled it at the sink. Slowly, to keep from sloshing, she carried it out and placed it before me. She knelt before me, raised my right foot, and set it in the warm water. When she leaned forward I saw that her upper chest was covered with red sun bumps and small pearlescent circles where the pigmentation had disappeared, leaving holes, empty places that looked like someone had erased parts of her. In the gap between her mottled flesh and the blue of her nightgown, her breasts appeared, white and round and close to each other. She lifted my left foot into the basin. As she waited for the sticky bits of shell and sand to loosen their hold on my feet, she dabbed her pinky in the thin layer of blood on my scraped knee, then on her tongue.

"You'll live," she said.

She bent toward me again, reaching under the water to brush the last, resistant particles free. Her freckled arms were strong and toned, like her legs. She was proud of her legs. In church, the deacons admired them as they passed the offering plate. Lawn-care men and grocery baggers whistled at them. Though they were speckled brown, strewn with white circles matching those on her chest, from a distance they looked like a teenager's. Except for bonier knees, I recognized mine as a copy of hers. Startled, I looked at her face to see if she had seen it too, but she was too busy scrubbing to notice me. She rubbed and brushed, scoured and scraped, attending to each nail until not a grain was left behind, separating the toes to make sure nothing remained hidden between them.

Satisfied that my skin was clean all over, she lifted my foot, dripping, onto her thighs and stroked it with the towel. When it was dry, tingling with blood and radiating warmth, she set it on the ground. Then she picked up my other foot and began again.

A Woman of Salt

Don't Look Back

In his *Commentary on Genesis,* John Calvin, reaping the wisdom of
Tertullian, Augustine, and Jerome, calls the death of Lot's wife "the
wonderful judgment of God, signal proof of divine vengeance." The
mercy of God falls on the just and the unjust, Calvin implies, but
God's vengeance is reserved for the deserving. Pulled by fond memories of her home and friends, Calvin imagines, the wife of Lot turned
around, disobeying God's commandment, and was punished for
it, her death a just price for her rebellion. How like a woman, he
implies, to let the mess of relationships stand in the way of immedi-
ate and unambiguous compliance with the just demands of God.
Like Eve, the wife of Lot fell into disobedience because of her weak
will; and for that she deserved to die, her salty form left behind as a
witness to the generations of the justice of God.

The wife of Lot had made her choice: she had fled the destruction
of God, never to return. All through the long night she ran from
the danger. She was safe with the angels and her husband and her
unmarried daughters. Yet at dawn, as the refugees approached safety
in the little city of Zoar, when smoke began drifting across the plain
and ash burned her eyes and she heard the screams and smelled the
terror and burning flesh, she turned round to look. Why? Why,
assaulted by this evidence confirming the angels' message of destruction, would she risk her life by looking back? What was so powerful
that it tempted her to defy the commandment of God and die?

Fond memories, Calvin says. The wife of Lot did not succumb to
woman's idle curiosity, as Josephus and others argued, transforming
her into a Hebrew Pandora; but she was a woman after all, a senti-
mental soul who could not let go of the past. Though she wanted

to escape destruction, she also wanted to be consoled. She turned around to look at her past one last time and fix it in her mind as a glowing bundle of kindnesses and joys she could carry with her to ease her exile.

If this is so, then the wife of Lot's sin in looking back was not rebellion. Greater than the sin of defying God's command is the sin of nostalgia: willfully refusing to accept the truth of the past and creating a beautiful lie to cover its horrors. The wife of Lot sinned because she could not overcome her desire to carry a lovely memory with her into the future instead of the burden of the truth.

But why name it *sin?* Why not call it *human,* this need to recover the past veiled in beauty? For to be human is to be deceived, as Eve quickly discovered. There is no escape from this, no matter how vigilant we discipline ourselves to be, for we are creatures of memory. As Augustine wrote in his *Confessions* (X), without memory we could not even speak of ourselves; yet our memory is tangled with forgetfulness so that we can never know the truth about ourselves and we become problems to ourselves, "like land which a farmer works only with difficulty and at the cost of much sweat."

The problem of the truth of our selves runs deeper than the tangle of memory and forgetfulness: it entails deceit. Our memory, Christa Wolf argues, inevitably creates calming fictions of the self that do away with ambiguity, contradiction, and pain. What we are in the habit of calling "remembering," is showing round our artistic self-creations as if they were genuine and expecting others to take them to be so.

> We seem to need the help and approval of the imagination in our lives; it means playing with the possibilities open to us. But something else goes on inside us at the same time, daily, hourly, a furtive process hard to avoid, a hardening, petrifying, habituating, that attacks the memory in particular.
>
> We all carry with us a collection of miniatures with captions, some quaint, some gruesome. These we occasionally bring out and show round, because we need confirmation of our own reassuringly clear feelings: beautiful or ugly, good or evil. These miniatures are for the memory what the calcified cavities are for

people with tuberculosis, what prejudices are for morals: patches of once active life now shut off. At one time one was afraid to touch them, afraid of burning one's fingers on them; now they are cool and smooth, some of them artistically polished, some especially valuable bits have cost years of work, for one must forget a great deal and re-think and re-interpret a great deal before one can see oneself in the best light everywhere and at all times. That is what you need them for, the miniatures.

(*The Reader and the Writer: Essays, Sketches, Memories,* 190–91).

Not one of us can help succumbing to the endemic power that eternally tempts us to re-create our past in a beauty that renders us tolerable to ourselves: to be human is to deceive ourselves.

Perhaps God had nothing to do with turning the wife of Lot into a pillar of salt. Perhaps the wife of Lot turned herself into salt, a daedal sculpture fashioned out of polished miniatures, a petrified self. Perhaps she stands on the edge of the plain as an eternal witness to our fallible selves, to the tangle of self and memory, truth and imagination, from which we cannot extricate ourselves.

Let us start again. Let us assume that Calvin is wrong not only about women's inherent weakness and the fundamental human requirement of obedience, but about the reason the wife of Lot turned as well.

Why would this wife want to linger over the place where her husband had volunteered to sacrifice her daughters to save his own neck? It was in Sodom only the night before that she had watched her husband bid two strange visitors welcome, stoop in kindness to wash their feet, bake them fresh bread with his own hands, and offer his two virgin daughters as sacrifices in their place. When the mob clamored outside to rape Lot's honored guests, Lot dragged his two little girls, Emet and Rachamim, to the front step. He was eager to cast them out to be gang-raped in order to save the lives of two strange men he called "my lords." "I beg you, my friends," her husband reasoned with the crush of neighbors as his daughters shook with fear in his grip, "do not commit such a wrong. Look, I have two daughters who have not known a man. Let me bring them out to you, and you may do to them as you please; but do not do anything to these men, since they have come under the shelter of my roof."

It wasn't altruism or loyalty to his Uncle Abraham's tradition of hospitality or even pure selfishness that emboldened her husband to make this evil offering to the God of judgment. It was the calculation of redemption: if the guests died, everyone would perish; but if Lot saved his two guests, he could at least save himself and a few others.

Why should the wife of Lot look back to the place where her two daughters had been offered as sacrifices on the altar of a vengeful God, when those same daughters, Emet and Rachamim, miraculously alive, were running ahead of her to Zoar?

At dawn, as they fled across the plain to Zoar, acrid ash in her nostrils and cries of anguish in her ears, the wife of Lot turned round to Sodom. She turned round not as John Calvin imagines, to sorrow over her past; nor did she turn round to wash her past in loveliness. The wife of Lot looked back to Sodom so that she might glory in the destruction of the place where she and her daughters had been betrayed. She looked back so that she might gloat at the annihilation of her enemies. She looked back in fury.

She looked back in fury. But when, gazing from a distance, the wife of Lot heard her neighbors screaming and calling out to one another, saw them drowning in a hot river, disintegrating in flames, buried alive under ash, her heart betrayed her: she felt pity for her enemies. Compassion swelled inside her and spilled out in tears, unwelcome, salty tears that ran down her face, her shoulders and limbs, shrouding her body. She tried to remember her enemies' many atrocities against her, to turn away from their suffering and dying, to stop her foolish tears, to clench her heart shut—"The heart is deceitful above all things, and desperately corrupt; who can understand it?" (Jeremiah 17:9)—but she could not; for her tears had hardened around her, fixing her in place so that she could no longer turn away from those she wanted to hate and was forced to keep staring at them, to the end and after, caught in an evil trance, her heart pumping tears of mercy within, everything else inert, deadened.

The wife of Lot is stuck there still today, unable to move in any direction, remembering the past and crying tears that harden around her as they fall. Imprisoned by her heart, she stands immobilized on the edge of the plain, a warning to all who see her: Don't look back.

A Hundred Fingers

The summer I was nine I knew a man with twelve fingers. He was the gardener at the motel where we lived, a thin, dusty-brown man who seemed to be everywhere. The day we moved into the Sea Ranch we saw him rolling a wheelbarrow across the lawn, carting a burlapped palm tree to a freshly dug hole. His hands and forearms were clenched tight with the load, the veins like rivers crossing a muddy plain. When the wheelbarrow hesitated or tilted over bumps, he kept it moving easily, never losing the calm in his shoulders and brow. Except for Tante Sien, my great aunt from Yerseke who visited us once and held me in her bosomy lap without saying a word, beaming at me, I had never seen a person so quiet in himself.

For the seven of us, arriving that first time, Florida was a feast of novelty. Seeking our fortune in a land of growth, we had left behind everything familiar: snow banks, Lake Michigan's numbing water, tornado shelters, all of our relatives, the Dutch Calvinist community my parents had been raised in and that ordered our days. In our new home we reveled in Spanish moss, palm trees, the Atlantic Ocean, six-foot

A Woman of Salt

rattlesnakes dead on the road, our first motel, our first time living so close to people who didn't look or sound Dutch, who hadn't ever heard of our church with its dominees and *preekstoels,* Canons of Dort and TULIP of true faith: Total depravity, Unconditional election, Limited atonement, Irresistible grace, and Perseverance of the saints.

Soon after we settled into the Sea Ranch I began following the gardener around, watching from a distance as he watered seedlings, snipped rebellious branches, gathered trash. The first day he nodded to me; the second, he smiled; the third, he set down his long-handled clippers by the bougainvillea hedge and stretched out his hands to me, palms up.

In the midday sun his palms glowed. I wanted to lay my head in one and listen, the way I held my ear against the inside of shiny pink conch shells to hear the ocean singing.

He flipped his hands face down, fingers extended like palmetto fronds. "Tell me what you see," he said.

On the outside edge of each hand, just below the pinky, an extra piece of flesh poked out. I had noticed the growths before, but assumed they were calluses like Opa Willem's. Now I saw they were miniature fingers, each about an inch long, with a crease across the middle and a tiny nail growing at the tip. Stiffer than the other fingers, they jutted crazily from the edge of his hand.

The gardener wiggled the stubs, making me giggle and feel like gagging all at once.

"They're little fingers," I said, glad to find my voice.

"The Lord gave me one for each tribe, each apostle, too." His voice was as unhurried as his movements.

"Do they hurt?"

"Mostly they help me."

I couldn't see how those skinny bits of flesh would be of much use. The way they stuck out, it looked like they'd get in the way more than anything else.

He twitched them again. "They're my seeing eyes. They tell me things, the insides of things, like when it's time to plant the lemon tree or when it's going to be a hurricane."

I looked up, thinking he had a glass eye like Mr. Boerhof, the elder

MARY POTTER ENGEL

who had examined our family's purity at our annual Home Visitation, but both of the gardener's eyes were soft and moist. Their stillness frightened me. I turned back to his tiny fingers.

"Can I touch them?" I asked.

"Suit yourself."

I brushed my index finger over the tip of one, ran it down the outside. The skin was smooth and hard, like polished stone.

After that, every morning, before my mother woke up, I would slip out to find Julian and we would work together until she yelled for me or sent my brother Calvin after me to come make the beds or mop the floor. Once she came to get me herself and on the way home told me to stay away from the gardener. "The world's full of mean people," she said. "You have to be careful."

"Julian likes me," I said, half innocent, half goad.

She grabbed my upper arms, fixed me with her eyes, metallic and green. "A girl who's lazy and sly? Who lies to her mother?"

Since my mother was always busy Lysoling the house or chasing after the three little kids, I visited Julian constantly. He taught me how to recognize oleanders and poinsettias, tell the difference between a coral and a milk snake, shake out my shoes before putting them on to make sure a scorpion wasn't hiding inside, sprinkle Epsom salts around the rose bushes to make them bloom longer and fuller, suck nectar from red star blossoms, find the night-blooming cactus. He let me help him tend his graveyard, the ground under the hibiscus bushes on the north side of the motel, where he buried crushed chameleons, birds that broke their necks on the sliding glass doors of ocean-view rooms, and the mice he caught in his traps. My job was to collect the shells and pieces of smooth-edged bottle glass that we mounded on each grave, to keep the blossoms in the markers fresh.

One morning, as we gathered fallen palm fronds and coconuts, Julian asked if I had ever seen a coconut fall during daylight. I told him no, not once.

"That's right," he said, satisfied. "That's the Lord's doing, His providence."

The word *providence* was familiar to me—from the dominee's sermons and Opa Willem's prayers, thanking God before and after every meal in his thick, sputtery English for "the abundant blessings of Your Providence"—and I was pleased to recognize it.

"Providence," I said, straightening up and articulating the word as if poised to win the Bible Spelling Bee. "P-R-O-V-I-D-E-N-C-E, Providence." Every night I put myself to sleep spelling. I liked the way the letters fitted against one another, crowding everything else out, the relief at the end, all the tricky places safely passed.

"The Lord makes it so coconuts fall only after dark," he said, "when all the little ones are to bed. You listen before you go to sleep. You'll hear them falling."

Looking first at the green nuts clustered under the branches above me, then back at Julian's sober face, I wondered if he was teasing me. He was full of tales about God and the Bible—like Jonah singing to the whale when he was inside it, enchanting it so its mouth yawned open in pleasure, freeing him.

"You're making that up," I said.

"The Bible says, 'He hides us in the shadow of His wings.'"

He handed another yellow-brown nut to me to stack in the bushel basket for his wife, who made a lemon-filled coconut cake Julian sometimes brought for our breakfast. As I laid it with the others, I decided to listen for coconuts dropping that night; but I already knew Julian was right, and the wonder of the world filled me up.

In mid-August that summer I overheard two women in the grocery store talking about the loggerhead turtle hatchings reported along our stretch of beach.

When the food had been put away, I headed straight for the beach. Crisscrossing my way to the pier and back, I imagined my gentle steps stirring the nests, calling the turtles awake.

I was determined to return to the beach that night—alone, if necessary. Julian would be gone long before dark, and since my mother and dad would be too tired or busy, Calvin was my best hope. Though two years older, he might think hunting in the dark for hatchling turtles a worthy adventure. I told him about it while we were doing the supper dishes and he agreed to come. We planned to ask permission, but as soon as the little kids went to bed, Mother and Dad started. She locked herself in the bathroom. He pounded on the door, shouting, "Show me the grocery receipts!" She screamed from inside, "Your daughter's got you wrapped around her little finger." He banged harder. "For Chrissake, let me in!" A lamp crashed to the floor, the bulb chinkling into pieces, and Calvin and I slipped out.

We ran across the patio to the beach, where a small crowd had gathered. We hurried toward it and within seconds we saw more turtles than we could count. Some were digging their way out of the sand, tiny head first, then flippers. Others, already free, lurched forward, dragging their eggshells with them. A few had already moved beyond the nest, jerking their new bodies across ridges and dips in the sand. Calvin grinned at me and I hugged him.

As we watched, the hatchlings spread farther and farther from the nest. We followed them to the water, where they hurried across the shiny wet sand into the surf and disappeared.

A wave threw several of the turtles back on shore, leaving them upside down on the sand, stranded. I picked one up. It waggled its flippers, tickling me, and I flipped it over and set it in the surf. The next wave tumbled it back onto the smooth, wet sand and it began scrambling toward the beach. Before it reached dry sand, I caught it and turned it in the right direction. The turtle was still for a moment, then pivoted and began thrusting itself back toward the beach.

Before I could turn it around again, Calvin ran up to me. "Come on," he said. "They're heading for the light."

We tracked turtles pushing through beach grass, piles of shells, abandoned chairs. Many had made it to the stand of rubber trees beside the motel. At the edge of the public parking lot, some were crawling into a lighted phone booth, stumbling against the hatchlings already piled inside. Others scooted around meters, over wheel stops, under cars, all heading toward Highway A1A, where a golden stream of headlights cut through a blaze of street lamps.

Careful where we stepped, we ran across the lot to the highway. In the heavy air, exhaust fumes mingled with DDT. Turtles crawled past us, through our legs and over the sidewalk. They slid down the curb into the road.

Under the wheels they made a small, cracking sound, like almond shells splitting at Christmastime. The night was full of their breaking. Flattened bodies littered the road. The metallic odor of blood, the smell of soft flesh already rotting rose from the asphalt. My hand slapped over my mouth to hold back the vomit. I wanted Julian to be there, to tell me what was happening, what to do, to calm me with his stillness.

"Neat," Calvin said. "Tomorrow they're gonna stink worse than a pail full of dead sea urchins."

"We have to save them!"

I turned and ran back across the parking lot. In seconds Calvin was panting alongside me. In the motel corridor we slowed down, crept on all fours to our parents' door, where our zori sandals and sand-dollar collecting buckets were lined up, and listened. She was accusing him of paying too much attention to a certain young woman at church; he was denying it, threatening to tell the dominee she wore mascara, to rub the forbidden stuff from her eyes himself if she didn't wipe it off right away. Calvin and I grabbed our buckets and ran.

On the beach there were turtles everywhere, hundreds of them, scattering in all directions.

We filled our buckets fast.

"What now?" Calvin asked, swinging his catch, proud.

"Take them home," I said. "Put them in the tub."

When we got back to our room, the lights were out and everything was quiet. We scrubbed our feet in the pan of water my mother kept by the door, turned the handle quietly, and crept inside.

"Where have you been?" my mother demanded. She had been lying on the bed with Debbie, in my place, and was now sitting up, her nightgown ballooning around her. "Sneaking out with that man?"

For a moment the hatred in her voice shook my rescuer's joy. I wanted to tell her that Julian followed the Bible like we did, that when I asked him if he had ever been bad growing up, he always answered, "The Lord says, 'Honor thy father and thy mother.'"

"Look what we found," I said to my mother, holding out my bucket.

She peered at the turtles wriggling over one another, trying to find a foothold.

MARY POTTER ENGEL

If you caught her just right, my mother could be as much fun as another kid. She would rip up old dresses and shirts to make enormous tails for our kites and then help us fly them, laughing and hollering down the beach. Or she would buy huge bags of chips and pretzels and cheese puffs, set them on the table with bottles of Orange Crush and Nehi Grape, piles of Milky Way and Three Musketeers bars, and let us snack as much as we wanted all day long. Sometimes, right in the middle of blasting us, she would stop, take a breath, then start singing funny songs to us, setting her punishing words to the music of "Old MacDonald" or "The Star Spangled Banner." By the second verse, we would all be laughing.

"There's lots more out there," I said. "Come and see."

She rubbed her index and middle finger over a turtle's back. When it kicked its flippers, trying to crawl away, she drew back.

"You're filthy," she said to me, wiping her fingers on her nightgown. "I'm not cleaning up after you, or those things either."

"Just let us keep them in the tub overnight," I said. "We'll take them away before you get up and we'll scour the tub." I was sure Julian would let us keep them in the huge galvanized steel basin that hung in his storeroom. He would find a shady spot for the basin, help us get food for the turtles, and figure out how to get them home.

"What's your father going to say when he finds a mess in his shower at five-thirty tomorrow morning? He works hard, you know."

I promised to tape notes on the bathroom door and shower curtain warning him, apologizing; do extra chores for a week, not complain about stomachaches when it was time for Sunday night church, tickle her feet twenty minutes every afternoon.

When she gave up and lay down to sleep, Calvin and I hauled our buckets to the bathroom. We counted twenty-seven turtles into the tub, took turns watching over them and running to the ocean for more water. We went to bed happy, dreaming of turtles whirling toward the moon.

In the morning my dad was in one of his rages. He stood over my mother, shouting in her face, "Helen, get up. You're not sleeping." He was pounding her shoulder against the pillow with one hand, clutching a towel around his waist with the other. "Wake up, for Chrissake," he yelled. "Can't you control those kids?"

Calvin and I kept very still, feigning sleep like mother.

Dad gave her a final rough shake and let her go. Her head flopped hard against the pillow, but her eyes did not open. He left muttering. We heard water in the bathroom, but we couldn't tell whether he was running hot water over our turtles or washing up in the sink. The second the door slammed behind him, we jumped up to see if he had left our prizes alone.

He had. All morning we showed off the turtles to Debbie and Mark and Paulie. When they went down for their nap with Mother, Calvin came up with a plan to race them and we sneaked to the dimestore to steal a bottle of red nail polish. Back on our patio, we marked Calvin's fourteen turtles with numbers and my thirteen with letters, then set up a course and started the competition. We each chose one turtle at a time to race, leaving the others in our buckets until we were ready for them. A few other kids wandered over to watch the fun, and soon everyone was hollering. The noise brought Julian to the far edge of the patio, where he stood half hidden behind the bougainvillea hedge, holding his rake and watching the commotion.

One of the boys scooped up my turtle from the finish line and tossed it to a tall kid near the start.

"Stop," I yelled. "You'll kill it."

The tall one caught it and threw it back.

I ran to Julian. "Make them stop," I said.

He stared at the ground, shook his head back and forth.

"Please," I begged, grabbing his arm, slick with sweat, and pulling him toward me.

He stepped back and stood the rake between us, ten fingers wrapped around the smooth wood, two jutting free.

I let go and stood by his side waiting for him to speak, to offer me one of his sayings from the Bible, like "You've got to live at the feet of the Lamb," "The mercy of God falls on the just and the unjust," or "There's an inside to everything that happens"—sayings that comforted me even though I didn't understand them. But he was silent.

While the boys whooped to each other, intent on their game, I

MARY POTTER ENGEL

snatched my bucket and ran behind the pool shed. When it seemed sure that they had not followed me, I hid the bucket under a dense growth of red star bushes and rushed around the back way to our room. My mother had walked the little kids to the Laundromat, so I didn't have to worry about her. It took only seconds to wriggle into my bathing suit, grab our inner tube and rope, and be on my way back to the turtles.

They were waiting for me, clambering over one another in the bucket. Their heads were still shiny, especially their tiny black eyes, blinking in the sunlight, but salt crystals had formed on their shells, making them look dusty and old. I leaned around the pool shed. The boys were busy racing again and Julian wasn't in sight. I grabbed the turtles and headed for the ocean.

At the shore I fastened the bucket on top of the inner tube and tied the rope around my ankle, then waded past the surf and dove in. I swam hard, pulling the tube after me. It seemed to take only a minute to reach the sand bar several hundred yards out where Calvin and I dove for sand dollars. After resting a moment, splashing water on the turtles to keep them happy, I pushed off again, toward the horizon, swimming out and away, farther than I had ever gone before. I felt strangely light and strong enough to reach the Gulf Stream.

The furious kicking made the rope chafe against my ankle and I stopped to try to loosen it. Slinging my arms over the inner tube, I remembered the sharks we sometimes saw cruising just beyond the sand bar. My knees jerked to my chest and my head wrenched round in all directions, blood pounding against my eardrums. I began hoisting myself onto the tube to paddle the turtles back to shore so they wouldn't be eaten.

I don't know what stopped me. I'd like to think I heard a voice telling me what to do. But there was no voice, mine or Julian's. There was only sky and water, a pail of turtles and my skinny nine-year-old body—worn out with fear and hoping and feelings I had no name for—all of us clinging to rubber bleached gray by the sun.

Julian's fingers weren't prophets or apostles or seeing eyes: they couldn't teach him the blessings of the world, show him the graced insides of things hidden to others. They couldn't tell him anything.

A Woman of Salt

They were useless. Because there were no insides to things. There was no sense in turtles losing their way when they were following God's directions; no reason why some were killed finding their way home; nothing to stop a hurricane from hurling coconuts through windows in the middle of the day; no voices to warn you, no use trying to save things, from the Devil or anyone.

Loneliness, that was all, and Julian had never said a word about that.

The sun beat on my face. A film of salt pulled the skin taut across my forehead and cheeks. I felt older than Methuselah. I thought if I didn't move, I would keep shrinking, dry up completely. Keeping one arm tight around the inner tube, I reached into the bucket for a turtle. I cupped it in my hand, kissed the salty green curve of its back, and lowered it into the ocean. When it was under water about six inches, I took my hand away. The turtle sank until it was almost out of sight, then caught itself with its flippers, stretched out its neck, and swam away. I lowered a second, and a third, until all twelve had been released, no longer praying, as I had when ferrying them out, that the deep would embrace them, but willing each one on its own, alone, to swim hard for the safety of the chains of sargasso grass that floated miles offshore. There—if they made it—they could hide, protected by shadows and debris, until they were big enough to swim wherever they wanted without fear.

Though desperate to rest my arms and cheek against the hot curve of rubber, as soon as the last turtle was on its way I set to work untying the rope from my ankle. When the tube drifted free, I began a determined crawl back to shore, afraid to look behind me. The water felt cold and the sky seemed darker. As I sank into the movement of my limbs and head, a song sang itself in my body to the rhythm of my strokes, the psalm we sang every Sunday morning after the dominee read the Ten Commandments:

> *In God will I trust, though my counselors say,*
> *O flee as a bird to your mountain away;*
> *The wicked are strong and the righteous are weak,*
> *Foundations are shaken, yet God will I seek.*

MARY POTTER ENGEL

Over and over it sang itself inside me, trying to calm me, but as it washed through me, endlessly repeating, I only grew more frightened, swimming faster, faster, until I was crying, throwing myself forward, panting toward land.

About a hundred yards from shore the singing stopped. The ache in my side sharpened and a heavy weight pressed on my neck and shoulders, pushing me down. Treading water, I squinted into the distance. On the beach was a dark figure, waving. My mother had an uncanny power to see through me, anticipate my actions and catch me in the moment of transgressing, as if she saw ahead to sins I hadn't imagined yet, and I knew it was her signaling me in.

I put my head back in the water and pulled myself forward, through the dark water to the green, until I was stumbling in the surf.

It was Julian who greeted me on shore. He had been watching me the whole time. If there had been trouble, I suppose he would have called the Shore Rescue Team; he couldn't swim: in that way he and my mother were alike.

"You all right?" he asked as I dropped to the sand.

I didn't want to look at him. I was afraid the kindness that always lurked around his eyes, the presence of those dark, unnecessary fingers would confuse me.

"Come on, Miss Moses," he said, picking me up under my knees and shoulders. "Your folks'll be worried about you."

He carried me back to the motel that way, my arms and legs dangling in exhaustion. At the end of our corridor, he set me down. "You go in and clean up now, take a rest. We got a job tomorrow transplanting those hyacinths by the office there."

As I approached our rooms, the jalousie door swung wide and my mother rushed to me. She clutched me to her, pressing my wet, sandy body hard against her warmth. She held me like that several moments, arms pinned, face buried in her chest, kissing the top of my head and whispering, *"Duiveltja, Duiveltja,"* little Devil, little Devil, "you could have been killed."

Then, her thumbs and fingers squeezing my shoulders, she stood

A Woman of Salt

over me, green eyes piercing, until she had wrung the whole story out of me. She wouldn't believe Julian had nothing to do with my disobedience. She had seen him carry me from the shore through the courtyard and blamed him for leading me astray, bringing me so close to drowning.

I didn't see Julian the next day. My mother wouldn't let me go out. After that, she kept me inside with her most of the day and close by her when we went out, always watching me.

From time to time I would see Julian through the jalousie windows, sweeping our corridor or pushing his wheelbarrow across the courtyard. He would raise his hand or nod to me, but I always ducked back inside where he couldn't see me, afraid of the sadness between us.

Once school started, it was more difficult to catch a glimpse of him. Our bus picked us up before he arrived and dropped us off after he had locked up his tools for the day and left. One Saturday morning, though, while my mother and dad were still sleeping, I saw him raking the front yard. He was wearing his soft khaki pants and white collared shirt with the sleeves rolled up and working as steadily as always, but with a droop to his shoulders, as if he had grown older or forgotten why he was working. And though he was close enough to hear me tap the window, he never glanced at our rooms.

In late October, just before Reformation Sunday, Mother took us back up north to live with Oma and Opa until my dad found another job and got back on his feet. Under Michigan's snows and eternally gray skies I forgot the sun and the ocean, the turtles and Julian.

When we returned to the Sea Ranch in February, he was gone. The lady in the office told me his diabetes had gone bad—he had almost lost a foot to gangrene—and right after Christmas he had quit. She was having a terrible time replacing him: He was dependable and hardworking, smart, too, not like some. I asked for his address, but she didn't know where he lived; his number, but he didn't have a phone. I thanked her and left in a hurry. Inside of me, everything was emptying, like a heavy canvas tent when the last pole is removed, collapsing, pushing out the air with a long sough.

I wandered to our graveyard. Everything was gone—the shells, bits of glass, wilted flowers. A rake had left neat furrows in the barren dirt.

MARY POTTER ENGEL

For a moment I wanted to kneel down and dig with my hands to see if I could find where he had buried the turtle the boys had killed. I thought I might take the cracked shell and hide it in the lining of my suitcase, so I could take it out and look at it sometimes, hold it in my hand and listen to it.

But by that time I was almost ten. I had mastered surfaces, living on the outside of the world, balancing on scaffolding built of correct spellings, perfect grades, chains of books, an angry righteousness that shut out disappointment and hope. If I had grown a hundred fingers like Julian's, all telling the graced insides of things, it wouldn't have been enough to call me back from the emptiness I had entered, wandering in a world without God, my mother's eyes everywhere, watching for the evil she saw inside me to emerge.

I left the graveyard and hid behind the suitcases stacked in the corner of the kids' bedroom to lose myself in a book. Sometimes it took her hours to find me.

A Woman of Salt

It Is Such a Little Place

If to look back is death, what then?

Choose Lot's way? Sever the past from oneself and live the rest of one's days mutilated, the phantom limb crying out to return?

"It is such a little place!" The first time Lot says this, he means to persuade the angels that the cozy town he wishes to flee to is of no consequence and that therefore it will cost them nothing to spare it along with him and his family. "What is Zoar?" he argues. "It is nothing."

The angels, who are guiding him to the mountains for refuge, do not reply.

"Let me flee *there*," Lot begs, adding again, "It is such a little place."

Four words—"Let me flee there"—separate the first "It is such a little place" from the second. Yet between the first utterance of this plea and its plaintive repetition Lot has traveled a great distance. His heart has entered the city of Zoar and seen the confinement of his life there.

The first time Lot says "It is such a little place," he is begging to go to Zoar because he is afraid of the wild and distant mountains the angels have counseled him to take refuge in. A city dweller, he is willing to leave doomed Sodom to save his life, but he is not ready to live life in the open. He wants the containment of fear, the security of walls, a place of predictabilities and guarantees. Why should he risk his life to bandits and beasts, starvation and loneliness, endless unknowns? Lot is willing to walk a long way off to escape dying, but he does not want to walk any farther away from the familiar than necessary: not to die seems the same to him as living.

Lot is a scheming man. He has finagled his way around God's commands before. Fleeing Sodom, he calculates that the angels will not deny him his wish to escape to Zoar instead of the mountains.

But in the moment he beseeches the angels, "Let me flee *there*," Lot senses that the angels will grant him his wish to escape to Zoar instead of to the mountains *and* that this concession to his fear will not be without great cost to him. The "there" where he wishes to live and where the angels will escort him will be his cage.

Because Lot is afraid to turn around to face the destruction of Sodom and Gomorrah, and because he cannot face the risk of fleeing to an unfamiliar place, he settles for a life built of small truths and certainties, the prison of the possible.

By the time Lot cries out again "It is such a little place," he has foreseen what it will mean for him not to flee to the hills but to take refuge in Zoar: He will enter the emptiness of a city walled by fear, where life is an unbroken calculation, a mastering of surfaces and living on the outside of the world, where they speak a language not of belonging but of what can be measured and contained, what can be bought and what can be sold, of debits and credits and knowing exactly where you stand, a tidy place where all roads are secured and all journeys mapped out in advance, a pinched place in which he will die every day and from which he will never return.

When Lot repeats "It is such a little place," he is mourning the fate he has chosen and been granted.

In the moment between the first and second utterance, Lot is transformed. He changes from a giddy man whose consuming fear gives birth to a limpid desire for Zoar, an unambiguous life, to a man heavy with the sorrowful knowing that the attainment of what he most wanted is itself fraught with ambiguity and contradiction and loss.

"It is such a little place": a lament the second time, no longer a plea.

Yet this is not Lot's tragedy: that he experiences the attainment of his desire as a loss. Eve learned as much in the garden when she tasted the fruit and was exiled from innocence. Lot's flaw is his own:

It lies in mourning the effects of satisfying his desire for Zoar and *nevertheless, still,* choosing Zoar out of fear.

He would have done better to turn around like his wife, hoping against hope to see, once before he died, the impossible: in the midst of destruction, a sign of God's mercy.

The apple tree never asks the beech how he shall grow;
nor the lion, the horse, how he shall take his prey.

WILLIAM BLAKE, "Proverbs of Hell"

Slipping Away

"Little Deuce Coupe" blasting over the radio, Neil drove the Bomb into the gravel lot at Howell Park, where our families were unloading their station wagons for the annual Vredeveld Avenue Church picnic. I ducked low in the backseat so my mother wouldn't see me and change her mind about letting me hang out with Neil and my brother Calvin for the day. She kept a close watch on me. "You can't trust Ruth," she would tell the aunts or my father if they tried to intervene. "Especially with boys. She's got the *Duivel* in her. I can see it in her eyes. I could see it when she was born."

While they finished unpacking, Calvin, Neil, and I stayed in the car to listen to a few more songs and finalize our plans to swim the length of the lake, which we had never done before. Driving to the park, the three of us had made a pact to get as far away from our families and the others as possible this year. Since the rest of them would be bunched at the east end of the park—the Calvin Cadets running three-legged races and the Calvinettes hunting for pennies in haystacks; the men

A Woman of Salt

pitching horseshoes and arguing about whether last week's sermon contradicted Article Six of the Canons of Dort on double predestination; the women plying black-suited Dominee Lachniet with *fet ballen* and pickled peaches, clucking about Reka Vlardingerbroek wearing a sleeveless dress to church, and yammering about who had been caught standing in line to see a movie or who watched TV or traveled or spent money *op Zondag,* the Lord's day—we decided to head for the west end, and the quickest route there was across the lake. We figured if we left as soon as we got there and swam fast, we could make it back in time for supper: hamburgs, pigs-in-the-blanket, homemade bread-and-butter pickles, seven-layer salad, and more desserts than appeared at any other time except Christmas Eve, when an elaborate buffet of sweets was spread after we had solemnly tasted the chocolate Cake of Sin, swallowed bites of the marble Cake of the Old Covenant with Israel, and eaten whole slices of the angel food Cake of the New Covenant in the Blood of Christ.

After the meal Calvin and Neil would haul picnic benches with the men and I would have to help clean up, serve coffee to behemoth-bosomed old ladies spluttering *"Dank u, meisje"* and widowers teasing that the weather was hotter than Dutch love. Though we might be able to sneak off for a cigarette, it would be impossible to escape the hymn-sing in the shelter. There, under beams strung with moth-pimpled lights, with Mr. Van Lonkhuyzen calling out page numbers and my mother pounding chords on the organ, the congregation would sing the songs *verboden* in church: American songs, gospel songs, songs whose tunes were too emotional for proper worship and whose words didn't come from the Bible; songs that tempted people to believe they could save themselves instead of depending absolutely on the sovereign God who, before creating the world, without regard to hearts or deeds, chose some to dwell with Him in glory and rejected the rest.

But while the congregation joined in praising their Savior—sent only for them, the elect—and thanking God for so freely giving them the gift of grace, Calvin and Neil and I would sit on the stone wall behind them and make up our own words to their melodies. Side by side, knees and shoulders touching, grinning into our songbooks and trying not to laugh when we caught one another's eye, we would croon "Just as I Am, with One Thousand Fleas"; "There Shall Be Showers of Guessings"; and our favorite, The Mary Magdalene Song:

What a friend I have in Jesus,
All my skin and briefs to bare.
What a privilege to carry,
Everything *to Him in prayer.*

The three of us never worried about being caught *spotten,* though trifling with what was sacred was one of the worst sins, second only to idleness and dancing. We were experts at keeping just the right distance from the dominee and the elders and at joking ourselves out of trouble with anyone else.

Our families reached the far end of the parking lot and trudged toward the picnic shelter. When the last baskets and coolers and cartons of hymnbooks and little kids were finally out of sight, Calvin, Neil, and I shook on our pact and were on our way to the far side of the lake.

To avoid suspicion we left separately, hiking past the roped-off swimming area to a spit of land beyond the boathouse. Hidden by racks of canoes, we dove in and started swimming. Since the shore was full of twists, each point thickly wooded, we were sure no one would spot us. Still, we turned around to check if anyone had followed us. My little sister Debbie, Mother's informer, was the likeliest spy, but her skirted pink bathing suit didn't appear among the trees.

The swim to the causeway spanning the water was easy—a third of a mile. We headed straight for the midpoint of the road bridge, where a culvert joined the two halves of the lake. Though Neil thrashed more than Calvin and I, we swam together evenly, well matched for strength and speed.

When the pipe was a body's length away, we dropped our feet to the bottom and rested. We could easily have hoisted ourselves onto the embankment and walked across the pavement to the other side of the lake, but Calvin said that would be cheating, since we had agreed to swim across the lake and not swim-walk-swim.

A Woman of Salt

"That's the pact," he said. "Through the pipe." He grinned at Neil. "Right, Neil?"

"Sure thing."

Calvin and Neil were masters of adventure. They were always trying to outdo each other—blasting firecrackers in rich people's pools, climbing out of their bedroom windows at night to race cars down farm roads, sneaking to the quarry and swinging into it on a rope, jumping as close to the underwater ledge as they dared, trying it after one beer, two—how many more I didn't know: they wouldn't tell me.

The three of us stood squishing our toes in the muddy bottom of Lake Howell, listening to the water gurgle through the opening of the culvert, slipping away to the other side.

We knew we had to do it. We wouldn't get another chance. In thirteen days Calvin was leaving for Dordrecht, our church college miles away. A week after that Neil would start Coast Guard training in Maine. And I would be left behind, taking special algebra classes at our crummy high school, babysitting Debbie and my little brothers, practicing organ-piano duets for church with my mother, washing windows for her over and over until she was satisfied they were spotless, feeling her scrape her thumb down my back before I left the house to make sure I was wearing a bra.

"All set?" Calvin asked.

"Ready," Neil said. "But the girl's not coming."

"What?" I asked.

"You can't do it," he said, shrugging. "That's all."

Neil was always trying to protect me, as if I were still twelve, as if Calvin and I hadn't been partners in crime years long before he moved in. It was Neil who refused to take me with them to the quarry. Calvin didn't care if I tagged along anywhere, as long as I kept my mouth shut. Neil worried more, about the Bomb, his grades, whether he would make it through training. When I told him on the way home from church one Sunday night that I didn't think I could make Profession of Faith with the other sixteen-year-olds next spring, because I hadn't had an "experience of the Lord," he started worrying about me, too.

"Why can't I do it?" I asked Neil.

He shrugged again.

"My lungs are better than both of yours," I said.

Calvin hooted with laughter, wiggled his eyebrows up and down at Neil.

Neil hung his head, watched his fingers drum the surface of the lake.

"You morons," I shouted, hoping they would take the flush spreading down my face and chest for anger. "I'm as strong as anybody. Stronger."

I glared at Calvin. "You want me to tell him?" I asked.

From the time we were in elementary school Calvin and I had competed to see who could swim the most laps underwater. We were both tall and skinny and strong as hell—people took us for twins—but I usually won, by a half-lap sure, but fair and square. I had never told anybody before—he made me swear not to—but I was ready to now.

"Don't be a dipstick," Calvin said. "Look."

He pointed to the entrance to the culvert. Most of the pipe was hidden in the darker water below, but the top third was visible, a ghostly curve under the surface, turning to stone in the air. Between the highest point of the circle and the stream of water flowing through it, there was only an inch or two of space. Waves slapped over the top of the concrete, soughed into it.

"Sure, you'd get in all right," Calvin said. "But what then?"

"It's just a two-lane road," I said. "No shoulder or anything. It's not that far."

"Forget the distance," Calvin said. "It's gonna be dark as the *Duivel* in there."

He thought if he said *Devil* in Dutch, the way Opa did when he was angry and wanted us to behave, he'd scare me off.

"It's not Doy-vul," I said. "It's Dai-vul."

"Same diff. Look, once you're inside, you won't know how much you have left to go. And you won't be able to come up for a breath."

"You're the one who's going to need the air."

"It's not the ten-meter platform," Neil said, looking directly at me. "You can't climb up and then decide you don't want to dive or jump. There's no room to back out."

"I'm the one who changes my mind?"

"What about snakes?" Neil asked.

A Woman of Salt

Every summer the park manager pulled two or three long snakes from the slime under the dock near the swimming area, and I would stay out of the water until I had forgotten them, shiny black and writhing.

"I'll let you go first," I said. I lowered myself underwater near the opening, stretching my arms to feel the sides of the culvert. It was about four feet across, maybe more, not wide enough for a full-power breaststroke, but big enough so we wouldn't have to dog-paddle.

Just as I was about to surface, one of them grabbed my waist from behind and pulled me from the pipe. He lifted me back and up until my head broke the water, then threw one arm across my chest and the other across my abdomen, pinning me tight against him. It was Neil. He was taking care not to hurt me, to use just enough force to restrain me, keep me from being the first one through, but I struggled and my right arm got wrenched a little.

"You're hurting me," I said over my shoulder.

I knew he'd let me go if I said that, and he did. Neil felt guilty because he thought I was still gone on him, *verkikkerd op de jonge,* as Opa Willem used to tease. In October, on the Youth Group hayride, Neil had made out with me the whole night, promising when we parted to ask me out on a real date—my first—soon. A few weeks later, Trina Holkeboer, a giggly senior with fleshy thighs and greasy black mascara lumped on her blond lashes, was wearing his ring around her neck. It lay between her breasts like a fallen boulder. Whenever I saw it I wondered whether I should have worn angora sweaters and brought home-made salted peanut cookies to Neil at football practice, like her, if he would have chosen me then.

"I was just measuring," I told Neil, massaging my shoulder where he had held me, though the pain had already gone.

Calvin moved closer, smiling one of his conspiratorial smiles. "Listen, I need you to go back and tell Mom and Dad we're hiking around the lake or something. I don't want them to come looking for us, okay?"

I didn't know what to do. I had never refused my brother before. If he said *Jump,* I jumped. If he said *Hide this in your room and don't look at it,* I hid it and didn't look. If he said *Lie,* I lied—to neighbors, to the police, to the dominee and the elders, even to Mother.

MARY POTTER ENGEL

"Come on, Rufus," Calvin said. "A favor. Not many more chances, pal."

"What if I go tell Dad what you two are up to?"

"Don't be a baby like Debbie. Listen, if you don't leave right now, I'll show Mom where you hide your diary."

"I hate you."

Calvin flicked water in my face the way he used to do when we were little. I splashed back, hard, trying to hold on to my anger, but I could already feel it evaporating, leaving me empty and brittle.

"Do this for me," Calvin said, "and we'll take you with us to the going-away party at the quarry next Saturday. Won't we, Neil?"

Neil cocked his head to the side and stared at me, his fingers still drumming the water. His hands stopped for a moment, then began tapping again. "Okay by me."

I couldn't tell if it was one of their tricks or not. The two of them were good at going back on their word and then denying they had made any promises to me because they hadn't sworn on the B-I-B-L-E or the Broken-Body-and-Blood-of-Our-Lord-and-Savior-Jesus-Christ. But this time there was a chance Calvin would follow through and, if he did, Neil was sure to go along with him.

"Okay, then," I said.

"Good girl," Calvin said.

"But if you're lying to me, I'll tell Mother the truth about the accident with her Mustang—the vodka, Neil driving, everything."

"It's a deal. Now go."

He and Neil grabbed each other by the forearms and shook themselves twice, the way they did before a big football play. They were all muscle and gristle and stupid grins.

I pushed off the bottom and threw myself belly first on the surface of the water, making as big a splash as I could, then began my most impressive butterfly toward the guarded swimming area. After a few yards I began a slow crawl, my head above water.

"See ya later," Calvin called.

"Thanks," Neil said.

"Jerks," I said, flipping on my back and beginning the backstroke.

The sureness of the movement calmed me. My mother had never

A Woman of Salt

learned how to swim and she couldn't understand my enjoyment of it. "You should spend your energy doing useful things like Debbie instead of showing off," she said. "Pride's a sign of the *Duivel.*" But I was a natural swimmer like my father. He traveled through water powerfully and elegantly, with the grace of an animal, and always emerged flush with pleasure. I loved to watch him. And when I was in the water, I became him; it was as if his power and instinct rushed through my body, my mind, making them one, no longer two pulling against each other. I didn't have to think about what I was doing or whether I should be doing it; everything, the perfect thing, came to me quickly and easily, and the water made way for me.

I switched to the sidestroke so I could sneak looks at the culvert. Calvin had already disappeared. Neil was scrambling onto the causeway. I stopped, let my feet touch bottom, and shaded my eyes with both hands. Neil ran to the other side of the road and knelt at the edge, his tanned body tensed with excitement. As he stared into the lake below, waves of heat rose from the road, wrapping him in shimmering bands of light. Suddenly he jumped up, punched both fists in the air. I lowered myself in the water, keeping only my eyes and nose above the surface, so he wouldn't see me. Too intent on meeting Calvin to glance in my direction, he rushed for my side of the road, leapt into the lake. He grasped the top of the culvert, hesitated a moment, and then he, too, was gone.

I stood up. Behind me, far away, I could hear mothers calling their children back to shallower water; kids screaming as they tumbled down the high slide; friends yelling to each other between the raft and the shore. The lifeguard blew his shrill whistle once, then again.

Ahead of me heat waves still hovered over the road, blurring everything. It looked as though the road had turned into the lake or the lake into the road, one quivering gray-blue wall rising between me and the sky, dividing the lake in half. The wall seemed translucent, but I couldn't see what was on the other side. I squinted, but the wall remained, undulating almost imperceptibly and shining too brightly in spite of its dull color, which made me dizzy, threw me off balance, and as I stood there trying to look through it, I felt myself grow heavy, sinking, the muddy bottom rising over my instep. Like the Egyptians

MARY POTTER ENGEL

in their chariots, I thought. I'm sinking like a dumb Egyptian, stuck mid-chase, trapped by my armor, dragged down by it. I'm drowning by the hand of an angry God, while God's favored ones walk through safely on dry land.

The mud kept rising, creeping toward my ankles, trying to bury me in its softness.

I yanked myself free, kicked off hard and swam straight for the road as fast as I could, not once letting my feet drift below the surface, for fear they would be sucked down again.

When I arrived at the culvert I was out of breath. I crossed my arms on top of the pipe and leaned my cheek on my wrists, resting—just for a second, to gather more strength, more air. My feet found the bottom of the hard circle and settled there. The concrete was cool and deliciously rough against the inside of my arms and soles of my feet. I unlocked my arms and drew in three long breaths, stretching my torso and throwing back my head and shoulders to expand my lungs. I was good at this. The distance—far shorter than any I had attempted since I was nine or ten—would be easy for me. And swimming through a pipe couldn't be that different from swimming across an open pool riddled with light. Calvin and Neil didn't want me to rob them of their glory, that was all. If I swam through the culvert, too, it would be a smaller thing; they couldn't brag about it the same way to their friends, even to themselves.

Gripping the rim of the pipe, I arched back so the top of my head touched the lake. I pulled in all the air around me until I thought I would burst, then folded myself up and plunged under the water into the entrance.

With the first full stroke my fingers and toes hit the walls. I pulled my arms and legs in tighter, changed to a flutter kick and tried to find a way to use the breaststroke without scraping my elbows. By the time I had figured out that I needed to keep my arms stretched in front and paddle from the wrist alone, I was already tired.

I couldn't feel a current. The water felt weighted, strangely unmoving, as if under pressure and darkness it had solidified. I kicked harder, maneuvered my arms to my hips and used them as flippers, but the water resisted me.

A Woman of Salt

I wiggled and willed my body forward, flapped my arms wildly, kicked so hard my instep slammed against the bottom of the tunnel, bruised. Sure that I had traveled at least three-quarters of the way, maybe more, I opened my eyes to see if I could glimpse any lightening in the water ahead.

It was dark everywhere. I couldn't tell my eyes were open and for a moment I was confused, thinking I had only dreamed them open. To startle myself awake, I squeezed them closed, tighter, tighter, then snapped them open, but open or shut, shut or open, there was only darkness. And a silence larger than the darkness, a silence that erased the drumming of my heart, rubbed out my determination, wiped away every thought as it formed in my head, making me feel as if I were dissolving into the nothingness around me, shedding my cumbrous female body, the body accused and accusing, the body of death, and entering a glorious freedom, the girl who became nothingness, who escaped the bondage of her flesh, and for some reason this amused me and I forgot where I was; I forgot Calvin and Neil, the doctrine-drunk men and sin-hunting women we were fleeing, the harmonizing of the faithful and the mute cries of those left behind, the Israelites and the Egyptians, my dad with his muscled arms and my mother unable to swim, my defiance and the water pushing against me, my mind, free of limits, and the woman-flesh insistently contrary to it, my campaign to be good enough and my mother's inexorable judgment against me, terror and longing, fleeing God everywhere and everywhere seeking God's face and, delivered from these daily dividings, I smiled, and in smiling almost took a breath.

I don't know why I didn't, why instead my body clenched itself shut against that tempting silence, kicked itself through the darkness more vehemently. My lungs were scorched and raw, growing hotter every moment, with each movement, until the will to breathe brought every cell alive with a terrible desire, all of them singing inside me a conquering chorus, "Air, Air, breathe and you shall live."

I maneuvered my arms forward and tried to drag myself along the walls of the tunnel. That slowed me down, used too much oxygen, so I straightened myself out and reached as far ahead as possible, stretching into the darkness, lightening inside, and I began to glide.

MARY POTTER ENGEL

Weightless, I drifted, through absence and longing, suspended in all that might have been—a body that would not betray me; a heart with no need to prove its worth; a mind not forced into exile; a self made whole, delivered from eternal rending; the mother who would welcome me just as I am, without one plea, who would gaze on me with kindness; the Savior and Friend I could never touch, never feel, though I searched for Him everywhere, sweet Master with the gentle yoke, who had not chosen me, never would choose me so I could be like Him and belong.

I can't say what it was that woke me, a current rippling over my skin, a school of minnows passing by, a sound of distant voices, a scent of air, a change in the quality of the darkness surrounding me or the light shining through the water, illuminating the opening of the tunnel. I opened my eyes and there was the entrance, round and white.

My body greedy for relief, I laid hold of the thick concrete rim with my hands and pulled. Divided once again, heavy with the self I would never be and weighted with mourning for the self I would become, I pulled myself toward the surface.

Being Yet Doubtful

Calvin offers another possibility: "Perhaps," he writes, "being yet doubtful, the wife of Lot wished to have more certain evidence before her eyes." She looked back because she lacked trust and it was for that sin that she was punished. He lays out the divine logic this way:

> Forasmuch as the deliverance of her, and her husband, was an incomparable instance of Divine compassion, it was right that her ingratitude should be thus punished.... First, the desire of looking back proceeded from incredulity; and no greater injury can be done to God, than when credit is denied to His word.

For Calvin, the glory of God is God's faithfulness; and the root of all evil is humankind's lack of trust in God.

Though Calvin, jealous for the uniqueness of Christianity, would cringe at the analogy, according to this interpretation the wife of Lot resembles Orpheus. Just as Orpheus looked behind him in impatient doubt—Was Eurydice really there, released from Hades?—and was punished by losing his love forever, so the wife of Lot looked back because she doubted God's mercy and was punished by being doomed to loneliness. Because she could not trust the compassion of God, she was left alone on the plain, isolated in her salt casing, the crust of suspicion, while her husband and Emet and Rachamim traveled on to begin a new life together.

But why shouldn't the wife of Lot have been mistrustful? Surely she was right not to trust her husband, a man of pinched imagination who sought refuge in little places that walled one's heart?

Why should she have believed the angels, creatures so unlike her?

Passionless beings, they knew nothing of the burden of longing or the terrors of rejection. While still within the gates of Sodom she hesitated, arguing with the angels over the contradictions between God's judgment and mercy, his providence and abandonment. Michael and Gabriel, impatient with her rending questions, eager to save her from herself, grabbed her hands and pulled her out of the house, just as they had pulled Lot into the house to save him from the angry mob. Against her will the angels dragged the wife of Lot through the city gate into the open country, away from her divisions toward redemption.

If the angels' lack of passion made the wife of Lot suspicious of their perception of danger and safety, their violence toward her persuaded her not to trust their fiery vision of God's righteous judgment and deliverance.

And why should the wife of Lot have trusted God? When she overheard God's messengers tell Lot that He was about to destroy the cities of the plain and they alone would be saved, she laughed the way Sarah had laughed in her tent when she heard God promise Abraham she would give birth in her old age. The wife of Lot knew what her life was. She knew she was worth nothing in the eyes of God. She might escape Sodom by clinging to her husband, but she was not dumb: the Compassionate Friend of Abraham and Merciful Savior of Lot had not chosen her, would never choose her to dwell with him in glory. She had already been consigned to judgment, already been marked for destruction. She had fought the terror of the damned and drifted through absence and longing long enough to know that.

On the way to Zoar, the wife of Lot looked back to see what she knew she would see: Sodom, the world she loved, shining as before, and God, absent as always.

It wasn't her husband or the angels or God that the wife of Lot doubted as the angels dragged her from the place she had made her home. It was herself.

She knew it was impossible to prevent her married daughters from staying with their husbands and that she could not have escaped her fate by leaving with Lot. She knew that even if she could have found a way to stay behind with her two married daughters, she would have been abandoning the unmarried ones to Lot, a father who had already proven himself eager to sacrifice them for his own gain and who might think it his right to use his daughters for his own pleasure once his lawful wife had deserted him by staying behind in Sodom.

She knew all this and still, as she breathlessly kept pace with the angels hurrying far from the cities of the plain, the wife of Lot wondered, Why did I follow Lot across the plain, hoping to be redeemed with him? Should I have left my married daughters behind, on the other side of God's electing grace, to be destroyed by the angry hand of a damning God? Shouldn't I have stayed behind to die with them?

In a turmoil of self-doubt, ripped with contradictions, the wife of Lot turned round. And from the edge of that plain of emptiness, looking across the distance, she saw herself, trapped within the gates of Sodom, burning in the fire of judgment: It was she who had abandoned her daughters, not they her.

The wife of Lot turned toward Sodom in repentance, weighted with mourning for the self she had become, heavy with the person she would never be.

But before she could call out to her daughters for forgiveness, grief swelled in her flesh, numbing her, leaving only the bitter salts of unshed tears.

He whose face gives no light,
shall never become a star.
WILLIAM BLAKE, "Proverbs of Hell"

Everything Returns

Ruth's friend Sandy helped herself to tampons in the grocery store. Eloise ripped off toilet paper from Big Boy Grills because she didn't like the owner's politics. Trix snatched mascara and lipstick anywhere she could. When Ruth's boyfriend, Lennie, needed paints or brushes, he slipped them into the pouch he had sewn inside the lining of his peacoat. Lennie's friends liberated watches, cameras, Pink Floyd and Miles Davis tapes, and sold them to Bart Van Kamp, an ex-seminarian who had left the Dutch Calvinist Church to champion the People's reappropriation of goods rightfully theirs, the theology of hope, and something called *prolepsis,* which justified acting *as if* the new order, when the mighty were brought low and the lowly raised up, had already begun.

Ruth wanted to show her solidarity. She would finger a pen or a bottle of kelp pills and skillfully slide it up her sleeve or down her pants. But as soon as the prize was hidden, she would feel the security camera trained on her, following her every movement, boring through her to the corrupt insides of her, like the metallic stare of her mother's eyes. Defeated, she would replace the item and walk out empty-handed.

Lennie suggested she try lifting a pack of Kools from the cashier's display at Reinsma's Family Restaurant, where she worked the dinner shift.

"It's a foolproof setup," Lennie said. "After you ring up a bill, you slip a pack into your apron pocket, behind your order pad."

"Mrs. Reinsma watches the dining room *every minute,*" Ruth said.

"Do it during the dinner rush."

"But she's always leaning through the pickup window and yelling at me, *Mr. Bonzelaar's coffee cup needs filling, Don't forget Mr. and Mrs. Wierenga's rolls, Pick up that napkin on the floor.* She sees everything; she's omniscient, like my mother."

"Not even the stingiest Dutchman is going to miss one pack. Besides, all food workers steal. The owners expect it, factor it into the wage."

For days Ruth worried herself into taking the cigarettes. Lying on the floor after work, her aching feet propped on the wall high over her head, she imagined her legs growing into wide, veiny columns like the legs of Minnie, the fifty-year-old lunch-shift waitress whose support hose was as thick as chain mail. She considered how little the Reinsmas paid her and the hours of work they demanded of her after closing every night, hauling cartons into the storeroom, wiping down the freezer, vacuuming, mopping, scrubbing walls; how Mrs. Reinsma scolded when she thought Ruth had been spying on her as she boiled sugar in vinegar for her trademark coleslaw or added the drop of vinegar to her famous piecrust dough; how Mr. Reinsma had followed her around the night Mrs. Reinsma left early, asking her to pose for "art shots" for his photography class assignment. She thought of the cheap tippers she had to serve, bridge groups reeking of perfume and gray-skinned salesmen in cheap suits; the customers who didn't believe in tipping, women like her mother who always found something wrong with the meal so they could stiff her in good conscience. Once a chatty couple from the Reinsma's church left a business card: "TAKE A TIP. How much better than gold it is to gain wisdom, and to gain discernment is better than pure silver. Proverbs 16:16."

MARY POTTER ENGEL

The next Thursday night, after Mr. Reinsma had left for his deacons' meeting and Mrs. Reinsma had begun assembling the next day's soup, Ruth hurried to the register. She covered the top and front of the display case with Windex and in slow, small circles began wiping the glass clear, waiting for her opportunity. But whenever she glanced up, Mrs. Reinsma's head was bent toward her in the pickup window, eyes squinted and lips pursed, her red-netted, brittle hair glowing under the heat lamps as if it were about to go up in flames.

Ruth polished the glass spotless and said goodnight to Mrs. Reinsma. On her way home she bought a pack of Kools and laid them on Lennie's sketch pad for him to find when he came in. Lennie didn't mention the cigarettes, but that night he invited her to Bart Van Kamp's weekly "Celebration of the People," which he had always attended without her before. "Don't mention you're still at Dordrecht," he coached Ruth before they left.

"Why would I? I despise the place."

Lennie knew it was true. At seventeen Ruth had won a four-year scholarship to Smith College that her parents had refused to let her accept. Her father had almost been won over by her arguments for tuition savings and an all-girls school, but her mother had insisted. "You know she can't be trusted, Clay," she said. "There's no curfew there. Who knows what she'll do, or what she'll learn from those worldly teachers and girls. It's Dordrecht or nowhere." When Ruth screamed at her, "You just want me to find a Dutch Calvinist husband!" her mother said coolly, "At least you have a choice. I had to work at the gas company so my brother could go to Dordrecht."

"Tell them you dropped out," Lennie said, "to become a waitress and a poet."

Ruth did her best to fit in at Bart's, though Lennie's artists and revolutionaries seemed more intent on getting high than discussing Marcuse, *Red Cats,* or Sartre's aesthetics. Even Bart valued the corporeal life more than intellectual pursuits. He explained ad nauseum why the People had a right to buy color televisions and Cadillacs when they were on food stamps, how a systemically violent class society justified the use of arms, why monogamy was an antirevolutionary concept.

After a few weeks, Ruth quit attending the Celebrations. She told

A Woman of Salt

Lennie she was too busy performing proletarian labor—as well as finishing an overdue paper on Plato's *Phaedrus*—to put up with self-gratifying Marxist hypocrisy. When Lennie left for Canada on an errand for Bart in December, she was happy to have the apartment to herself. She studied in bed whenever she pleased, burying herself under books for days at a time.

The third week Lennie was in Toronto—Ruth had expected him back in a few days and still had not heard from him—a new customer showed up at Reinsma's. He stood near the entrance, considering the room, his flecked brown suit tapering perfectly to his slender body, a wine-colored scarf billowing inside the white shirt at his throat. Small gold spectacles accented his beautifully lined face. He removed his hat, exposing delicate white hair, and bowed to the scattered diners. A few nodded hesitantly in return. Seating himself in the corner booth, he placed his hat on the seat and surveyed the menu. He ordered with gracious formality and ate his stuffed cabbage rolls and lemon meringue pie in continental fashion, fork in left hand, knife in right. Afterward, he fitted a Balkan Sobranie into an ebony cigarette holder and smoked it as if it were his only task in the world.

Here was a man, Ruth thought, sure of himself and his place in the world.

She refilled his coffee cup, admiring the oval pin in his silk scarf. It was gold, inlaid with onyx, with a small diamond at the center. She tried to imagine her grandfather sporting such an elegant pin when he left the Netherlands before the war, but the thought of Opa Willem wearing an ascot was ridiculous. A squat man with muscled arms boasting anchors and serpents and callused hands missing one and a half fingers, Opa Willem was no gentleman. He spoke spluttery English, wore janitor's coveralls everywhere and wooden shoes in the yard, rolled his own cigarettes, gave Oma pop beads for her birthday. He never bought silk anything, thought it crazy, *heel, heel gek,* to waste money on anything not heavy and rough, serviceable.

"How old is your pin?" Ruth asked as she finished pouring.

The man's eyes lit up. He slid to the end of the booth and stood next to her. "Please, permit me," he said, bowing. "I am Stefan Ciperas."

MARY POTTER ENGEL

"Ruth VanderZicht."

He took her hand and kissed it. *"Enchanté, Mademoiselle."*

When he smiled at her with his lively eyes, she grew conscious of the dirt collecting in the tucks of her white uniform, the paint worn off the front zipper pull.

Stefan stayed after the other customers left, sipping his coffee and talking to Ruth as she bused and wiped tables. He told her that the pin had belonged to his grandfather and that it was the only thing he had escaped with during the war; that he had been an officer in the Royal Prussian Army; that after his wife had died, his son moved into his house and sent him to live in the senior high-rise across from Reinsma's, among people with whom he had nothing in common, old busybodies incapable of elevated conversation. She told him she was studying philosophy, that she wanted to go to Paris, live in the Latin Quarter, write poetry.

After that, Stefan dined at Reinsma's every Tuesday and Thursday. He would order the special and eat it unhurriedly. Coffee and pie, always with his Sobranies, he would make last until closing. As Ruth collected ketchup bottles, emptied creamers, and rolled silverware in napkins, he would muse about poetry, the trappings of the Catholic Church, the wonders of theosophy, the unequaled beauty of the Baltic Sea. When he left, he would bow to her from the doorway. On his table, beside the tip, she would find a gift for her—a long-stemmed red rose, a pamphlet by Madame Blavatsky, or a Polish poem he had translated and written out in his spidery script, *The greenness of the meadows is the greenness in my heart.*

One evening as Ruth handed Stefan his check, he asked, "Would you honor me by attending a small mandolin concert at my apartment this Sunday?"

Imagining Bohemian dances, tapestry gowns, courtyards under the stars, Ruth said yes at once.

"If you please," Stefan said, "you must not come without a chaperone. A man and a woman alone, it would not be proper."

Ruth persuaded Lennie to escort her. During the concert Ruth was captivated by Stefan's professional performance and the melancholy music so unlike the hymns and organ preludes she had grown up with.

A Woman of Salt

Lennie—Mr. Plaggemars, as Stefan insisted on calling him—was impressed by Stefan's jade chess set and shortwave radio. But, as he told Ruth as they walked home, he couldn't understand what she saw in a paper-skinned, paranoid elitist who jumped to his peephole at every sound in the hall, smelled like garlic, and served bitter tea. "He treats me like a *mind*," she said. "He likes it that I think like a man."

Lennie never went back to Stefan's. When Ruth started visiting Stefan every Wednesday after work, bringing a loaf of bread she had baked for him, Lennie began calling him Old Man Stef-fan, her Project Man. She insisted that she wasn't helping Stefan; she liked him. He played ballads and mazurkas for her on his mandolin, served her crushed raw garlic on hardtack and shavings of dry green cheese on cold boiled potatoes. He gave her chess lessons—"Chess is a mystery, like woman"—and Russian lessons, his fingers pressing against her throat as she struggled to form the impossible gutturals. He taught her things no one in her family of *boers* had ever heard of: graciousness, the authority of expensive shoes, and foot reflexology. "Can you feel it inside?" he would ask, pressing his thumbs deftly into her arch. "Yes," she would say, as the cramp in her stomach released.

While she drank slippery elm infusions to soothe her stomach or alfalfa tonic for her blood, he told her stories. How after he sent a letter to President Eisenhower containing plans he had drawn for an anti-Russian submarine, Secret Service Agents started surveilling him. How once, in the early nineteen hundreds, after Russia had shifted the border into Prussia yet again, he was called upon to deliver a secret message to agents stationed in what used to be his country. The border guards, all peasants who switched loyalties with the wind, stopped him and searched his boots, inside his heels, the lining of his hat. When one of them reached into his pocket and took out his tobacco pouch, squeezing and sniffing it greedily, Stefan told him, "Help yourself. It is finer than anything you have ever tasted or will ever taste again." Shamed, the guard threw the pouch back to him, sent him on his way. He knew how to handle peasants, he said. That's why the Germans had put him in charge of the labor camp outside his village in Poland, a flour mill. He had done an honorable job there—not like some—and could show Ruth official documents proving it.

MARY POTTER ENGEL

Stefan read Ruth's aura, took her to a Theosophical Society meeting in his building, revealed to her cryptic Rosicrucian teachings reserved for members of the highest order, spent hours discussing metaphysics with her. "What you call God," he explained, "cannot be described or defined. It is like an electric current pulsing through the universe, connecting everything in the unity of Mind. It energizes the world. It lights up everyone who knows how to plug into it, so they shine like the stars."

Once, Stefan asked her, "Do you believe in Eternal Life?"

"Lennie's Marxist friends," Ruth said, "say the afterlife is a con to get the people to ignore unjust social conditions, that when you die, it's over, so you have to make a lot of noise now."

"And you?"

"'I believe in the resurrection of the body and the life everlasting,'" Ruth recited sarcastically. "That's what I had to say every Sunday, the Apostles' Creed, but I *don't* believe it."

Stefan pulled a dollar bill from a change pouch he kept in his vest pocket and unfolded it. "Eternal Life is the Eternal in each moment." He pointed to the pyramid on the back of the bill. "Like that all-seeing eye, bathing everything in light, so we see the world in its unity and essence. Do you understand 'essence'"?

"That which makes a thing what it is."

"*Charosho.* Good. If we see the essence, we are not fooled by the many manifestations."

He disappeared into his bedroom and returned with a strongbox. He opened it and removed a sheaf of papers. "My cremation papers," he said, holding them up. "Do you know why I will be cremated? To save my son money and trouble, yes. But truly because the spirit is all that lasts."

"My Opa Willem believes cremation is an abomination," Ruth said, "because the body belongs to Christ and at the resurrection it will be raised and be made like the glorious body of Christ." She deepened her voice and affected a Dutch accent. "'If *ve* are not raised, then *Chrrist* is not raised.'"

"'We shall all be changed,'" Stefan said quietly, "'in the twinkling of an eye, at the last trumpet.' This is Saint Paul, too, yes?"

"Exactly."

Stefan filed the papers and rejoined her. "It is true. Nothing is ever lost; everything returns. When I die, my son and his American wife will throw away my herbs, burn my papers and books, sell my furniture, my mandolins, too. But my spirit will be released into the highest heaven, and when I have enjoyed a few days there, I will come back for a visit. Do you know what I will do?" He smiled impishly, waiting for her reply.

She shrugged her shoulders and shook her head, smiling back.

"I will enter the electric circuitry in my son's house. Every day I will make something blink off at a most inconvenient time, the lights in the den one day, the shaver or hair dryer the next, their new oven the day after that—to remind them. I will visit you, too."

The first evening of summer Ruth arrived at Stefan's apartment with a round loaf of Russian rye. She undid the wrapper and held it out for him to smell.

"Let's eat it now, while it's warm," she said, handing the loaf to him. "I'll slice it while you make tea."

He looked at the dark bread in his hands, then at her. "Each time after you leave—please, you must forgive me—I put your bread in the garbage disposer."

"What?"

"I grind it. Around and around." He swirled his index finger. "Until it is nothing, gone."

"You're teasing."

"Poison, maybe."

"But I would never hurt you."

"One must be careful. You, too." He handed the loaf back to her. "Please."

She took the bread from him. "What if you went with me to buy the ingredients, came home with me and watched me bake the bread?"

"First I must see if you are a friend who will not tarnish."

All summer Ruth worked on Stefan. They rode the bus to the farmer's market and returned to his pocket kitchen to eat raw salads—the intestinal broom, he called them. He let her buy him lunch at a vegetarian cafeteria called Eat Here Now, where the busboys wore vintage dresses and the busgirls wore mechanic's coveralls and combat boots—a protest against the gender confines of a sexist society. She took him to the health food store to buy organic flour and unfiltered honey. When Lennie went away on another job for Bart, Stefan came to her apartment to watch her bake sprouted wheat bread. The last week of August he invited her to bring a loaf of bread to their next meeting.

Wednesday afternoon Ruth wrapped a milk-and-honey loaf in a dish towel, hid it in a paper bag, and carried it to Reinsma's. The minute her shift was over she hurried to Stefan's apartment. She knocked, making a face in the peephole. The door opened a crack and she squeezed through.

"*Svezhyy khleb,*" she said, uncovering the braided loaf and holding it up. Stefan bowed to her, as always, though this time when he rose he smelled not of garlic but of cologne.

"*Svezhyy khleb,*" he said. "Fresh bread."

She raised the loaf to her nose, breathed in its fragrance, then held it out to Stefan. "It is especially *charosho,* I assure you, sir."

"*Spacibo,*" Stefan said, accepting it.

In his open-back leather slippers and blue paisley silk robe, Stefan looked more elegant than ever, like an aristocrat in an old movie. It was the first time she had seen him without his ascot. His neck was a delta of thin blue veins.

"You slice and serve it," she said, setting her apron, heavy and jingling with tips, by the door. "I'll eat my piece first, so you'll be sure no one's tampered with it."

Stefan cut two slices of bread, put them on china plates feathered with cracks, and carried them to the table.

They spread the bread with butter and raw tupelo honey. Stefan took the first bite, smiling at her with his eyes. Ruth smiled in return and bit into her piece. She was so happy she hardly tasted the bread. Her mother, her aunts, the Mrs. Reinsmas of the world, everyone who watched her, waiting for the *Duivel* they saw inside her to show itself so they could chastise it out of her—they were all were wrong: she was not a devil; she could be trusted.

When they finished eating, Stefan stood up and bowed to her. His robe loosened and he pulled the sides together, carefully lapping the left over the right and securing the belt.

"Now a gift for you," he said, reaching for his mandolin on the wall. "I will play a song I wrote for you. It is called, 'My Jewel.'"

He sat on a chair facing her and played a fragile, lonely song.

"Beautiful, beautiful," she said as he stood and bowed. "No one's ever written a song for me before. *Spacibo.*"

"*Pozhaluysta!* And now we will have a lesson on the mandolin so you can play for me. Come, sit," he said, patting the sofa, "if you please."

Ruth sat on the end of the sofa. Stefan sat next to her, so close she could feel his wiry arm through the thin silk of his robe. His cologne tickled her nose and she pinched it, sniffling.

"You do not like my toilet water," he said. "I will remove it." He leaned forward as if to rise.

"It's okay," she said. "It reminds me of my grandpa, Opa Willem. On Sundays he wears Old Spice."

"He is a good man, your *lel?*"

"He's stubborn. You can't change his mind. But he's kind."

"Like you, is it not?" His soft gray eyes glittered with amusement.

"*Touché,*" she said.

Stefan placed the mandolin gently on Ruth's lap. His left arm slid around her back to help her adjust the position, his left hand closing over her left on the mandolin's neck and his right embracing hers over the sound hole.

She studied the golden-brown curve of the mandolin against her white uniform, his liver-blurred hand surrounding hers.

"First we will play a folk song." Leaning closer, he guided her fingers over the strings. As they plucked the simple melody, the mandolin pressed against her breasts.

Ruth straightened her back and pushed out her elbows.

Stefan gripped his arms tighter around her.

His strength surprised her; she thought of him as frail.

"Music heals the soul," he said. "I have not yet explained this to you. Each soul vibrates to its own note. For its harmony in the universe. Mine is here." He closed his eyes and struck the low E string, sending out a rich, resonant sound. "I feel it here," he said, releasing her and cupping his hand on his heart. "Now we must find yours. If you please, close your eyes and listen."

Ruth closed her eyes. She could feel him watching her intently. He stroked the A string. She could feel him straining to feel inside her for a response. He played the string a second time. The vibration tingled the base of her neck.

"There is something? Yes?" he asked.

She opened her eyes, and as she turned to him to tell him no, she couldn't feel anything, she didn't want a music lesson, she wanted to go home, he kissed her, full on the lips.

His lips were thin and hard, as dry as onion skins.

She twisted away from him and stood up, gripping the mandolin's neck. She thrust it toward him.

"I have to use the bathroom."

"Of course."

He rose slowly, his eyes crinkled in happiness. Color shone through his translucent skin, lighting up the web of wrinkles crossing his thin face. He took the instrument from her.

Ruth hurried into the next room, past the military-perfect hospital bed and nightstand crowded with pills and syrups. In the bathroom she locked the door, hiked up her uniform, and peed. The first time Lennie had joked about what Stefan wanted from her, she had been furious. "You're not the measure of all men," she had yelled at him. "Stefan's interested in higher things. He believes in *spiritual* relationships. The body's not important to him. I'm a consciousness to him, neither male nor female."

Washing her hands, she saw Stefan's gold pin was lying on the glass shelf above the sink, next to his shaving brush and mug. She dried her hands, looked again, then unzipped the front of her uniform, snatched the pin, and laid it inside her bra along the underwire. She zipped up and walked out.

Stefan met her in the bedroom. He gazed at her, his eyes still shining. Ruth wondered whether he was reading her aura—black now, or a horrid orange.

"An experiment," Stefan announced proudly, his Adam's apple bulging. "I tested. To see if I was still alive."

A Woman of Salt

She waited, not trusting herself to speak.

"You understand? In that . . . delicate area." He nodded discreetly to his penis, which made no appearance in his carefully closed robe. He smiled at her again, as if proud of them both. "Not one woman in my theosophy group could help me. They are too old and unforgiving." He took her hand and kissed it. "Thank you, my friend."

Ruth withdrew her hand. "I promised to help Lennie frame one of his paintings tonight." She walked past Stefan to the living room, stopping by the door to pick up her apron. "I have to go. Sorry."

He followed her. "Forgive me for not escorting you to the elevator today. In my robe," he laid two bony fingers across the fraying collar, "it is not proper."

Ruth stepped into the hallway, clipped past the elevator to the end of the hall, and hurtled down the five flights of stairs. She dashed through the parking lot and across the street toward Reinsma's. The CLOSED sign hung on the front door of the restaurant and every light was out. Though Mr. Reinsma periodically reminded his wife that keeping the big sign lit over the front door was free advertising and a deterrent to burglars, Mrs. Reinsma refused to waste electricity to illuminate an empty space. Ruth hurried past the deserted building.

She hadn't gone far up her street when she thought she heard a car following her. Its lights off, the car crept along several yards behind her as she walked, keeping pace with her. She walked purposefully, her head high. The car began closing the distance. Ruth sprinted ahead and darted between two houses. Breathing hard, her heart knocking against her chest like a fist against a locked door, she ran toward the back. A dog flung itself against a chain-link fence, barking at her. She ran past it and threw herself into the hedge behind the neighboring house.

Crouching as low as she could, her fingertips resting lightly on the ground, she caught her breath and listened.

The dog stopped barking. There was no sound—no engine whirring, no wheels snapping over loose gravel, no faint whistling of brakes, no car doors clicking open. Only blood pounding in her ears.

She waited, readjusting her balance every few minutes, afraid her leg would go to sleep. The houses around her had closed in on themselves for the night, their windows unlit. A dense cloud cover hid the stars, so that even the metal garbage can standing alongside the shed in the backyard reflected no light. The darkness calmed her.

When her heart had slowed, Ruth peered around the corner of the house.

The street looked empty.

Bracing her back against the rough brick of the house, she slipped her hand down her uniform and took out the pin. In her palm it looked enormous. The diamond in the center of the gold-rimmed black oval flickered like a wakeful eye.

She crushed her hand around it to blind it.

Obdurate, it bit into her flesh.

Scrabbling to her feet, she threw the pin in the garbage can and rushed away, sneaking between darkened houses to her apartment, running as fast as her skirt would allow, afraid to look back to see what might be behind her.

The Allurements of the World

Not content to blame the wife of Lot for weakness, disobedience, ingratitude, and lack of trust in God (the root of all sin, Calvin argues in the *Institutes of the Christian Religion*), in his *Commentary on Genesis* Calvin offers yet another explanation for her turning toward the destruction of Sodom.

> [W]e infer that . . . she was moved by some evil desire . . . for we know He commands us to remember Lot's wife, lest, indeed the allurements of the world should draw us aside from the meditation on the heavenly life.

In pitting meditation on the heavenly life against the pleasures of the corporeal life, Calvin has exposed his deep Augustinian roots: fear of desire. What are Augustine's *Confessions* but the narrative of the soul's weaning from the desires of the body? Why else would he, in *The City of God,* identify the wife of Lot as "a solemn and sacred warning that no one who starts on the path to salvation should ever yearn for the things that he has left behind" (X, 8) and declare her saltiness "a condiment by which to savor this warning" (XVI, 30)?

Given that Calvin assumes with Augustine that the corporeal world is fraught with temptations, what is it that he thinks the wife of Lot longed for so much that she would turn round to see in spite of the divine prohibition? Her beautiful house and furnishings? Her oil lamps and olive jars, vials of fragrant oils? Her horn comb and silver mirror? The heavy cloak of camel hair and the ruby earrings she left behind, forgotten in her haste? Could she have been so in thrall to these things that she would risk her life to catch a final glimpse of them?

Not likely. It is more probable that it is *Calvin* who has suc-cumbed to the temptations of the world here: he has let the cultural association of "Woman" with the lower, material world and the ubiquitous negative stereotype of the greedy, unsatisfiable "Woman" color his exegesis of the wife of Lot.

Consider this: It wasn't the things of the world that the wife of Lot loved, but the world itself, the loud confusion, the crowding mess of it; its constant re-creation of color and texture and warmth; its profligate ways, spilling over constantly in glorious abundance and waste; the way everything in it arises and slips away, so dear in its disappearing.

If she so loved *this* world, the world of inexhaustible life, a world far removed from Lot's God of death and judgment, why wouldn't she have given her life to see it one last time?

Purge the flesh and you canker the spirit.

EDWARD DAHLBERG, *Can These Bones Live?*

Refuge

It was mescaline that drove Ruth to live with Baptist missionaries in Switzerland.

After she and her boyfriend, Lennie Plaggemars, were expelled from Dordrecht College for "conduct unbecoming a Christian," they renewed their pursuit of Blake's promise in *The Marriage of Heaven and Hell:* "If the doors of perception were cleansed every thing would appear to man as it is, infinite. For man has closed himself up, till he sees all things thro' narrow chinks of his cavern." Reading Huxley convinced them that *only* mescaline's "infernal, corrosive method" could destroy the cavern of piety they had inherited and reveal a world shining with the Oneness of Being.

She and Lennie had both grown up prisoners to the grum dualism of Dutch Calvinism—total depravity *or* the glory of God, flesh *athwart* spirit, Christ *against* Culture, faith *or* reason, those washed in the blood of Jesus Christ *versus* those drowning in the World of Devil cards, alcohol, dancing, Cat Stevens lyrics, and other unspeakable evils. Ruth struggled to break free through reason, practicing suspicion of the unfaithful body and heart and giving herself wholly to the certainties of the mind. Lennie painted. "Like Blake says," he argued, "'there's no body distinct from soul and no soul distinct from body. The path to the infinite is through the sensual.'"

That every one of Ruth's previous experiments with drugs had ended in disaster only strengthened her resolve to find Oneness of Being. Hers was not the perseverance of the Synod of Dort's TULIP of faith she had been raised on: Total depravity, Unconditional election, Limited atonement, Irresistible grace, and Perseverance of the saints; it was the cussedness of desire, a longing to have her mind opened up to everything and to have everything open unto her, an unquenchable thirst that burned stronger with each failure. More than ever, still, she wanted to leave behind her torn self and lose herself in the glorious possibilities of the Infinite, the plenitude of the mind of God; she wanted to drown in God.

Ruth swallowed the mescaline eagerly. Not that she counted on becoming one of Huxley's "happily transfigured majority." Lennie had a better chance to encounter "St. Michael and all the angels" because he was an artist, Protean by nature. She was brittle, anxious. She had no imagination.

As soon as they took it, they drove to Lake Michigan, where they ran along the shore flying Lennie's thirty-foot dragon kite. Once they were warm, they walked onto the lake, crawling and sliding among the gnarled ice hills, searching for a ship. The winter before, they had found a freighter trapped in the ice, hulking in the frozen waves, listing to one side, cold metal glinting with moonlight.

Lennie was on fire. He saw each star pulsing with its own glorious color and raved about the holiness of colors, how it felt to be inside all of them at once. "Huxley wasn't exaggerating," he said. "Mescaline *is* the fruit of the tree of life. It turns you back into Adam, lets you see what he saw that first morning, 'the miracle, moment by moment, of naked existence.'"

Ruth saw nothing. The forsaken hills they struggled over one after the other, the blackened sky bearing down—everything seemed empty, emptying.

Driving home from the lake, her bones cold, the drug bitter on her

A Woman of Salt

tongue, Ruth willed herself to believe Huxley was right: Mescaline *would* help a poor visualizer like herself see what artists see every moment, everything shining with the manifest light of Is-ness. The night wasn't over. She still had a chance to see the world without splitting or tearing—no self *and* world, no self *or* other, no body *against* mind—everything united in the mind of God.

Back at their apartment Lennie tacked a bedsheet to the wall and began painting. As undulating ice-blue hills spread across the blankness, Ruth sank into the easy chair, her body growing heavier until she pulled free from it and drifted above it. Looking down, she saw Lennie dipping his brush, spreading paint, switching from one corner of the painting to the other and back again in a frenzied bliss. The girl in the chair was still except for her breathing. Ruth counted the breaths, sure that if she missed one, the girl in the chair would die. One hundred and twenty-one, one hundred and twenty-two, one hundred and twenty-three.

A string rose from the girl's head. More strings were attached to her chin, elbows, hands, knees, and feet. Lennie, too, had sprouted strings. As he waved his brush back and forth and swung around for paint, they crossed and separated, a furor of dancing lines. Ruth followed Lennie's strings into the dark space above, where they ended in two square wooden crosses. A giant hand held each wooden cross, working the strings. The right hand was busy. It tilted its cross, wiggled it, stopped, moved back, and Lennie brushed paint on the sheet, stared at the stroke for a moment, and stepped back to appraise it. The hand dipped forward, Lennie bent down. The hand drew up, Lennie stood. The left hand was still. The strings trailing to the girl were slack, leaving her slumped in the chair.

Ruth drifted above the giant hands. A thicker set of strings rose from the fingers and wrists and led to a second set of wooden crosses twice as large as the first. These crosses in turn were held by a pair of hands larger than the pair below, and the larger pair was manipulated by still thicker strings and larger hands. Back and back, as far as she could see, there were strings and puppeteers' hands.

"Sounds like your mother," Lennie said when Ruth told him what she had seen. "Doomsday Report," he said, "Helen of Hell Controls the World."

"That's not funny."

"It's just infinite regression, Ruth. Some old lady once told William James that the world rested on turtles all the way down, no way out. I could do a strip like that. Not a stack of Yertle the Turtles, but your predestination nightmare—no free will, just a chain of puppeteers."

"Do you think the world is real?"

"'Do what you like, this life's a fiction / and is made up of contradiction.'"

"Fuck you and your fucking Blake."

"Settle down, Ruth. You had a bad trip, that's all. Forget it. The world *is* real. We don't make it up."

"So *we're* the ones who aren't real?"

"Why do you have to choose between them, as if they're enemies? It's not self *or* world, it's *both*. They're bound up together."

"How? Tell me how."

"Imagination binds everything up—self and world, mind and body, spirit and flesh, whatever you want to call the two sides. It creates a space for both to cohabit long enough to transform one another; it makes a container in which spirit and flesh can become one, here and now, continually *becoming* one as they meet in the imagination, a kind of dynamic eternity in *this* world. That's what I believe, anyway, misguided ex-Calvinist Blakean that I am."

"Who or what pulled your strings to make you say that right now?"

Lennie put his arms around her and kissed the top of her head. "People aren't determined, Ruth. They *care* about each other. Sometimes in fucked-up ways, but it's still real." He held her closer, kissed her eyes, which were squeezed shut. "Let's make love, call you back from hell or wherever you went."

Hours later, when Ruth woke screaming, Lennie held her and predicted the mescaline's effects would fade in a day or two. "God's not punishing you," he said. "Stop torturing yourself."

The drug's grip on Ruth tightened, clamping her mind shut against all logical maneuvering. She was convinced that the only choice left to

A Woman of Salt

her—if it was a choice—was believing that the drug had permanently altered her thinking patterns or that it had uncovered the true structure of the world. Both possibilities left her daydreaming about stepping in front of buses or falling through the ice.

When a letter from her mother arrived, offering to send her to Switzerland for a year, Ruth took it as a sign. Though she hated herself for doing it, she had been crouching over her Bible every night after work, sitting cross-legged on the floor in her fishnet stockings, hot-pants, and halter, letting the pages fall open at random, and seizing upon the first words her eyes fell upon.

She was desperate for a message like the one Saint Augustine had received. Frustrated over knowing that truth is incorporeal yet remaining unable to submit his fleshly desires to the life of the mind, Augustine overheard a child singing, "Take it and read, take it and read." Immediately he opened the Scriptures *sortes Virgilianus* and read the first passage on which his eyes fell: *Not in reveling and drunkenness, not in lust and wantonness, not in quarrels and rivalries. Rather, arm yourselves with the Lord Jesus Christ; spend no more thought on nature and nature's appetites.* Within days he had fulfilled his mother's prayers for him: he abandoned his beloved concubine and son and submitted to baptism. Released from the drag of the flesh and devoted to the life of the spirit, he escaped his torment: "Our hearts are restless 'til they find their rest in Thee."

To find such a refuge in a life of the mind unencumbered by the body was what Ruth had longed for since she was a child. From the beginning she fled God everywhere and everywhere she longed for God's presence—an intolerable tearing within her, rending body from mind, spirit from flesh, self from self. She learned how to save herself from the torment of dividings by choosing one side of the split to live in wholly and casting off the other. Faced with a choice between a rejecting righteous God or the forgiving mess of the World, she chose the World; between being chosen to share a judgmental God's glory or to live with the damned, the damned; between divine determinism or human freedom, freedom; between her mother or her father, her father; between the treacherous body or the certainties of the mind, the mind; between her mother or her self—that one was harder.

MARY POTTER ENGEL

Even allowing for rhetorical flourish—"Who can recall to me the sins I committed as a baby?" he asked when recounting his immoderate sucking at his mother's breast—Augustine's conversion was more dramatic than anything Ruth hoped for. She would have been satisfied with Paul's wedding nostrum, *Though I speak with the tongue of angels and have not love. . . .* But in spite of jiggling and slanting, her Bible invariably opened to divine retribution, prophecies of destruction, people fleeing in terror from friends, fathers, enemies, God. "Whatever God has brought to pass," she read, "will recur evermore"; "They hatch adder's eggs and weave spider webs; He who eats of those eggs will die, and if one is crushed, it hatches out a viper."

Ruth regretted eating the egg of wonders with Lennie.

The night she received her mother's offer, her Bible opened to "Take to the hills like a bird!" She called immediately. Though she could hear Helen gloating at having enticed her daughter away from bartending and fornication by appealing to her love of adventure, Ruth went ahead with the arrangements. And though Lennie accused Ruth of selling out, two days later she was on her way to Lausanne.

Dr. Campbell, a Scottish evangelical working for the Wycliffe Society, met Ruth at the Geneva airport. Mrs. Campbell, Dutch-American like the VanderZichts and a friend of Ruth's mother, welcomed her at their tiny apartment with a big-boned hug. The Campbell's three children, who had grown up swimming in crocodile-infested rivers in Africa and now rode rapid transit and chattered in perfect French, smiled shyly at her.

After supper every night, Dr. Campbell read a chapter of the Bible at the table, the way Ruth's father did at home, working in a continuous chain from Genesis 1, "In the beginning God created the heavens and the earth," through Revelation 22, "The grace of the Lord Jesus Christ be with all the saints. Amen." But unlike in Ruth's family, at the end of the chapter Dr. Campbell did not choose one of the children at random to repeat the last verse, word for word, and then read the entire chapter over again if the child could not repeat the verse exactly. Instead, every evening after the reading the Campbells prayed out loud together until the spirit moved—close to an hour usually, twenty minutes if Ruth was lucky. If Ruth hadn't been captive to apathy, she would have found their warm sincerity and cheer unbearable. During the day Dr. Campbell trained young missionaries to evangelize the world; Mrs. Campbell ran a free clinic; and the three kids attended school. Ruth wandered the tidy streets in her work boots, velvet bell-bottoms, and sharkskin ski parka, looking for the university where she was supposed to study French literature. Everywhere she turned, from the measured *bonjours* of the impeccably dressed burghers to the gold timepieces in the shop windows, Swiss formality and calculation met her, tightening the determining bands of puppet logic around her.

Less than three weeks after arriving at the Campbell's house, Ruth contacted The Refuge, a retreat for renegade Christians and other searchers not far from Lausanne, just below the village of Champs des Fleurs. The community was run by Dr. Dietrich, a scholar with a reputation for demonstrating that it was possible to be intelligent *and* Christian. His books had been required by a hip philosophy professor at Dordrecht College, and Ruth had been impressed enough to remember Dietrich's arguments against the trap of false reason and for a leap of faith. The day she received the letter from Dietrich's secretary inviting her to join the community, Ruth told the Campbells she was leaving the next morning.

On the train, speeding toward mountains shining with snow, a crack opened in the puppet vision and Ruth began to hope she would find a way out. Lennie and his friends would have a good laugh about The Refuge, mock it as antirevolutionary, naïve, a cop-out—and her as well. She didn't care; she wanted to breathe.

In Orsières a Refuge resident overheard her asking where to catch the bus to Champs des Fleurs and offered to show her the way. A biologist from London, Adrian had spent the day shopping in Martigny— he showed her the early French edition of Pascal's *Pensées* he had picked up—and was heading back to Dr. D's Mountaintop, as he called it.

As the bus wound steadily up the mountain, Adrian deluged Ruth with information. There was a ski resort five kilometers above The Refuge and many community members wandered up there for a glass of mulled wine, a *gâteau,* or a run down the slopes. The food was dreadful—all muesli yogurt, cold porridge, soybean loaves, and ruined tea.

Helmut's and Jim's chalets were the best—not as regimented as Dietrich's and his sons-in-law's households. Most of the American guests were witless—their minds a complete muddle—the Germans silly, the Dutch messy, the Swiss crazed, the Asians altogether too cheery, the French absent—the food, you understand—and the bloody English always behaving *comme en pays conquis*. Dr. Dietrich couldn't speak French worth a damn and fancied himself an exorcist: people from all over Switzerland—worse than England in its fascination with demons and Satanology—came to him to be healed. Mrs. Dietrich was another matter altogether, a dear and a saint. The Dietrichs' son was a brat who was always off skiing or *faisant l'amour* with one of female guests in a villager's barn or field. There had been quite a few rows over him. *Les Americains,* Adrian said wistfully, *ils sont libres sous le ciel, pas comme les Anglais et les Suisses.*

Ruth did not tell Adrian that she had come to live in Dietrich's World-denying community because of mescaline and that she had come to mescaline by loving the World and God and wanting to lose herself in them; that she had fled to the mountains seeking a fortress from them and from herself, a purity of spirit that would eat away the torn self she had struggled so hard to escape. Who knew how Adrian would capsulize her to the Refuge regulars?

The bus let them off and Adrian walked her to the Dietrichs' chalet at the summit of the community. As they climbed the icy paths, Ruth's breathing grew labored. To get more air, she unzipped her parka and pulled her sweater away from her neck. She felt dizzy and though the sun had begun to set, the snow shone with a harsh light that made her head hurt.

At the door to the Dietrichs' chalet, Adrian waved cheerio. Immediately Ruth found herself sitting down to dinner with twenty others. "Ben-ven-new a La Rayfoodge," Dr. Dietrich called to her from the head of the table. Though he was a large man, his voice was high and scratchy, as if something were permanently squeezing his throat, pinching the sounds out. The tiny voice emerging from the hulking body reminded Ruth of Lennie's high-pitched voiceovers to muted television shows and she smiled. Lennie would have had a great time impersonating Dr. Dietrich.

A Woman of Salt

During the meal Dr. Dietrich discoursed and everyone not invited to answer his questions kept silent. As he talked he furrowed his brow and narrowed his eyes to slits. His face was a confusion of sadness and severity and arrogance. There were more conflicting lines in his cheeks alone than in an El Greco painting and Ruth felt queasy looking at them. His subject was *des spectacles,* the world as the theater of God's glory, our lives a mystery play enjoyed by God and the angels. He rambled. What Ruth could follow she found obvious, though everyone else at the table seemed spellbound. When he announced after the prayer that he would be leaving soon for a four-week tour of the States, she was not disappointed.

After supper Ruth sat cross-legged on the chapel floor to hear a lecture by Colin Byrnes, Dietrich's right-hand man. The lecture, connecting Sartre to the phenomenologists and existentialists, analyzing his main concepts, and critiquing his rationalism from a Christian point of view, was brilliant. Ruth clapped heartily with the others when it was over.

Adrian stood up, interrupting the applause. "It's easy enough, isn't it," he said to Byrnes, "to pick off a rationalist committed primarily to his own brilliance. Much harder, I should think, to dismiss a philosopher whose thoughts arise out of the suffering of the world. Why not have a go at Camus and his novels of compassion?"

Colin gave a lengthy answer outlining the limits of all reason and immanentist thinking, even in its most humane forms, when it was not tied to the Archimedean point of Christ.

A black-haired, delicate young man stood up. Palms pressed together, he bowed to Colin, then to the audience. "In my country," he said, smiling sweetly, "good hot peppers, but no Christ."

There was uncertain laughter.

"Before met Dr. Dietrich, I was a kite flying in sky, free. Every wind rip me, push me off course. Now have Christ. Dr. Dietrich tied my string to Christ this rock. Now I float high in the heaven, but never disappear."

He bowed again and sat down.

While everyone was clapping, Ruth left the chapel. Kite strings,

MARY POTTER ENGEL

puppet strings—it made no difference: they all tied you to someone else's whims, strangled you.

She hurried through the starry darkness to Jim and Monica's chalet, where she had been assigned a bunk in a lower-level room. The room felt chilly when she entered, and she was glad she had brought two pairs of wool underwear. She hadn't needed them in the Campbell's apartment, which was so warm she had to remove her nightgown once she was under the sheet.

Ruth hoisted her suitcase onto the bunk. While she was unpacking, three of her roommates came in. Margaret and Deirdre, who shared the bunk across from Ruth, were from England, traveling with a Christian rock group. The lead guitarist was Margaret's husband, who had been assigned to another chalet. Annie, who slept on the bunk below Ruth's, had been sent to The Refuge by her Iowa family two years ago because of some trouble she wouldn't reveal. She had advanced to serving as Mrs. Dietrich's assistant. She adored Mrs. Dietrich, whom she called "the mother I never had" and "a spiritual genius, very grounded, revolutionary."

"Mrs. Dietrich says 'Everything that lives is holy,'" Annie said.

"She stole that from Blake," Ruth said. "The last line of 'A Song of Liberty.'"

A half hour after curfew the cot against the outside wall, under the window, was still empty. Annie had told Ruth that Cynthia had arrived from California three months ago with another witch, who had slept in the bed Ruth occupied now, and a warlock. The three kept to themselves and were rumored to have private appointments with Dr. Dietrich. Cynthia's friends had left abruptly a few weeks ago. Occasionally in the night Annie and Margaret heard Cynthia opening vials of liquids that she sniffed, dabbed on her wrists, or mixed while chanting. Best to leave her alone, they said.

The next morning Ruth got up in the dark, splashed freezing water on her face in the tiny sink by the door, went upstairs for oatmeal and hot cocoa, and began the daily work-study-prayer discipline of monastic communities that The Refuge prided itself on. In the morning, half the community reported for duties while the other half studied. After

A Woman of Salt

lunch they switched. In the evenings everyone gathered in the chapel for lectures.

Ruth was assigned to Mrs. Dietrich's kitchen. When she showed up the first day, Annie was peeling carrots. She taught Ruth to wash her hands like a nurse, splaying the fingers and rubbing soap between them, and told her to peel and mince a ten pound bag of onions. When Ruth was halfway through the mound, Mrs. Dietrich arrived to explain the rules of the kitchen and to examine Ruth's work.

She was not chopping the onions properly. She was holding the knife incorrectly, starting with a vertical instead of a horizontal cut, and not attending to the width of the slices, consequently ending up with irregular pieces. "Ugly, undercooked chunks call attention to themselves in the stew and ruin the composition of the whole," Mrs. Dietrich said. Ruth tried again but could not make pieces of uniform size. Mrs. Dietrich took the knife from her and showed her how to do it, saying, "Those who prove themselves faithful in small things will show themselves faithful in the large." Ruth began again. After a moment Mrs. Dietrich took the knife from her. "I'll finish these," she said. "You may clean out the ovens. You'll find rags and cleaners under the sink."

Ruth spent the next two hours with her head inside an oven that hadn't been cleaned in years. The sides were covered by a thick layer of annealed grease. Charred hills rose across the bottom. She sprayed cleaner everywhere, waited, then began scraping furiously. The fumes from the cleaner made her dizzy, and every few seconds she drew her head out for fresh air. "Good work," Mrs. Dietrich said. "Don't forget to wipe all the chemical residue off the elements and the bulb when you're finished, so the odor won't taint the food."

When the oven was spotless and Ruth stood before her covered with black grease, Mrs. Dietrich put her arm around her and beamed at her. "Lovely job," she said.

Ruth stepped away from her, trying not to show her revulsion.

"I know you don't agree," Mrs. Dietrich said quietly. "You want to forget about the body and its burdens so you can pursue the life of the mind. But I believe the body is not inferior to the mind. In fact, it's necessary to it. If you try to separate the two, you corrupt them both.

For either one to be hallowed, the two have to be joined together in our daily living. Wisdom comes when the two are in harmony. That's where joy is born."

She paused, waiting for Ruth to argue, but Ruth said nothing. She stood there with her arms crossed over her stomach, chewing her lower lip and looking to the side so she wouldn't have to meet her eye.

"Don't forget the life of the body, Ruth," Mrs. Dietrich said, her voice even softer now. "You need it to be whole."

Ruth nodded, not trusting herself to speak. Annie had said Mrs. Dietrich was writing a book. Probably *The Joy of Keeping House for Christ*, Ruth thought.

"Off you go, then," Mrs. Dietrich said, furtively touching Ruth's forearm. "And don't forget to eat a good lunch before you study."

That afternoon Ruth sat in a cubicle in the Study Room kneading her sore forearms while listening to a tape on the Parousia. As Dr. Dietrich droned on, she thought of how ridiculous it was for the men to be assigned to help with carpentry, plumbing, electronics, and farming, while the women had to clean toilets and mop floors; how much Mrs. Dietrich reminded her of her mother, relentlessly domestic, commanding, and critical. After supper she asked Annie to assign her to another job, and the next morning she was transferred to housekeeping at Donna and Rich's chalet.

On her day off, Tuesdays, Ruth walked to Champs des Fleurs below, the ski village above, or the farms in between. The roads and trails were immaculately kept—she once came upon a worker walking behind a logging truck sweeping up dead branches and other natural debris from the logging road. The mountains themselves seemed perversely domesticated—fields neatly fenced off, watering troughs carefully placed, cows adorned with clanging bells, outlying huts strategically placed for maximum beauty and function. The tidiness set her on edge. She gave up exploring to read in her bunk.

Sundays Ruth volunteered to stay behind to clean up the breakfast mess while everyone else went to services. She took her time washing the dishes, relishing the solitude and silence.

As she was finishing the pots and pans one Sunday, the bell on the doorknob jingled, then stopped suddenly. The door closed quietly.

Thinking Monica's husband had run back for his organ music, she called out, "Jim?"

A drop of water from the faucet splashed into the sink. Soap bubbles snuffed out one by one. It was foolish to be afraid, she told herself. Though the villagers complained occasionally about *les Americains* getting drunk in town, the only danger at The Refuge was falling on the icy paths.

Ruth resumed scrubbing. She scraped a spatula against the blackened bottom of the oatmeal pot. Deciding to try her mother's trick, she poured in a few tablespoons of baking soda and added a little vinegar and water to boil off the charred pieces. As she turned to place the pot on the burner, she saw a man standing a few feet from her, watching her intently.

She sucked in her breath. "Fuckin' A."

The man stared at her, his half-smile not wavering.

"Who are you?" she asked. "How long have you been there?"

"Trois minutes, à peu près."

He was slight, like her, as if everything in him had concentrated in his thoughts, causing the flesh to atrophy. Dark brown hair shagged over his ears. His face was fine-boned, long and thin, with the smoothest skin she had ever seen. Though he was clean shaven, a dark shadow covered his cheeks, upper lip, and chin. He was exactly her height, which made it hard to avoid looking him in the eye. Behind his gold wire-rims a tight web of blood veins spread across the blue-white surface, reaching for the blurred rim of the irises. The irises were a brown she had never seen before, almost as black as hers, but flecked with red and gold, the colors pulsing around the dark swallow-hole in the center.

"Et vous ne l'avez pas su," he added with matter-of-fact triumph.

She wanted to return to her cleaning, to let him know he did not intimidate her, but she could not turn her back to him.

"Qui êtes vous?" Though she knew he understood English, Ruth spoke in French to let him know that she, too, was a force to be reckoned with.

"Je suis Jean-Pierre," he answered. "Like the apostles." He gave a small laugh.

The sound of his voice, speaking and laughing, was like a stream purling over loose stones.

Drying her hands, she told him she was walking to church and he could come with her if he wanted. He nodded agreement and she ran downstairs to grab her *Sainte Bible,* a nineteenth-century leather edition whose smell she loved. She threw on her parka and they began walking in the bright sun.

Jean-Pierre wore only a black vest over a white shirt with sleeves rolled to the elbow, exposing his fragile forearms. The long bones so thinly covered with flesh made Ruth want to cry. She offered her Bible to him, thinking he would prefer it to the English translations in the chapel.

"This belongs to *you?*" he asked in disbelief.

"Yes," she said. "Why not?"

He studied the cover without taking the book from her. *"Le Seigneur du monde,"* he said, with a grunt of a laugh.

At the entrance to the chapel, they stopped to stomp the snow off their boots. Inside the congregation was singing "Fairest Lord Jesus."

"They're singing Jesus Christ," Jean-Pierre said, "the incarnate one!"

"We're not too late," Ruth said, opening the door.

The chapel was packed. People from outside the community often came to The Refuge on Sunday to hear Dr. Dietrich or Colin preach. She squeezed herself into the crowd by the door and motioned Jean-Pierre to follow.

Jean-Pierre put one foot on the threshold, but quickly withdrew it, backing out the doorway onto the cement walkway.

"There's plenty of room for both of us," Ruth whispered.

"It's against my religion," he muttered.

Ruth watched him hurry away, then found a seat on the floor, by the bank of windows that overlooked the Dents du Midi. With the sun warming her shoulders and head, she thought of Lennie joking about neckties, over-boiled potatoes, tortured pot roast, bloodless abstractions, intellectual snobs being against his religion. "The religion of life! The religion of exuberance!" he would shout, stabbing his arms in the air. Then he would throw his arms around her and dance her until she was giddy, singing "'The cistern contains: the fountain overflows!'"

A Woman of Salt

Lennie believed in dancing. He believed in pounding his feet on the earth and smearing his hands with colors and feeling the forms of things with his fingers and palms. "'The head Sublime,'" he would say, reciting his favorite proverb from Blake, "'the heart Pathos, the genitals Beauty, the hands & feet Proportion.'" Sometimes he made Ruth forget her fear of her body, forget to keep her distance from it, and she would slip back for a moment, return home to the joy of her flesh moving through the world like a graceful swimmer, her body and her mind one, not two pulling against each other. She missed him.

Ruth didn't mention meeting Jean-Pierre to anyone. If he was a stranger, it was better not to say anything about him, since the Dietrichs were suspicious of the local people. If he was a Refuge regular, she didn't want to be told anything about him. She wanted to figure him out herself.

For two weeks she did not see Jean-Pierre again. She went on as usual, housekeeping in the morning, listening to tapes in the afternoon, attending lectures after supper. One evening Colin organized a talent show in the chapel. Margaret's band played, a woman read a poem, and an Indonesian man announced he would dance a portion of the *Ramayana*.

"You will see in my dance," Ved said, "how Ravana, the Great Tormentor, the Great Deceiver and Tempter, steals Sita and imprisons her in the underworld and how Rama searches for Sita and at last kills Ravana with arrows to rescue his love so she can rule with him once again." He bowed to Colin. "Rama is Christ, who rescues our soul from the torment of separation from him to dwell with him on the throne of God's glory."

As Ved danced, the graceful love of Rama and Sita, Sita's beauty, Rama's longing for Sita, his torment when she was ripped from his side, and the joy of their reunion filled the room. Ruth thought of how happy Lennie would be watching the drama. "It's a celebration of the union of God and world, spirit and flesh, soul and body," she could hear him whispering excitedly to her, "the soul's need for the body, its love for the body, and vice versa. Without either one there's no life, no art, no joy. Body is dead without soul, mind is barren without body."

Immediately after the performance he would cut shadow puppets of Rama and Sita out of cardboard, paint them, make them dance on sticks behind a row of candles and marvel out loud at how two-dimensional dolls could convey the rounded truth of life.

Ved brought his palms together and bowed to the audience. Ruth bowed back, desolate that the story had ended.

As the crowd gathered coats and backpacks, Colin took the microphone.

"Before we leave," he said, "there is a matter we must discuss."

The crowd groaned, thinking it another scolding about offending the villagers or not keeping the tape library neat.

"The dance we have just seen," Colin said, "for which we are very grateful, indeed," he smiled and nodded at Ved, "was lovely. Nonetheless, it contains some rather troubling ideas which Dr. Dietrich and I would like to call your attention to."

As far as Ruth knew, Dr. Dietrich was still in the States lecturing.

"True Christianity is not a philosophy, like Buddhism. It cannot be merged with other religions. Neither is it a syncretist religion, able to absorb other myths or coexist with them. True Christianity is a strict monotheism which excludes worship of all other gods and drives out all myths. Although Ved's intentions are honorable, the strain of pantheism in his dance must be refuted. The truth of Christ, the cosmic Christ or Logos of John's gospel, is not that God *is* the World, that God *is* the rocks and the rivers and trees and should be worshipped in them, but that God, though omnipresent, transcends the finite world and must be worshipped as qualitatively distinct from the world. We do not worship creation but the Creator. I say this not to criticize Ved or to make him feel that his conversion is not authentic, but to remind all of us of a difficult concept. Thank you."

Ved bowed to the audience. "Please, forgive my ignorance," he said. Turning to Colin, he bowed and said, "Thank you, sir. I want to learn."

Everyone clapped.

Adrian stood up, but Ruth couldn't stay to listen to him argue with Colin. She walked out in a fury, as much because Colin had humiliated Ved as because he was spouting the same destructive dualism she had fled: God *or* the world, Christianity *against* culture. Like her Calvinist family and ancestors, Colin insisted that the two sides were doomed to battle each other unceasingly, tearing everything apart.

Ruth was tired of battling, tired of the intolerable tearing within. She was tired of choosing and of the fear of not being chosen, tired of running between anger and hopelessness, exhausted by promises of wholeness and belonging that were never fulfilled. When she reached her bunk, she collapsed into sleep.

That night she dreamed of Rama searching for Sita. He found her chained at the bottom of a dark stone stairway. As he stood at the top of the stairs, water began rising, swiftly flooding the dungeon. Sita stood up, her body straining against the manacles, every cell calling out to him. Rama leaned toward her to free her, but Ravana's eyes, green and metallic, fixed him to the spot. The waters reached Sita's neck. She tilted back her head and lifted her chin, higher, higher, her eyes seeking Rama's. The water kept rising. It lapped against the stone walls, over Sita's face. She held her nostrils above the surface, fighting to breathe, but the water covered them, silent and cold.

On her next Tuesday off, Ruth found a copy of Narayan's translation of the *Ramayana* in Martigny. In study hall the rest of the week, headphones on and a tape spinning, she read the story hidden inside her notebook. After her evening chores, she lay on her bunk musing, imagining Rama and Sita inseparable as children, Rama in exile once Sita has been torn from him, Rama searching for his love, uncovering Ravana's deceits, plunging arrows into Ravana's evil heart, releasing Sita from captivity, Rama and Sita ascending together. She felt Rama's longing for Sita and Sita's for him. It surged in her blood, expanding her cells, crowding out her thoughts. What if God and the world, soul and body, belonged to each other the way Rama and Sita did, so that when apart they longed for each other, when separated they found their way back to each other?

Jean-Pierre showed up that Saturday morning, intercepting Ruth on her way to her morning chores. Excited, he invited her to come to the flea market in Martigny to hunt for old books. Adrian, headed for the study chalet, passed them at a distance and waved. Ruth looked at her watch, hoping he wouldn't come over to chat.

"Are you all right?" Adrian called.

MARY POTTER ENGEL

"Yeah," Ruth said, nodding vigorously.

"You look as if you're deep in thought."

"The mystery of the Parousia and all that. You know."

"Do you want to have a cup of tea?" Adrian asked, walking toward her.

"Can't now, thanks," she said, hurrying away and waving good-bye. "Late for work. See you later."

Ruth would have left with Jean-Pierre right away, but the thought of being reprimanded by Mrs. Dietrich held her back. She asked Jean-Pierre to wait an hour. She'd complete as much work as she could and then tell Donna she had to lie down because she wasn't feeling well. No one would miss her until bedtime.

By nine-thirty she and Jean-Pierre were on their way down the mountain. He wouldn't take the bus, so they hitchhiked. By ten-thirty they were ambling through stalls cluttered with jars of antique buttons, piles of silk velvets and lace, cut-glass chandeliers, Turkish coffee pots and enormous bowls made of copper, thick cotton underwear and wool socks, leather purses and belts from Florence, junky key chains and statues of the Virgin Mary. Everyone was shouting the rarity of their wares and the bargain prices. The smell of *frites* and beignets was everywhere. Ruth hadn't been as happy since she was a child.

Just before the booksellers, they passed a woman selling old clothes. Ruth stopped to rifle through a pile of French navy sweaters. Slung over a chair nearby was a long fur coat. She stroked the sleeve.

"How much is this?" she asked the vendor.

"Seven hundred francs," the woman said.

Ruth picked it up. The coat weighed at least twenty pounds. The skin was denser and tougher than any leather she had ever seen. It seemed impenetrable. The collar, cuffs, and belt were tanned smooth, but the rest was covered in long, thick fur. There was a patch on the top front and on one of the sleeves where the fur had worn away, but they were not that noticeable. She lifted the coat to her nose, expecting the odor of mothballs and un-aired closets. It smelled like a freshly uprooted tree trunk, damp and faintly pungent. She slipped out of her parka to try it on. From the fitted waist the coat angled out to form an A-line skirt that came down to her ankles. The sleeves covered her

A Woman of Salt

hands, leaving her fingers exposed. The coat hung heavily on her. It seemed to pull her toward the ground. To her surprise, the weight calmed her. She had spent most of her life seaching for weightlessness, but the way the thick hide hung about her, wrapping her in a firm embrace, made her feel at rest. She stood the collar up, folded one flap of the coat over the other, and cinched the belt tight. She couldn't imagine being warmer.

"What kind of fur is this?"

"I don't know, *Mademoiselle*."

"Bearskin," Jean-Pierre said, watching Ruth model the coat.

"It looks very nice on you," the vendor said, shaking her head approvingly toward Ruth.

Ruth took off the coat and examined the inside. The label gave a Rotterdam address. She held the coat up to the woman. "What about this tear here, in the back, and this mildew patch by the hem?"

"Six hundred and fifty francs, *Mademoiselle,* no less."

Ruth had less than half that amount hidden inside her bra and she wanted that coat. She laid it over the chair and walked away.

"It's smelly," Jean-Pierre said, following her. "Mold is something you can never get rid of."

"I know. But I have to have that coat."

"That ridiculous thing? It weighs more than an anchor."

"I can't explain it. I just have to have it. I wish I had enough money. Maybe I should bargain for it?"

"The vendors here are very clever. Leave it."

They wandered through the other stalls, fingering shell buttons and brass candelabra, sheepskin slippers and Parisian scarves, but Ruth could not shake the lovely feel of the coat's weight, its heat. Lennie would have loved her in it. He would have spun her around until she was dizzy, growled in pleasure at her, and begun a giant painting of a yellow-and-red bear-woman in his head. He would have insisted she buy the coat, conned the vendor into trading it for a charcoal portrait of herself.

"Back in a minute," Ruth said to Jean-Pierre.

She offered the woman all her cash plus her coat, the fashionable faux-sharkskin parka her mother had sent her before she left for the Campbells'.

Ruth walked away wearing the fur coat. Thrilled with its smell, the way its weight pressed her toward the earth, and the hard flap of the hem against her ankles when she moved, she twirled around and gave Jean-Pierre a quick hug. They wandered hand-in-hand through the market to a café, where they drank cups of thick coffee and discussed the books they had bought, Bergson for her, Baudelaire for him. As he spoke of Baudelaire's dark genius, Jean-Pierre's face was in continual motion, his eyes shining behind his wire-rims and his hair, such a soft brown, falling into greater disarray each time he ran his hand through it excitedly or shook his head to emphasize a point. His intensity made Ruth feel at home. At last she had met a person whose energy matched hers, who wasn't frightened of it. Lennie was obsessed with the power of the imagination, but he wasn't strung tightly enough. He seemed worn by her energy at times, wary of it. Jean-Pierre fed on it.

At nine they parted at the Orsières bus station. Jean-Pierre wanted her to stay longer, but Ruth didn't dare risk Mrs. Dietrich's fury by coming in past curfew.

When the bus for Champs des Fleurs pulled into the quai, Ruth turned to hug Jean-Pierre good-bye, but he was already gone. Loneliness rushed into her. She felt everything in the station disconnecting, moving farther apart, opening into a pit that was swallowing her. The noise of voices and coughs and shoe heels and bundles echoed in the emptiness. She hugged her coat to her more tightly, buried her nose in the musky fur.

Back at the chalet she didn't hang the coat in the entryway with the others. She spread it across the end of her bunk and fell into a deep sleep.

She woke with a start, fully alert. The room was horribly cold and still. No shifting under blankets, no hoarse breathing. Even Margaret, who had been coughing constantly the last week, was silent. Ruth wanted to reach for her gold wire-rims to look into the darkness and dispel her fear, but the cold held her back. She opened her eyes wide, trying to absorb everything in the room. Moonlight fell through the

A Woman of Salt

narrow window above Cynthia's cot. The streaming light seemed to make the room colder. The cold hung over her, surrounded her, pressed itself hard against her, forcing her down the way an ocean breaker holds bodies under water until all breath is gone and they rise to the surface dead. She welcomed it, yet felt unsettled by it. She held absolutely still, afraid that at the slightest movement she would be devoured by it. It increased the pressure, moving closer, pressing deep inside her, as if taking the measure of her spirit.

Ruth felt as if her body had dissolved into the air. She was no longer resting on the mattress, but hovering near it. She existed without limitation; there was no membrane to contain her cells, no weight to resist her will, and she floated in a giddiness born of the absolute identity of willing and acting. She was certain that whatever she could conceive she could do. Relieved of the drag of her flesh, she was pure energy, omnipotent. She felt wonderful.

Annie's voice brought the edges and weightedness of her body back.

"'O Lord, my God, in You I seek refuge.'" Shaky at first, her voice strengthened as she continued. "'Deliver me from all my pursuers and save me.'" She paused, began again. "'For you the Lord is a safe retreat; you have made the Most High your refuge. When he calls upon me, I will answer; I will be with him in times of trouble; I will rescue him and bring him to honor.'"

As she prayed, the presence seemed to hesitate, lighten its pressure. When she reached "When he calls upon me," it had begun to release its hold.

It left without hurrying, passing first from inside Ruth, then from her body, her bunk, and finally the room, leaving by the narrow window.

Ruth was bereft. Emptiness rushed into the space it left inside her.

"I *felt* it," Deirdre said. "I felt it touch my skin."

"It was looking for something," Margaret said.

They were quiet for a few moments, not sure they had understood what she had said, but certain it was true. They kept silent a while longer, guarding against its return.

"Thanks, Annie." Cynthia's voice was small.

"The Holy Spirit did it," Annie said.

Deirdre began praising and thanking God for "delivering us from evil." One by one the others joined her, each adding her thankfulness for safety.

Their credulity exasperated Ruth. They had woken up in unison and felt cold, that was all, yet their minds leaped to the Devil. Were they innocents who believed the spirit was palpable? Couldn't they conceive of a God whose disembodied truth lifted them out of the world of limits and deceptions?

"It's a chilly night," Ruth said to the women in the chalet. "Let's go back to sleep."

She turned on her stomach and buried her head in the pillow. The emptiness rumbled inside her, making her queasy. She had lost her appetite the last few weeks and grown thin enough for Mrs. Dietrich to ask if she were ill. "It's not good to spend so much time alone, dear," Mrs. Dietrich had said to her. Ruth assured her she felt fine. Still, her thermostat had been off lately. She was either burning up or shivering with cold. Now in the dark she was shaking under the blankets. Remembering the bear coat, she drew it from the end of the bunk and pulled it over her.

Ruth woke up exhausted, but she made it through her morning chores and the long afternoon by hoping Jean-Pierre would surprise her after supper.

In the next few weeks Jean-Pierre spent more and more time with her. They would walk the mountain paths discussing God and philosophy, freedom and determinism, dreams and betrayals, or planning mountain hikes, a trip to the Montreux Jazz festival, a bicycle tour through northern Italy. They were together so often Ruth was concerned that Adrian would make a snide remark when he passed, or that Annie or one of the other Refuge loyals would scold her. But no one mentioned Jean-Pierre to her.

The days Jean-Pierre did not come, The Refuge seemed crabbed and provincial. Ruth missed his intensity, his brilliantly analytical mind, the way he mocked Dr. Dietrich's and Colin's simpleminded readings of non-Christian thinkers, his piercing eyes. He was like the brother she had always wanted, the long lost other half of her originally hermaphroditic soul—closer to her than Lennie. He understood her suspicion of the body and its desires; he wasn't interested in sex and "the incarnate truth of the world," like Lennie; he fueled her love, her need, for soaring thoughts; he relieved the burden of her eternally contradicting self by meeting her completely in the mind. She felt free with him, herself.

The third week in May, Jean-Pierre announced that the time was right to hike over the mountain pass to the lake, a two-day journey from Champs des Fleurs. Ruth told Annie she had to go Lausanne for a few days to visit the Campbells. The next morning she met Jean-Pierre at the bus station in Champs des Fleurs. They transferred several times, always going higher, until they reached a small village. From the station they walked up a winding, heavily wooded road until they reached an old barn and large cow pasture.

Already hot, Ruth rolled her bear coat tightly and stuffed it into her knapsack. Jean-Pierre smiled. He didn't like to see her in the coat. Her "bad bargain," he called it. "Why carry around a dead body?" he would ask. "You can move so much more freely without it."

The path led between two fences, alongside a rocky stream. For six hours they walked, encountering no one, and by afternoon they had reached the high meadows. Snow covered the peaks around them, lay in great patches along the trail. Mountain goats stood on outcroppings along both sides of the meadows. Hawks flew overhead. In the soft grasses flowers of all colors appeared. They stopped at the high point to rest on a boulder and drink some water from the stream. The sun was starting to go down as they shouldered their packs to continue the climb. They had to cross the rest of the pass, make their way down a trail leading to a small inn beside Lac Diamant.

By seven they had crossed the pass and begun the descent. It was much more slow-going than they had expected. The path was steep and rocky, slippery with melting snow and ice. They had to stay close together to help each other when they slid. Jean-Pierre, who had filled out over the last months, with muscled forearms and ruddy cheeks, had no trouble catching Ruth.

By dusk they had not yet found the place where the path leveled off. Jean-Pierre insisted they were not lost. The wind blew up and it began to rain, making the way more difficult. Below them they saw a herder's stone hut built into the side of the mountain. They scrambled to it and knelt to look in the narrow doorway. It was dark inside and empty. Jean-Pierre crawled in. Ruth hesitated. She didn't like being trapped in tight spaces with another person.

"Come inside," Jean-Pierre called.

She shook off her fear and entered. The air was moist and the smell of earth was everywhere. The hut was just high enough for them to sit with their backs against the far wall. They sat side by side watching the storm through the doorway and listening to the thunder move across Les Diablerets.

"Hungry?" Jean-Pierre asked, holding up the rest of the baguette.

"Famished."

They ate the bread with an ashy cheese and a bottle of wine. The storm blew around them. From time to time rocks tumbled down the mountain.

"It's one of Ravana's tricks," Ruth said, hearing a close crack of thunder.

"You don't take that myth seriously."

"It's a beautiful story."

"Even a beautiful falsehood is fit only for primitive minds."

"Don't tease."

"Once you give power to fictions, you're trapped."

"What about the Buddhist concept of useful fictions?" she asked. "The notion that though the enlightened ones live in the truth, they use fictions to help lead those wandering in the world of illusion to the light?"

"That's for those deceived by the material world. For those who see the truth of the spirit without the veil of the body, there's a direct path."

"How?"

"With the pure mind, purely. Mind to mind. No distortion from the physical world."

"You see this way?"

"Me. You."

The wine and fresh air and exercise mingled in Ruth's head to confuse her. All day she had waited for the right moment to tell Jean-Pierre about her vision of the puppets and the giant hands, but now she was not sure. The temperature had dropped several degrees since they had

A Woman of Salt

come inside and she was cold to the bone. She removed the bearskin coat from her pack and spread it on the ground, sure that however ugly Jean-Pierre thought it, he would appreciate the thick hide's insulating them from the cold below.

"What are you doing?" he asked.

"Getting ready for bed. This thin air makes me tired."

"You're going to sleep with the fleas?"

"You, too. We'll keep each other warm."

Ruth lay on the coat, leaving room for him. He stared at her, shaking his head.

"I'm not asking you to make love," she said angrily, "just to keep me warm in this godforsaken place. What's wrong with you?"

He sat in the corner, arms resting on his bent knees, staring at her.

Ruth turned away, pulled the coat tight around her, and fell asleep.

She dreamed Rama had been chained in a tower by Ravana. Through the tiny window high above the earth he could see more than he had ever seen. From that height everything stood out clearly enough to be understood. He could see Sita far below in the enchanted circle and her severance from him seemed right, as it should be. Contained within his mind, the world was at rest. Rama wanted to stay up there forever looking down on the world and grasping its meaning. The force of this desire aroused Ruth and she woke up.

She lifted her head and listened. The rain had stopped. She reached for Jean-Pierre. He was not next to her. She edged around the hut, feeling for him. She crawled out the doorway, thinking he had gone to pee. The sky was clear, with a full moon, the air crisp and full of silence. She stumbled away from the hut and peed.

"Jean-Pierre?" Ruth whispered, standing up. "Are you there?" *"Tu est là?"* she called into the night. *"Où est tu? Dites-moi."*

She listened but heard nothing, no bird calling, no animal rustling.

The air was chilly and clear. The wind picked up. She felt it grazing her cheeks, searching under her clothes. It blew inside her, whirling, emptying her, lifting her over the mountain to the clouds, to the stars, rushing her among them, willy-nilly, whipping her up and down, in mad whirlpools and veering lines, widening spirals and sudden plunges, until she lost aboveness and belowness, inside and outside, self and world, and was drowning in the Oneness of Being, emptied and alone, terrified she would disappear in nothingness and be lost forever, drifting at the whim of the world, because there was nothing to hold her to the ground.

Chilled, she wrapped her arms around herself, pressing her hands into her ribs and the bony hollows of her shoulder. She scrambled back inside the hut, thinking she had missed Jean-Pierre in her first search.

He was not there. His pack was gone, too.

Ruth wrapped herself in the coat and sat with her back against the stone wall, watching the doorway and trying to keep herself awake by taking small bites of the hard, half-bitter chocolate. If Jean-Pierre was outside hiding, waiting for her to fall asleep so he could scare her, he would be disappointed. She watched for him until dawn.

When it was light enough not to stumble, Ruth cinched her coat tightly around her, hoisted her pack, and found the path to the glacial lake. The lake came into view an hour later. She looked into the brilliant turquoise water for a moment, then turned and headed back toward the pass. Approaching the hut, she stopped and stuffed her coat into her pack. She edged quietly to the door and poked her head inside. Jean-Pierre was not there. She climbed the rocky ledges to the pass, working fast so she would be sure to get back to The Refuge by nightfall. All day she walked, looking behind every tree and boulder for Jean-Pierre and stopping only to fill her water bottle in the stream or to catch her breath. Her knees ached. Her toes burned where they rubbed against the front of her boots.

She arrived at the chalet long after supper. Annie gave her two of Mrs. Dietrich's whole-grain rolls and the carton of yogurt she had saved from lunch. Ruth shredded one roll on her napkin and left the other untouched.

"Don't you feel well?" Annie asked. "You're very pale."

"Just tired," Ruth said, "unbelievably tired."

For the next several weeks Ruth gave herself over to the comfort of routine: cleaning toilets in the morning, listening to tapes after lunch, attending the evening gatherings, and retiring early to lose herself in the *Ramayana*. One afternoon in the study chalet she started an angry letter to Jean-Pierre, but she abandoned it and wrote to Lennie instead.

A Woman of Salt

Lennie had written her every week since she had left. *Hey there, Heidi, any good dope over there? Bart's in the state pen for armed robbery. I'm thinking of moving to Toronto. You'd like it, lots of far-out galleries and divine Chinese food.* Every letter incorporated his doodlings. Around the border of one sketch of her lying on her side he had written, "'The nakedness of woman is the work of God.' Blake. I miss you." Across the bottom of a drawing of her swimming in Lake Michigan he had printed, "Blake's Devil says, 'Man has no Body distinct from his Soul; for that call'd Body is a portion of Soul discern'd by the five Senses, the chief inlets of Soul in this age.' YOUR BODY / SOUL IS LUSCIOUS. COME HOME SO I CAN PAINT YOU."

Ruth wanted to tell Lennie about Rama and Sita and let him draw them as she talked. She felt if she could see his drawings of them, she would understand her dreams of them. *I know you're in love with the absurdity of Amerika,* she wrote him, *but why not have a look at Europe? The dope is first-class and there's a museum on every corner. We could hitchhike across Europe sleeping in hostels and eating in open-air markets. You sell sketches to tourists, I lead tours in English. You nose out adventures, I get us back on track—like before. Please come.*

Jean-Pierre didn't show up for almost a month. He surprised Ruth in a remote Alpine meadow one sunny afternoon, where she lay reading Heidegger's *What Is Called Thinking?* His face had lost some of the ruddiness and he seemed thinner and slacker than he had on their last hike.

"I hardly recognized you without your flea-catcher," he said.

"It's too hot to wear it now."

"What'd you do with it?"

"Stashed it in a box under my bunk."

He sat beside her, picked up the book, and searched the fifth lecture. "'The destiny of our fateful-historic Western nature,'" he read, "'shows itself in the fact that our sojourn in this world rests upon thinking, even where this sojourn is determined by the Christian faith.'" Flipping to the last lecture, he continued, "'The saying "For it is the same thing to think and to be" becomes the basic theme of all Western European thinking.'"

"Yeah, yeah," Ruth said, "Descartes. *Cogito ergo sum.*"

"No, Descartes meant logical analysis. Heidegger means tapping into the essence of Being." Jean-Pierre turned to the last page and read, "'We have learned to see that the essential nature of thinking is determined by what there is to be thought about; the presence of what is present, the Being of beings.' He doesn't mean some part of being or any being among beings, but the power of Being itself. If you know how to open yourself up through thinking, you can tap into the power of Being, the Oneness of Being, and accomplish amazing things."

"Like what?" she asked.

"Anything you want. Learn languages fast, write brilliant books, convince people to follow your ideas."

"Sounds good."

"It is."

The sound of accordions and singing drifted to them from a large chalet high in the meadow.

"Farmers," he said. "The village is taking lunch together and resting. Primitive minds, you know, slaves to their stomachs and muscles."

The song was a happy one and the chorus of well-fed voices slid over it in perfect rhythm. As they sang, Ruth became nauseated. She put her head between her knees and breathed deeply.

"Let's take a walk," Jean-Pierre said.

Dizzy from the thin air and their conversation, Ruth rose to follow him. They climbed away from the chalet to a stream rushing over stones. Hiking higher, they let themselves over a fence and entered another pasture. They walked slowly, discussing thinking and the phenomenology of Being. As they neared the next fence, they surprised a bull eating in the shade. It raised its head and snorted at them. They both stood still. It pawed the ground, staring at them. Ruth turned white. She glanced at Jean-Pierre, who seemed amused. She ran for the fence. Safe on the other side, she turned around. Jean-Pierre was standing next to the bull.

"Be careful," she said.

He laughed and walked slowly toward the fence. The second his feet hit the ground on her side he bowed his head and, using his index fingers as horns, rushed toward her.

A Woman of Salt

Stepping back from him, Ruth fell over a stone.

At once he was contrite. "You okay?" he asked, reaching to help her.

"Yeah. Sorry. It's getting dark. I need to head back."

"Of course," he said. "Shall I accompany you all the way back to your chalet this time?"

Ruth watched the sun disappearing behind the mountain.

"We could continue our discussion as we walked," Jean-Pierre said.

"Annie's waiting up for me."

"Let me walk the rest of the way with you."

"Mrs. Dietrich will be furious if I come in past curfew again."

"She's not your mother. She's not God, is she?"

Ruth counted the eyelets in her boots, in pairs, singly.

"Don't be afraid of them. They're not like you and me. They're trapped in their bodies and know nothing of the spirit."

"Maybe next time."

"Perhaps you are ashamed of me," Jean-Pierre said.

She shook her head.

"Why not, then?"

"I don't know." She shook her head as if fighting off a heavy sleep. "Because it's already dark. Because I'm tired. Because I'm confused."

"Confused or scared?"

"Confused."

"But it's very clear that I can help you. You want to cut away the strings, don't you, and end the life of manipulation and emptiness. Yes?"

"Yes."

"You want to cast off the body and fly free."

"Yes. *Yes.* More than anything."

"Then you must be courageous. You must risk a great solitude. I will show you the way. Now, if you like."

Fatigue rushed through Ruth. She wanted to fall to the ground where she stood and rest forever.

"I can show you the way to true freedom of the spirit in Being itself."

"I just want to crawl into my bunk and get warm." She turned from him and headed down the path to Champs des Fleurs. "See you tomorrow night," she said over her shoulder, "after supper."

"I'll come help with your morning chores," he called after her. "When we are together always, we will not waste time with mundane things."

When Ruth returned to The Refuge, a postcard of Nixon grinning and flashing the victory sign lay on her pillow. *Ruth, Ruth, Ruth! Can't make it, sorry, moving to Toronto. V's setting me up. Come as soon as you get back. Call me and I'll come get you. 912–474–0095. Crazy love, L.*

She closed her eyes and laid her head against the scratchy blanket tucked into her bunk. Her head whirled and she felt as if she were losing her balance. Fighting the urge to vomit, she put the card under her pillow and crawled into bed with her clothes on. In seconds she was asleep. In her dreams Rama stood outside the enchanted circle where Ravana held Sita prisoner. Ravana was devouring her, swallowing her flesh in a storm of wind and cold. Rama leaped into the circle to save her, but when his feet touched the earth, Sita was not there.

Jean-Pierre did not appear again until the ache of loneliness had filled Ruth completely. He showed up near dusk in her favorite spot, a small forest clearing a mile from The Refuge. He had spent the weeks apart from her, he told her, preparing a real mountain journey for them. This time they would climb even higher, to a place of astonishing beauty. They would hitchhike to Poulin and walk to the trail that led to an abandoned summer herding station in the high meadows of Mont Vevey. No tourists went there and the sturdy Swiss rarely hiked there. The path was rocky and dangerous in places, but the view was well worth the climb.

"It's so beautiful you won't be the same once you've seen it," he said.

"You won't desert me again? You'll stay with me the whole time?"

"If that's what you choose."

"Yes or no?" she demanded.

"If you ask me to," he said, "I will, yes."

"I'm asking you."

"Then I will not leave you."

A Woman of Salt

"Will it be cold that high up?"

"Fresh. But no need for a coat. A sweater will do."

They left early Friday morning. Ruth told Annie the Campbells had invited her to join them for a revival Dr. Campbell was leading in a stadium on the outskirts of Paris. Jean-Pierre met her in Orsières and they had no trouble catching rides to Poulin. By early afternoon they had reached the trail. They walked quickly, planning to reach the high meadow by dark.

They arrived at the small wooden shelter as night fell. Ruth made a fire while Jean-Pierre scouted the area. Exhausted, Ruth went to bed, leaving Jean-Pierre to tend the fire. She fell asleep as soon as she rolled out her sleeping bag on the wooden bunk built into the wall of the shelter.

Late in the morning she grumbled awake. Jean-Pierre teased her about sleeping so late. She blamed it on a crushing headache.

"A hike in the fresh air will clear your head!" he said. "The view I want you to see is a few hours' climb from here. It's spectacular. You can see many peaks, like a jaw full of teeth."

Groggy from too much sleep, Ruth put on her daypack and followed him. Jean-Pierre walked faster than usual and she had a hard time keeping up. Her headache worsened. It felt as if every vein were clenching. Dizzy, she stumbled over a root on the path. When she righted herself she seemed to be moving even more slowly. Her chest and throat tightened, making it hard to breathe. She grabbed the collar of her T-shirt and yanked it away from her body. She sucked at the air, but her lungs wouldn't fill. She stopped, sat down, and pulled her T-shirt farther away from her chest. Jean-Pierre was a few hundred yards ahead now.

"Wait," she called.

He turned round.

"What's wrong?" he asked when he drew near.

"Can't breathe." She waited for more breath. "Altitude sickness?"

"Impossible. It's only ten thousand feet here."

"Never been this high."

"But the viewpoint is still an hour's climb. You can see everything from there, the whole universe. It's only another thousand feet higher. Rest here a moment to acclimate, then we'll continue. I know you can do it."

He sat beside her and leaned his head against her shoulder. His coldness against her sweaty heat seemed to clear her head.

"Come on, then," he said after a few moments. Grinning, he helped her up. "I'll pull you up the mountain. I'll carry you if you like. Here, let me take your pack."

Without the pack Ruth climbed a few hundred yards higher. But her breath became increasingly labored. Her limbs grew sluggish. She had to stop to rest every few minutes, her head swimming. They were climbing now in a wind corridor. The wind had picked up and was rushing past them from the valley below to the clouds. Ruth sat down on a rocky ledge jutting high over the valley.

"Resting so soon?" Jean-Pierre asked.

"Have to."

"Lean on me."

"Can't."

The glare of the sun hurt her eyes. She could hardly see Jean-Pierre, the light was so strong.

"You go ahead," she said.

"Without you? Impossible!"

"I'll take a nap here and catch my breath, while you climb the rest of the way. You'll make better time without me. You can describe the view to me."

"But you *must* come."

"Please," she begged.

"You said you wanted to escape the puppet vision and the emptiness inside you that separates you from the world."

"I do."

"And you want to be free?"

"Yes. *Yes.*"

"Then come with me and see all things from that high point, where the power of Being and the power of non-Being appear as one. That's freedom."

A Woman of Salt

Ruth pulled herself up and stood at the tip of the ledge. The wind, coming from behind her, seemed to lift her up, and she felt a great space opening above and below her, inviting her.

"Fly," Jean-Pierre said. "Fly. You'll be happier than you ever imagined. No strings, no weight, no body; pure movement, pure freedom, pure energy."

"I don't know," she said, her face troubled, her head turning slowly from side to side.

"You don't believe me." Jean-Pierre was visibly angry now.

She fell more than sat. The ground was hard against her hipbones and elbows. She had lost more weight than she had thought.

Ruth didn't want to miss the view she had worked so hard to reach. She dreaded making Jean-Pierre angrier, but her body refused to let her get up.

"That is your decision, then?" he asked curtly.

She nodded.

"I'm sorry," she said.

"It may take me a while to get back," he said. "You'll be alone. And the night is coming."

"I'm sorry. I just can't."

It didn't take long for Jean-Pierre to disappear behind an outcropping. Still holding her shirt out from her chest, Ruth lay her head on the ground and closed her eyes. She wanted to sleep for centuries.

Ravana was sitting on her chest. He stared at her, his green, lashless eyes boring through her, pursuing her secrets. His body began to wither and his eyes began to grow until he was nothing but eyes watching her, fixing her in place. She wanted to run away, but she couldn't move. She closed her eyes so he wouldn't see her, but his eyes covered the inside of her lids. His eyes lifted her and carried her to the top of the mountain, where she stood on the edge of a precipice. Below her stretched the entire world. Everything, everything was contained in her vision, all of it in sharp relief, from the atoms of the rocks through the alpine flowers to the laws of generativity and entropy. Nothing was hidden from her. The sun began to set in the ring of mountains. In the darkened sky it became an ocean of blood being swallowed by a giant jaw. The darkening, bloody expanse called to her in a voice that was a deafening infinity of voices, saying, "Jump. Jump and you will fly free forever." She stretched out her arms and stood on her toes on the edge, raised her face to the spacious darkness and breathed it in, ready to rise into it.

She didn't know what stopped her. She shifted her weight back almost imperceptibly and a pebble slipped under her toes, throwing her backward onto the ledge. The back of her head struck a rock and she lay as she had fallen all night, the cold traveling inside her.

When she woke, the sun was blazing. It blinded her.

Adrian found her sitting by a stream just above the Refuge that afternoon, her head in her hands. She told him she was listening to the water running over the stones. He wrapped an arm around her and began walking her back. It wasn't long before he stopped, knelt down, and told her to climb on his back.

"I'll hurt you," Ruth said.

"Unlikely. You're a wraith. The greater danger is that you'll blow away."

He helped her on, secured his hands around her wrists, shifted her weight on his back, and carried her to her chalet.

For six days Ruth lay in her bunk in a fever. Adrian checked on her hourly. Annie and Mrs. Dietrich fed her honeyed tea and sugared toast wedges, changed her soaked blankets, sponged her face with cool water, bathed her, sprinkled her pillow with orangeflower water to remove the smell of decay that hung about her. Ruth grew thinner and thinner, weaker and weaker. Veins mapped her eyelids. Tremors ran through her body as she dozed. On the seventh day, Mrs. Dietrich called the Campbells. "She's quite ill," she said. "I'll see that she gets to the airport and on the plane all right. Tell her parents they *must* meet her when she gets off the plane. She is very weak."

The Campbells were unable to locate the VanderZichts. They offered to nurse Ruth at their house, but Mrs. Dietrich said it would be better for Ruth to go home. She had had enough of the mountains. Mrs. Dietrich found Lennie's number in Ruth's wallet and called him. "She'll need some tending to," she told Lennie. "It would be good if you could take her to the ocean, let her sun on the sand, swim in salt water."

A Woman of Salt

Lennie assured Mrs. Dietrich he would meet Ruth at the airport and care for her.

As they waited for her flight to be announced, Mrs. Dietrich sat beside Ruth with one arm around her back and the other on her arm, to support her.

Ruth shivered in the air-conditioned chill of the waiting room.

Mrs. Dietrich removed the large, intricately patterned red wool shawl she was wearing and helped Ruth wind it around her black pullover sweater.

"This will keep you warm on the plane," Mrs. Dietrich said. "I found it years ago in an outdoor market and I've worn it ever since, summer and winter. It's the perfect weight. You can send it back once you're well."

"Thank you," Ruth said.

"Ruth," she said, "I packed all your things, books and journals. too, everything except your coat."

Ruth turned to her in fear.

"Don't worry," Mrs. Dietrich said, laughing gently. "I bundled it safely away in my closet. Write me as soon as you're settled and I'll send it to you, wherever you are. It's a lovely coat, Ruth. Don't forget it. You'll be wanting it someday."

She Looked Behind Him

Calvin's exegesis of Genesis 19 builds on the tradition of the Latin church fathers. For all his Renaissance skill in Hebrew and training in rhetoric, he ends up interpreting the story of the wife of Lot through the Western theological grid of law and disobedience. Many of the Eastern church fathers—Irenaeus, Origen, and John Chrysostom—take a less abstract approach, following the rabbinic path of midrashic interpretation, narrative exploration of the meaning hidden in the silences of the text.

According to one rabbinic midrash, Lot was following his wife, not she him. She looked back behind him, not behind her, the rabbis say, drawing meaning from every word and its position in the text. They make of this observation a story with Lot as the protagonist. That Lot follows his wife and not she him confirms that Lot was up to his lingering tricks, like the hesitant soul that God must drag into redemption. But let us take the rabbis' observation and see what else can be made of it when we do not assume Lot as the center of the story.

Let us wonder, for example, why Lot would permit his wife to walk ahead of him. Why, when he is so obviously nervous for his own skin and comfort and salvation, would he let his wife precede him and thus be always one step farther removed from destruction and one step nearer to redemption than himself? Surely the Lot who a few sentences ago so eagerly offered up his virgin daughters to save his own life would not act in such salvific chivalry. Why, then?

Perhaps Lot followed his wife not to protect her, but to make sure she didn't change her mind and run back to Sodom without him, leaving him alone.

Lot was right not to trust his wife: she would have bolted in an instant. But not to Sodom or Gomorrah, not to her things or her friends or the daughters she left behind. Given a chance, the wife of Lot would have run outside the story of Abraham and the God mindful of him. What was there for her in the relentless dividings between the chosen and the damned?

Given a chance, the wife of Lot would have fled to the mountains for refuge to write her own story of redemption.

Imagine: She left Lot and the two angels and the God of Abraham and her two young daughters and ran breathless toward the mountains for refuge. She scrambled up the rocks, shedding her body as she climbed. Rising into thinning air, she sloughed off, cell by cell, the body that imprisoned her in a hell of determinism, the body that tangled her in lies, the body that confused her with shame, the body that betrayed the freedom of her mind, the body that chained her to her mother, the body of a woman, the body of death. And when, weightless, she reached the farthest point from the earth, the summit where spirit empties itself of flesh and flesh absents itself from spirit, all longing between them severed, she flung herself into the air to fly unencumbered; she died to her body and rose her true, discarnate self.

The wife of Lot fled to the hills to leave behind the burden of her flesh, to escape the world in which body and spirit were embrangled within her.

The journey to freedom the wife of Lot desired was a journey like Saint Augustine's: from suspect body to liberating intellect, from flesh to spirit.

She did not know, she could not have guessed the truth that Edward Dahlberg witnesses to in *Can These Bones Live?*: "Purge the flesh and you canker the spirit."

The wife of Lot was not turned into a pillar of salt as a punishment—for disobedience to her husband, defiance of God, lack of trust in God or herself, inordinate love of the world, triviality, or revenge.

By turning her to salt, God weighted her to the earth forever. Forever without end she became body. Impossible now to escape her fleshly self or to deny it.

In the moment she became salt, the wife of Lot left off shedding flesh to become spirit and turned in a new direction: spirit enlivening flesh.

God transformed the wife of Lot into a pillar of salt to save her from cankering her spirit.

A Long Way Off

In a sanctuary of white walls, unadorned save for the verse "Worship the Lord in the Beauty of Holiness" painted black high above the pulpit, a father is bent in the pew, crying. He started during the New Testament reading, Luke 15, the Prodigal Son, every parent's fantasy: A selfish and unloving son earnestly repents of his sins; he is welcomed back with kisses, and a fatted calf is killed to clinch the deal.

When the dominee reached verse 18, *Father, I have sinned against heaven and against you, I no longer deserve to be called your son,* the father turned to his daughter, then lowered his head and began crying. He's weeping with joy for the return of his daughter's lost soul. He thinks because she's in church beside him, bowing for prayers, rising and being seated for hymns, in rhythm with the holy congregation, that she has come back to seek his favor.

But he's wrong. This daughter, eyes fixed straight ahead, forehead wrinkled in concentration, is not lost. She was never lost. She was away, seeking her own way. And she refuses to return, under any conditions.

The Bible tells us, the dominee begins his sermon, bellowing so the

MARY POTTER ENGEL

congregation will know his words are *God's* Word, *a man had two sons,* *a dutiful son and a foolish son.*

What a fool this daughter was to agree to meet her father on a Sunday morning, to let him catch her off guard on the phone Saturday night.

"In town for business," he said, "but tomorrow I'm free. I'll pick you up, nine sharp. Wear something nice, a skirt. I located one of our churches on the West Side, not too far out. After the service I'll take you out for lunch downtown."

Hearing his voice after so long an absence bewildered the daughter.

When she didn't respond, he said, so quietly it was hard to be sure she had heard it, "I'd like to see you, Ruthie."

Voices mobbed inside her, shouting one another down, The bastard hang up how did he find me Lennie promised not to tell them I got into graduate school what does he want don't be afraid what if he's generous like the time in college he bought me a radio saying don't tell your mother when Mother finds out he took me out to lunch there'll be hell to pay say yes.

To silence their clamoring, she said to him, "6514 Irondale Avenue, south of the university, I'll be on the front steps," and hung up.

What was this daughter hoping for when she made that bargain? A meal of pâté and lamb, crème brûlée and Grand Marnier, over which he would confess his failure as a father, hand her a check for her rent, offer to buy her a chocolate suede suit for job interviews? A long walk along the lakefront afterward, just the two of them, discussing labor and management, World War II and Viet Nam, LBJ's tragic rise and fall? Her asking him if he was happy now that he had given up trying to start his own business and achieved success working for someone else? Asking him if he had in fact disinherited her or ever threatened to, or if that was another of her mother's lies?

Childish fantasies. As naïve as the restless boy to her left who accepts the Dutch peppermint his grandfather hands him to buy his silence. He thinks if he places the hard white disk between his lower teeth and lip and sucks it very slowly, its sweetness will last through the sermon.

The younger son, the dominee continues, *the foolish one, said, "Father,* *let me have the share of the estate that would come to me."*

A Woman of Salt

When this daughter, left she didn't ask for anything because there was nothing she was willing to pay for.

"Let me fall on my own face," she screamed at her father. "That's all I want from you."

"Ruthie, Ruthie," he said, shaking his head. "There's so much pain in the world. Let's not add to it."

Without hesitating, the father divided his property between his sons. The foolish son quickly gathered his belongings and left for a distant country. He ran halfway round the world to squander his inheritance on drunkenness, devil cards, dancing, women of ill repute.

What does this dominee know of women of ill repute? She should stand up and teach him, say, Here I am, Dominee. Look at me. I am a woman who has been arrested for shoplifting, stolen from a friend, smuggled dope, swallowed Quaaludes mescaline LSD cocaine speed always speed—whatever promised the most distance—posed nude for artists, slept with armed revolutionaries who read Neruda, men with thick lips who bragged of murder and running from the law, strangers whose names I did not know; a woman familiar with demons, intoxicated by death; a woman with eyes in the back of her head, twin horns of perception that feel out the darkness and warn me when to run. I am proud of my past; it's all the capital I have to set myself up in the world. Why should anyone cry over it?

. . . famine in that far-off land. Willingly would the son, destitute now, have filled his belly with the slop he fed a stranger's pigs.

Eyes on the dominee, jaw set, the father picks at a hangnail on his thumb until it bleeds.

The daughter crosses her legs, points them toward the boy with the peppermint. He's banging his knees together, rustling his pant legs. Without taking his eyes off the pulpit, the boy's grandfather jabs him in the thigh to make him stop.

But no one offered him anything. This is the way of the World: to promise everything and offer nothing. Be wary of worldly things.

This daughter loves the World, the loud confusion, the crowding mess of it; its profligate ways, spilling over constantly in glorious abundance and waste; the way everything arises and slips away, so dear in its disappearing; the way it resists control, a worthy opponent for both

MARY POTTER ENGEL

will and reason; the way the World attacks, honestly, out to crush her in its path, never hypocritical, beating her down to lift up her soul. Whenever the dominee or elders or Sunday School teachers, their faces anguished, asked her, Don't you love the Lord? she would answer, "I love the *World*. 'This is my Father's world': that's what we sing in church, isn't it?" And they would slump away, sorrowing over her.

. . . and forsaking the life of idleness, the true mark of the Devil, the son set out for home to beg his father to hire him as a servant.

A *slave*, the dominee means. The runaway son should never have come back: the price was too great. Nothing should cost that much. And why should this daughter crawl home on bloodied knees, when her father never did? Her father never begged forgiveness for leaving his family, for denying his father, an ignorant laborer with a mangled tongue, not good enough to polish his son's wingtips.

Consider this verse, the dominee says. *"While his son was yet a long way off." Listen. "While his son was* yet a long way off, *his father saw him and was moved with pity and ran down the road to meet him, weeping with joy."*

Her second year in college, her father flew halfway across the world to chastise her: his Christian duty. He searched her out in the bar where she worked to burn the Devil out of her with his wrath. Friends told her later he pushed through pool players and tables of drinkers, shoved aside a waitress, demanded that the bartender tell him where his daughter was.

She was in bed, immobilized by a crushing headache. She had left the bar an hour before, an uncanny weight pressing her shoulders and neck, shimmering at the edges of her vision, the eyes in the back of her head elongated and prickling with danger.

Her father bounded up the stairs to the attic apartment she shared with her boyfriend Lennie. He banged on the thick wooden door with the butt of his fist, shouting, "Open up, Ruth. Let me in."

It felt as if he were pounding on her chest. She couldn't breathe.

"I know you're in there," he called. "Open up. Now."

She pressed her eyebrows toward her cheeks to stanch the pain and saw his tall, muscular frame filling the narrow hallway outside her door, his swarthy face flushed with righteousness.

A Woman of Salt

The door shook with his battering. "I'm banging on the gates of hell for you, Ruth." His voice reverberated in the hall, rang inside the tiny apartment.

She lay as if dead, sure that he was preparing to ram the door open with his powerful shoulder, kick a hole through it, reach in and undo the lock, unclasp the chain.

The handle rattled, stopped, rattled harder. The door thundered in the jamb.

"Ruth!" he called out, almost sobbing. "Come back."

After a moment there was silence. Every pore in her listened, but she heard only a faint crackling in her skull.

When the pounding resumed, it was more rhythmic, as if his dogged insistence, like the trumpets around Jericho, would make the door crumble.

Afraid the door would not hold against his thick fists, she inched off the bed toward the open window.

"Let me in," he yelled.

Carefully she hoisted herself onto the roof, behind the dormer, where Lennie liked to smoke dope and watch the stars perform. She clutched the edge of the dormer, her hands and arms growing tenser each moment until they were burning with the strain.

A siren blared in the distance, grew louder. She looked down the street, sure it was screaming toward her. A car drove by, disappeared.

A cold spring rain was falling. She couldn't stop shivering. The numbness in her hands loosened her grip and her fishnet stockings, swollen with water, began slipping down the shingles. To stop sliding, she shifted her weight back, against the roof.

A taxi pulled up in front of her house, honked twice.

She huddled closer to the dormer.

Below her, the storm door squeaked open, thudded shut. Her father ran across the front walk, feet splashing in the puddles, suit jacket pulled over his head. He climbed into the taxi and rode away.

When the brake lights had disappeared, she counted to three hundred to make sure he wasn't circling back, then lowered herself down to the window and crawled inside. She stuffed her wallet and cigarettes into Lennie's rain poncho, threw on shoes, and ran downstairs, flying out the back door and down the alley, through the next and the next, not stopping until she had reached the all-night doughnut shop downtown.

She spent the rest of the night there, chain-smoking and watching the cream swirl into her coffee, wondering how he had found out she wasn't living in the dorm, praying that the clarifying hatred coursing through her would not disappear when morning came.

When the sun rose, she left, walking for hours, her feet drubbing the sidewalks.

That evening her father called from Yugoslavia. Between silences, his words crawling across lines buried deep in the ocean, he told her he was tied up in a meeting with officials in Tito's government, negotiating the first business contract between a capitalist nation and a communist country, or he would have stayed to talk with her. Postponing the meeting to chase after her had almost cost him the deal. "Use your head, Ruth," he said. "One mistake can ruin your life. Think about the consequences. Promise me that."

Her mother called later that night and ordered her to see a Christian shrink recommended by Dominee Wierenga. Ruth refused. Helen threatened to call the president of the college and have her expelled for living in sin. "When your father was at Dordrecht," she said, "he was suspended for two weeks because a professor saw him standing in line to see a movie. Don't think it won't happen to you." Ruth hung up on her.

Later that week, Ruth's cousin Rink, a city police officer, showed up at the apartment with her brother Calvin and a search warrant. She hadn't seen Calvin in two years, though he and his Bible-crazy wife lived in the same town. "God tell you to betray your sister?" she asked him. Calvin watched in silence as Rink arrested them for possession of a controlled substance and an unregistered weapon—a pistol Ruth hadn't known Lennie kept hidden behind the bookcase. Lennie's parents posted bail for him the next morning and took him away. Ruth got out a few hours later, the charges dropped. The following day the dean notified her she had been expelled from Dordrecht for "cohabitation," and that weekend a registered letter arrived from her mother:

A Woman of Salt

Ruth Helen,

"Can the Ethiopian change his skin, or the leopard his spots? And you, can you do what is right, you so accustomed to wrong? I will scatter you like chaff driven by the desert wind. This is your share, the wage of your apostasy. This comes from me—it is Jehovah who speaks—" Jeremiah 13: 23–25. You are a daughter of wickedness and a whore of Babylon. We're tired of your lies. You've broken your father's heart over and over again and you don't even care. He's been too patient with you. We've had enough. Your father's taken you out of the will. We don't want you to ever speak to us again. If you must communicate something to us, contact our attorney, Jim VanderPloeg, 618–722–4893.

Helen VanderZicht

Ruth tore the letter to bits, casting the pieces from a bus window.

So our Heavenly Father runs down the road to meet us, weeping with joy at our return. In this we see the grace of God, the grace of God.

He says "Gawt" and not "God," so no one will imagine he means a lesser being, a soft, never terrifying presence who would embrace His children without first lashing them to convict them of their sin.

This daughter knows too well the refrain this dominee is after with his fierce "Gawts" and freighted repetitions; years of two sermons a Sunday, weekly Heidelberg Catechism classes, and countless arguments over the Canons of Dort have worn it into her skull: There is no good in us; we depend absolutely on God; God's glory is all; think therefore nothing of yourself; be grateful He has justified a worm like you. She doesn't want to hear another thick-headed Dutchman bleat the gospel, scathe the Arminians for their devilish free will and proclaim the Truth of divine election and limited atonement—salvation for the chosen few through Christ, eternal damnation for the rest. Her Opa Willem and Oma Reka were punished, cut off forever, and why? Because they loved each other.

Like Oma and Opa, she's not one of the worthy. She doesn't care to be. That's her father's dream. In this country her father wasn't a bastard. Though his parents lived in a ghetto of Dutch factory workers, no one in America knew they had had to get married—in a civil ceremony, the church refusing to bless the union of fornicators. Here her father was free to invent himself. He bought himself a car in high school, went to movies, enlisted in the navy, moved to the West Coast to study engineering, changed his name to Clay.

This Father runs down the road eager to embrace his beloved son, to shower him with gifts—fine robes and a precious ring—to welcome him to the feast he had prepared for him. So God, our Father . . .

Her father didn't embrace her when she jumped into the rental car at nine sharp. He reached toward her, but withdrew his hand before touching her face. "Thank you, Ruth," he said.

He wouldn't even do that much for Oma and Opa. Oma and Opa were always waiting for him to show up, sure he would, though he never did. He refused to step foot in their house. When they visited every May for the Tulip Parade, to see Ruth and the other grandchildren wash the streets in their wooden shoes and the Dutch costumes Oma had made for them, he made sure he was away on business. He couldn't stand their calling him Kees instead of Clay, the way they said "me-lek" for milk, "broat" for bread, "ja" instead of yes. He made his children change their yeahs to yesses, vocalize the *s* strongly, the American way. He told them to write on all forms that he was born in the United States. Afraid to lie, Ruth scribbled "U. S. citizen" in the blanks.

After they took Oma to the nursing home, her fingers ceaselessly unraveling the hem of her robe, Opa moved into the front room of their tiny house. He lay on the couch, a glass of Tang and a stack of rusks near him on the floor, searching his Dutch Bible and sifting through pictures—Reka in her Sunday apron, white lace hat with gold blinders, and coral beads; Kees with Reka on the boat to America; Kees in his sailor whites. When Ruth came to clean and cook for him— sweet-and-sour red cabbage with pickled peaches from the cellar, *hutspot,* buttermilk-barley soup, *banket* for dessert—he told her stories: Oma hired out at ten to a farm in Zeeland, scrubbing and ironing for rich Dutch *vrouwen* in America, eating lunch at the kitchen table while they sat in the dining room; Kees bringing the paddle to Oma and insisting she spank him because he had hurt his brother, buying his

A Woman of Salt

own clothes at ten, hiding in the closet when the Salvation Army delivered the Christmas basket, refusing to open his packages. Afterward, Opa would press Ruth with questions: "Are you happy to live here in America? *Ja,* your *vader,* a big man now, *is niet? Waarom* he won't look at us? Why? Tell me, Ru-tie, was it worth it, that I move to America?"

Once he, too, was in the nursing home, a few rooms down from Oma, who no longer knew him, Opa's heart weakened rapidly, though the doctors found no disease. When the elders came to sing psalms in Dutch round his bed, to ease his way, trusting, to the Lord, he waved them away. He was waiting for Kees.

Kees or Clay, this father has no business crying for his daughter. Let him cry for his own failures.

The door to our Father's house stands open, ready for our return.

The father's head bows and his arm moves up to blot his cheeks. In the dampness of his shirt there is the smell of hours spent ironing his dress shirts, pajamas, underwear.

The daughter slides away from him across the hard wood. Her skirt brushes the leg of the boy. He stares at her, sticks the thin disk of peppermint at her between his teeth, then snaps it in half.

This son of mine was dead and has come back to life; he was lost and now is found.

Her father went back to the Netherlands with his parents only once, when he was twelve. It had been a bad year there for farming and mussel-fishing and his parents packed a trunk with coffee and sugar, sheets and blankets, hoping to appease their families. Oma's family took the gifts, but wouldn't speak to them. Down the street, Opa's father slammed the door on them, crushing the boy's hand.

Her father didn't tell her this; her mother whispered it when Ruth, still a girl, asked why the last two fingers on her father's left hand bent in upon themselves. "Don't ever mention the fingers to anyone," her mother said, "or anything about his nervous breakdowns after the war, either. No one's supposed to know—not even me."

Merciful Father, make us acceptable in Thy sight. May we come before Thee . . .

The dominee's voice has fallen into the rhythmic softness of prayer. Ruth's mother also told her, when she complained that her dad recited

MARY POTTER ENGEL

the prayers before and after meals by rote—"May we come before Thee holy and unblemished"—that her father prayed beautifully, with more feeling than the dominee or elders, and that he loved to pray, but only in private, when the two of them were alone. Whenever he was asked to pray in public, he refused. "Such a strong man," her mother said, "afraid of a thing like that."

Hide not Thy face from us, we beseech Thee. Amen.

The congregation echoes the dominee's amen and rises to sing "How Blest Is He Whose Trespass Has Freely Been Forgiven." When they sit again, to wait for the deacons to file down the rows distributing the collection plates, the father's shoulder brushes against the daughter's. She draws her arm closer to her ribs, locks it in place by clutching her waist, then holds very still, waiting for the memory of his touch, like thousands of small bubbles breaking over the surface of her skin, to fade.

The boy's grandfather leans over him and nudges Ruth with the heavy wooden plate. She passes it, adding nothing to the jumble of change and pledge cards. Her father drops in a bill for himself and something extra, for her. He takes the piled offerings from her and hands them to the deacon in the aisle.

What does this deacon see when he bends to receive the plate from her father? A stranger in an expensive suit and tie? A handsome father with his look-alike daughter? Does he see his square chin, broad forehead, and brilliantly white hair against his dark and youthful face and think him a righteous man? A man who sits on the consistory of his home church, soberly dispensing harsh wisdom to those who have strayed? Does he notice his tears, and say to himself, There's a truly contrite heart?

The first time her father came to visit her at Dordrecht, he picked her up at the dorm and they walked miles around the campus together. "What did you want to do most in your life?" she asked him. He answered softly, without hesitating. "I always wanted to build a bridge."

The organ swells into the doxology and the congregation stands, singing "Praise God from Whom All Blessings Flow," while the deacons parade the gifts up the center aisle and lay them before the dominee.

A Woman of Salt

The people in the congregation bow their heads, close their eyes, and as the dominee begins the prayer of thanksgiving, Ruth's father reaches for her hand, surrounds it with his. He squeezes it gently and lets go.

She turns to look at him.

He smiles sadly at her from a great distance she doesn't recognize. It's as if he's trying to remember who she is, where they are.

Doesn't he know that *he's* the one who cut himself off, *he's* the one who's lost—lost his parents, wife, children, his daughter, himself? Let him cry for *that,* and for what he loses every day he stays in that country he fled to when he ran away from his father in America: a hard country, where the stony earth does not yield to planting and the only way to prosper is to build on what is predictable, guaranteed; a faraway country, where they speak a language not of belonging but of what can be bought and what can be sold, of debits and credits and knowing exactly where you stand; a country of judgment where all roads are secured and all journeys mapped out in advance; a safe country, free from the risks of mercy and from which he refused and refuses to return and maybe her father is crying now not for her but for the boy who ran away because he couldn't help his father, couldn't save him, though he wanted to desperately, maybe he is crying for the boy who left so long ago for that distant, hard place and never came back, who refused to crawl back across the chasm that opened between him and his father, refused not out of pride or stubbornness or habit or hopelessness or fear but terror, terror of his father's strangeness to him on the other side of that abyss, terror of his own strangeness, so far away, terror of falling, terror there would be no bridge, terror there would be and maybe he is crying for that boy and for how much it cost him to run away to such a little place and for his father, who, disoriented in a new world, unsure of his footing, unable to read the signs, never set off in search of him, never came rushing over the breach to meet him, when that was all he longed for.

The dominee steps down from the pulpit to the communion table centered just beyond the front pews. The elders rise to join him, flanking the table. Across the front of the table is carved DO THIS IN REMEMBRANCE OF ME. Fingers of red- and blue-stained light reach across the

MARY POTTER ENGEL

white linen runner, over the plate of bread and the silver pitcher of grape juice. The dominee pulls himself up to issue the warning to his flock to examine their worthiness to partake of the Lord's Supper lest they condemn themselves by eating.

Let every one consider by himself his sins and accursedness, that he may abhor himself and humble himself before God . . . walk sincerely before His face, without any hypocrisy, enmity, hatred . . . Those who do not feel this testimony in their hearts eat and drink judgment unto themselves.

Gravely the dominee lifts the bread toward the congregation. *Take, eat, remember, and believe the body of our Lord Jesus Christ was broken unto a complete remission of all our sins.*

He sets the bread down and stretches his arms wide in welcome.

Come, he calls, *all is ready.*

The elders wait until each has received a plate mounded with squares of bread, soft and snowy, then disperse. When they have finished serving Christ's squared body, they will return the emptied plates to the table and swing out to the congregation again, more slowly this time, bearing deep, round trays heavy with tiny cups clattering in their holders, brimming with the blood of the covenant that links fathers and sons.

Sometimes Ruth's father does not take communion, though it comes only once every three months and to refuse it raises suspicion among the faithful and the possibility of a home visitation by the elders, to probe for the hidden sin. She has seen her father do this, let the plate pass without taking a piece of Christ's flesh for himself, the rattling tray go by without removing a cup of Christ's blood—once when she was a little girl, still buoyant enough to make her neighbor spill his wine, and again when she was older, more disciplined and reserved. It is not pious restraint, as she once thought, but an agony of the heart. He is a man torn in two, caught between being condemned forever for longing to be accepted as he is and condemning himself eternally because he refuses to ask for acceptance from another.

While the deacons glide through the congregation, the organist directs the expectant silence with a subdued anthem, played in a whisper. The boy with the minty breath rolls the hem of his tie toward his chin. At the pew ahead of them, a deacon, taut with solemn duty,

A Woman of Salt

passes the dwindled mound of bread to the man nearest the aisle, then steps back a pew. Hands clasped, face expressionless, he waits for the plate to travel to the other side, then back, hand to hand, down the father and daughter's row, back to him.

The boy elbows Ruth hard. She scowls at him and he drops the plate of bread on her lap. Without pausing she passes it to her father.

Her father considers the body broken for the remission of his sins. His thumb, bristling with black hairs, presses against the plate, the yellowed nail and dark skin yellower and darker next to the bleached white of the bread. Then, without meeting the deacon's eyes, he hands the plate to him.

The deacon thrusts the plate back, urging the gift upon him.

Ruth's father lets his head fall, stares at his legs. His face is spent— mouth defeated, eyes shrinking, robbed of their luster. It's the face of a man hunted, pursued within and without, weary with anger and running—the face not of King David but of Saul.

The deacon leans forward, taps him on the shoulder, jabs the plate at him again, adding a curt nod.

Eyes cast down, bent fingers nervously plucking invisible lint from his coat sleeve, Ruth's father turns farther away from the broken body.

Reaching past him toward the proffered plate, Ruth takes a portion of bread for herself and with it held aloft in three fingers motions the deacon to move on, begging him to pass over her dad without judgment, to allow him his unworthiness, to grant her dad that freedom.

MARY POTTER ENGEL

Mother Love

Another example of rabbinic exegesis of the narrative in Genesis 19 appears in the following midrash, quoted through the centuries by a chain of Jews and Christians: Philo, Josephus, Saint Luke, Irenaeus, and John Chrysostom.

> The wife of Lot could not control herself. Her mother love made her look behind to see if her married daughters were following.

According to this midrash, as the wife of Lot fled Sodom, she did not look back with the self-deceiving eyes of nostalgia; she did not turn around because she was foolish or curious or mistrustful; she did not turn round in disobedience to her husband or in defiance of a vengeful God; she did not turn round ungrateful for the gift of heavenly life or lusting after the corporeal life she had left behind; she did not look back in anger to gloat over her enemies' destruction or in joy to see her sister's wild triumph. Listening to the silence of the text, these rabbis hear a different truth: The wife of Lot turned around because she was unable to control her desire and looked back in love at her daughters.

This midrash may intend to honor motherhood in order to imprison women within it. But what other wisdom can be drawn from the direction the rabbis' search for meaning takes here?

Imagine the wife of Lot being dragged away from Sodom across the barren plain by two razor-winged angels. Her body sinks in fatigue: she was awake all night, holding her daughters as the mob shouted for Lot to send them out as he had promised, and turning over and over in her mind whether to escape with her sister in a different direction or to flee across the rocky plain with Lot. The angels yank at her arms. Rocks cut her feet. The wind whips her legs and face. Sand stings her eyes. She is angry at her husband, dawdling behind her. It was his lingering, his cowardice, his foolish bargaining with the angels that brought them to the edge of destruction and forced them to this flight into pain.

She is angry at her sons-in-law. When Lot came to warn them, "Up, get out of this place, for the Lord is about to destroy the city," they ridiculed him, saying, "O thou fool! Violins, cymbals, and flutes resound in the city, and thou sayest Sodom will be destroyed!" When she came to beg them to allow her daughters to leave the city with her, they did not answer her. Why should they take note of a woman?

The wife of Lot rankles at the thought of her married daughters. Why had Dini and Chesed not defied their husbands and followed her? Why had they abandoned her?

She is furious with the angels. They are dragging her out of her home against her will, their cold fingers burning her flesh. They are forcing her toward Zoar, a place for pinched hearts.

And, as the angels drag her away from Sodom toward redemption, the wife of Lot rages at the God of Abraham, a god unable to imagine a freer, more graceful end to the world he supposedly created in love.

Just so she flees the city of Sodom, in a fury.

But beyond the city gate, in the middle of the desolate plain, the wife of Lot looks up from the barren ground and sees Emet and Rachamim, her two unmarried daughters, running ahead of her. They whimper as they run, holding hands and stumbling with fear. They are so small, she thinks. Seeing their smallness she remembers her two daughters left behind. Looking at Emet and Rachamim running ahead of the angels, she sees Dini and Chesed. She sees them chasing after the lambs when they were girls. She sees them washing each other's hair by the cistern, playing tricks on their father, squealing with joy. She sees them drawing water for their husbands-to-be, baking unleavened bread, nursing their newborns, crying and clinging as they kiss her good-bye.

The wife of Lot dreads turning around. She fights violently

against her desire, trembling like a woman in labor. She does not want to watch her daughters being destroyed, dying, their hair like torches, flesh consumed, bones exposed, mouths open in voiceless screams.

For a moment hope buoys her. She thinks, maybe Dini and Chesed have changed their minds and are following me after all. And she is tempted to look back to see if what she desires is true.

But she smells the burning flesh and she hears the screams.

She knows her daughters are dying.

Overtaken by an unquenchable longing to see them once more before they die, her little girls, blood of her blood, flesh of her flesh, she hesitates. If she could see them just once more, carry a vision of them with her into exile, perhaps her heart would not shatter.

And she looks back to Sodom, forced round by love.

The rabbis have called the wife of Lot by the name Irit, sometimes Idit, *ornament.*

Her name is תְּשׁוּקָה, T'shukah, *longing.*

The crow wish'd every thing was black,
the owl that every thing was white.

WILLIAM BLAKE, "Proverbs of Hell"

The Inhabitants of Sodom

*H*elen parked the rental car at a shopping center near a busy intersection and walked the last half-mile to her daughter's house. Though she had on her most comfortable shoes and a pair of roomy pants, she hadn't walked more than a few blocks for years and the strain of the heat and the hill made her dizzy. She would have blisters the next day and both hips would be inflamed, but she would hardly notice them if her visit was a success.

Every few minutes she stopped to catch her breath. When a car sped by, throwing dust and stones, she turned aside and covered her mouth and nose with the linen handkerchief Ruth had tatted for her in high school. No one slowed down to offer her a ride and she was not surprised at this: people were out to take advantage of others.

When she saw her daughter's mailbox at the crest of the hill, she removed the camouflage vest and hat from a plastic bag. She had found them at a discount store the day before and hidden them inside her robe so her husband wouldn't discover them in the suitcase. She put both on, crushed the bag into the vest pocket, and slogged up the hill.

MARY POTTER ENGEL

At the property line she hid behind a fir tree to gather her strength. She had to run a hundred yards in the open to the shed at the back of the house. Her daughter's boyfriend—a dirty man, *vies, vies,* from Argentina, who looked more like a drug dealer than the professor and poet Ruth claimed he was—had already left; Helen had made sure of that by following him to the college at seven o'clock. Her daughter had gone to the park at eight to take her morning run and driven directly home from there an hour later. Her car was in the driveway now. Good. It would block sight of her as she ran. She gathered her breath and ran, not glancing at the house with its many windows but looking straight ahead, as if by fixing her eyes on her hiding place she could make herself invisible to her daughter.

Behind the shed she knelt in the bushes, hands on the ground, head raised, struggling to catch her breath. If it weren't for her lungs, she would be fine. Her energy had always been prodigious. It had only begun to diminish after her sixtieth birthday, and most days she hardly noticed the difference; she could still get up at eight, clean the entire house, make three meals, do the shopping, and stay up past midnight designing and sewing her quilts, without feeling exhausted. She was good about keeping busy; Clay left for work at four-thirty in the morning, went to bed at eight, never talked unless there was a financial matter that required her signature. Ruth knew nothing of the costs of marriage.

She stood up and leaned around the corner of the shed to observe the house. If her daughter had been at the kitchen sink, she would have seen her running past the house. The headstrong girl would have jumped in her car, locked the doors, and squealed away as if running from the police—the way she had done two days ago, the first time she and Clay had knocked on the door asking to be let in so they could talk, just talk, with her, tell her how much they loved her. Ruth usually relented when Clay spoke with her—she adored her father. That's why Helen had brought Clay with her the first time. But when Ruth saw them on her front porch, she slammed the door on them and bolted out the back to her car.

If Ruth escaped this morning, she probably wouldn't return until long after dark, with that *vies* man right behind her. This was a

A Woman of Salt

respectable neighborhood, with well-tended houses and wide lawns, a place Russell had chosen. What did the neighbors think of this strange car parked in her daughter's driveway night after night? Ruth had never cared what others thought; she always did as she pleased. This man was sure to have a wife and children down in Venezuela or whatever filthy country he was from. If he went back to them, there was a chance that Russell would take Ruth back, though the elders had assured Helen that according to Matthew 5:31 a husband could put away an adulterous wife in good conscience.

But Russell wasn't made of stone, like Ruth. Helen had seen that at the wedding. Russell cried through the ceremony, Ruth was a sphinx. During the reception he beamed at Ruth and couldn't bear being separated from her for an instant. She flitted among the guests making indecent jokes and laughing, drinking more than her share of champagne, pulling everyone—even the dominee!—onto the dance floor, jumping about whorishly in front of the aunts and uncles, nieces and nephews.

The house was quiet. No lights visible. Ruth was probably upstairs, showering or studying at her desk—she was forever burying herself in books, avoiding people, refusing to talk or help with the housework.

She was safe, then, her mission undiscovered. She still had a chance to get to her daughter and plead with her to be saved.

Because she had never been a match for her daughter in arguments, even when Ruth was a child, last night Helen had memorized the words of Dr. Farber: "A man is not an adulterer because he commits adultery. He commits adultery because he's an adulterer. Deceit, theft, covetousness, wickedness, lasciviousness and fornications—all these evil things come from within and defile the man. And where did you get this lust? You were born with a sin nature that you received from your spiritual father, the devil. Jesus said to the unsaved, 'Ye are of your father the devil, and the lusts of your father ye will do' (John 8:44)."

Ruth always repented, eventually, when confronted with her unrighteousness. The moment her daughter wavered when hearing Dr. Farber's words, the second she showed the slightest softening, a downcast look or a forehead furrowed with confusion, Helen would throw her arms around her. She would hold her daughter as she shook with

MARY POTTER ENGEL

124

tears like a chastened child. Reconciled, Ruth would drive her to the rental car and they would caravan to the Holiday Inn to get Clay, celebrate with a fancy lunch. Later Helen would call her sisters, let all four know that she had chastised Ruth and returned her to the fold—the child they constantly faulted her for not controlling. "That girl's headed for damnation, Helen," they would say. "*Do* something with her."

It was a lovely day, clear and dry with a cool breeze, and not one of her daughter's windows was open. How could she stand living without fresh air?

All the doors were probably locked. Ruth always kept her doors locked: the bathroom when she was little, her bedroom when she was a teenager, her apartment in college. A strange girl. Ruth never looked her in the eyes. Even as a baby she hadn't. And she would never talk to her. No matter how much she pleaded with her or tried to befriend her, took her to lunch or bought her valuable first editions, her daughter never offered her anything but trivialities or lies. If she asked an innocent question, "Why are you so late?" Ruth would shrug and say "There was a National Junior Honor Society Meeting after school," not mentioning that her Catholic boyfriend Steve was there and that she had sat close to him, breathing in the scent of his unlawful flesh, opening herself to him. Ruth was just like her father, secretive and cold. The two of them had to be watched. Helen had been forced to search Clay's stacks of papers, call hotels across the United States, follow her husband to meetings. If she wanted to know what Ruth was thinking and doing so she could help her, save her from herself, she had no choice but to check her drawers while she was in school, dig in her hamper for the spiral diary wrapped in a sour-smelling sweatshirt.

She would skim the inconsequential parts:

The Viet Nam war, the Israel-Egypt crisis, the fires in Detroit and riots between the races, constant bitterness and distrust of man toward his fellowman—all these make me think the end of the world is near. . . .

Been cleaning the house all morning. . . .

Steve says I'm beautiful. Why does he lie to me???

I'm never sure about anything. I was made to be confused. . . .

Steve and I talked about the catechism book I gave him. I told him I didn't like to hurt people, that I'd rather be hurt myself, that when people hurt me I believed it was my fault, that I had only had four happy hours in my life, all of them with him. . . .

Some things take longer to heal than others. Calvin says suicide is the unforgivable sin, but I can't find that in the Bible and I wonder why God would hate a heart so battered it could no longer contain hope. . . .

When Helen's interest was piqued, she would slow down, struggling to decipher the light pencil strokes and her daughter's impossible writing:

I should have listened to my mother. She's on the ball with things like this. She told me I was too aggressive. . . .

After Mother went antiquing with Mrs. Noteboom, Steve cruised by the house and I jumped in the car. I think Mr. Van Nuys saw us drive off. If he tells Mother, I'm dead. Anyway, we drove to the Heckla bridge and talked and talked. We agreed that if we ever spent the night together, we would just be with each other and talk, not sleep or do any of that kind of stuff! He and I have too many scruples to do anything else. . . .

Steve said he wouldn't use my body unless my mind and soul came along with it in marriage and that he was giving me a ladder for Christmas so we could elope. . . .

Mother went on a tear when I wasn't home from school by 5:30 on the dot for supper. She told Debbie, "I know where your sister is and what she's doing! She's been living a lie to us! I should never have agreed to let her see that boy 'just once.' My parents wouldn't let me even say hello to a boy who wasn't Dutch. Debbie, you will never, never date a Catholic! Do you hear me?"

Even with a magnifying glass certain words were hard for Helen to make out—was it "breath" or "breasts," "our faiths" or "our future"?—and the ends of some sentences disappeared altogether—*I have to ask God to forgive me for even thinking. . . .* These gaps would have frustrated her if she hadn't had a talent for guessing what was missing. No matter how Ruth hid in silence, evasion, or trickery, her secrets, like Clay's, were always revealed to her in the end. Just like this time. When Ruth called two weeks ago, saying Russell had moved in with a friend temporarily and that they were seeing a counselor, she had sensed something was up. Tracking down Russell had paid off: he told her about José or Pablo or whatever he was.

Crouching, Helen ran to the back of the house and tried the door. The knob clicked from side to side, refusing to turn open. She expelled her breath, faulting herself for not taking a credit card with her to slide inside the jamb and release the lock. From inside came the scent of potatoes fried in olive oil and rosemary, Ruth's favorite breakfast. Russell was a gourmet cook. He spent hours preparing Florentine chicken, mulligatawny stew, scallops in wine sauce for Ruth. Clay refused to boil water. Why couldn't her daughter be content with what she had? That was the secret. Dr. Farber had said it in the tract she had ordered two weeks ago from Love Worth Finding Ministries, "The Secret of Satisfaction." He proved from Exodus 20:17 that covetousness leads to whoremongering, destruction, and other debasements. All of Ruth's degrees had blinded her to this simple logic, that the end of desiring what was unlawful for one to have or to be was always a renewed loneliness. Knowing that had saved *her*. If she wanted to save Ruth, she would have to make her see it, too.

Keeping low, she hurried to the side of the house and flattened herself against the siding between two windows. Her heart banged in her chest and sweat dripped round the rim of her hat. The vest was stifling and the gnats at her face and throat were devilish. I'm too old for this misery, she thought. It isn't right. I've got to make her see. If she won't listen this time, I'll drive to the college and tell her dean the whole story, let him know my daughter wasn't raised to behave this way, have him tell Ruth she'll lose her job if she doesn't give up this foolishness. That's all that's ever mattered to Ruth, her books and her work.

She leaned to the left, jerked her face to the window and back again. The den and kitchen were empty. For once she was glad her daughter didn't believe in curtains or blinds. She tried to push up the window, but it wouldn't budge. She dropped to her hands and knees and crawled along the foundation to the dining room at the front of the house, keeping low beneath the window ledges. Her silk palazzo pants would be ruined, stains and tears at the knees and cuffs, but what would that matter once Ruth was back with Russell and leading a normal married life?

At the window nearest the corner of the house she stood and peered into the dining room. The vitrine she had given Russell and her daugh-

A Woman of Salt

ter as a wedding present, filled with gifts of Lladro and cranberry glass and malachite, stood against the far wall. The glass needed cleaning and a halo of dust had formed along the top curve. Her daughter had never taken care of her things, and this hurt as much as anything else. She had tolerated the years Ruth lived like a gypsy at school, reading God-knows-what in bare apartments infested with roaches, befriending priests and Jews. But she had hoped that the girl would change once she was finally married. When Ruth called her out of the blue to tell her that she was marrying Russell, an old friend from Dordrecht College, Helen was sure that her daughter had at last matured beyond rebelliousness. Russell was one of their own, from the Dutch Church. He came from a prominent church family, the Krommendyks! And he was so pleasant. He took time to chat with Helen every time he visited Ruth at their home. When Helen heard the good news about the wedding, she said, "Don't hurt that boy."

But Ruth broke Russell's heart. Before their first anniversary she told him she had made a mistake, and to salvage his dignity Russell moved out.

Why did she have to ruin everything? Ruth had had better luck in marrying than Helen had. Russell wasn't as good-looking or ambitious as Clay, but he was from a wealthy family and he was charming and gracious. The whole family loved Russell. Maybe he didn't talk to her exactly the way Ruth wanted. Maybe he had a hair-trigger temper. So what if he told her what size to rip the lettuce, complained she used too much toilet paper, criticized the sag of her *dikke eind*? What difference did that make? Everyone made a bargain when they married and the price had to be paid. Why couldn't Ruth accept that?

Ruth appeared in the hallway carrying a bucket, a squeegee, and newspapers. The mother ducked away, waited a few moments, then looked again. Her daughter had stationed herself near the hallway, at the front of the living room, and was sponging the window near the door with ammonia water from her bucket. She looked gaunt and unkempt in her jeans and wrinkled T-shirt, and her straggly hair was far too long for a woman almost thirty. What did men see in her daughter? she wondered. Ruth made no attempt to care for her looks or to be accommodating; she thought nothing of their happiness, only her own.

MARY POTTER ENGEL

When the glass was wet everywhere, Ruth dropped the sponge in the bucket and ran the squeegee down the window, across it, and down once more, patiently wiping away the excess water with a rag after each stroke. Crumpling a piece of newspaper, she began rubbing the glass, angling her head this way and that to check for spots she had missed, the way she had been shown. "Spray bottles of Windex, paper towels, and a few quick swipes won't do," Helen had always told her daughter as she checked her work for streaks every Saturday, making her wipe the windows over and over until she was satisfied they were perfectly transparent. It was a good sign. If, after all the evil she had done, Ruth still washed windows the way she had been taught, perhaps she was not lost yet; perhaps she could still be reached. She was glad that she had come. It would be worth the week she would spend in bed recovering after they returned home. Once it was over and things were back the way they should be—Russell in charge, Ruth repentant, grateful and loving to her mother for keeping her from throwing away a bearable life for the false hope of something better—even Clay would agree that it was a good thing she had come back this morning.

When they had returned to their room at the Holiday Inn after knocking on Ruth's door the second day, Clay had been angry at their daughter's refusal to speak to them.

"You've tried twice already," he said to her. "Leave it alone now."

"You agreed it was our duty, Clay. You left your work for this."

"We're wasting our time."

"If she could just see that if you're a child of God, twice born and blood bought, you desire nothing beside God and God's—"

"It's her life," Clay said. "Let her ruin it."

"But we traveled so far to see her," Helen said.

"It's not worth your agony, Helen. We're flying home in the morning. That's the end of it."

Helen persuaded Clay to stay one more day. That evening in the restaurant she told him that she was leaving very early in the morning to drive an hour or two to an antique mall she had heard about, to look for a special present to drop off at Ruth's house before their flight, a sign of reconciliation and their willingness to help. She might spend the rest of the day hunting for quilt shops that sold specialty items she needed and couldn't find at home, so he shouldn't worry if she didn't come back until late afternoon. He could walk downtown, visit the library, have a swim and a sauna, stay in the room and catch up on his paperwork. They would meet for dinner and call from their room to arrange to drop off the gift on their way to the airport. If Ruth wouldn't answer her phone, they would leave the package at her office with a note.

At the front window her daughter crushed a clean sheet of newspaper into a ball and polished the glass again, rubbing one spot over and over, straining to see if the marks were on the inside or the outside. She picked up the bucket and moved to the next window, away from the front door.

The mother retreated along the side of the house and circled around the back to the other side. When she approached the living room windows near the front, she slunk down and advanced more slowly. At the corner of the house, she was on her belly, wriggling under the shrubbery, boxwood scratching her arms and face. When she was directly under the window her daughter was washing, she rested. Only a second, she told herself, just until my heart stops hurting, or the girl will move on and I'll miss my chance. Careful not to make a sound, she folded her knees into position and braced her hands on the ground. She rocked onto her toes and took several long breaths.

In a rush of motion she turned and stood so that she was looking directly into the face of her daughter on the other side of the window.

Ruth's face was hard, hard. Even as a child she had tried to mask her feelings, but she had never been good at it. Helen could always read her daughter's face. Now Ruth's jaw was clenched. Her cheeks pulled tight across the bone. Her forehead scowled over narrowed eyes. She was ugly with hate. From the minute she was born Ruth had hated her. Those dark eyes that Clay thought sparkled with joy flamed with contempt for her. Burning ice, they fixed themselves on her and bored through her, accusing her. "I know you, Mother," they said, "and there is no good in you."

"Mother," Ruth said, her voice wobbly through the glass, "don't do this. Don't come in my house."

"Come out, then," she called to her. "Come out so I can talk to you."

The daughter threw down her rag and ran from the window.

She'll lock herself in the upstairs bathroom, the mother thought. Ruth was as dumb about hiding as Clay was. During one of their fights after the kids had left home, she had ditched her car in the neighbor's back field and hidden in the house a whole week and Clay had never discovered her. Frantic, he kept calling Debbie to find out where she was. When she stole next to the bed late one night and stood over him, he woke with a start, yelling and taking the Lord's name in vain.

Helen took Clay's Swiss Army knife out of her vest pocket and slit her daughter's window screen. She reached in and undid the latches, removed the aluminum frame, and tried to push up the window. It wouldn't budge. She slid the longest blade between the halves of the window, trying to release the lock, and sliced the tip of her left index finger. She pinched the flesh together with her thumb and wound the handkerchief around it. It turned bright red in seconds. She took off her hat, wrapped it around her right fist, and smashed through the glass. The pointed shards that remained, like an inverse star, she broke away with the butt of the knife. When the hole was big enough, she reached in and undid the lock. Pieces of glass fell as she pushed up the window, covering the sill with diamonds. She brushed them aside and tried to hoist herself up. The ledge was higher than she had thought and she fell to the ground. One of her shoes dropped off, but she didn't care. She would come back for it later, when everything was set-tled, once and for all, after her daughter had admitted her fault and begged her forgiveness. She managed a firmer grip, took a deep breath, and tried again, this time dragging her waist to rest against the sill. A piece of glass dug into her right palm, but there was no time to remove it. She pulled her lower body over the sill. Her stomach caught on a sharp point, but she pulled herself free and tumbled headfirst into the room, knocking against the bucket. Ammonia water sloshed over the sides, burning into her cuts. I'm in, she thought. That's something to be grateful for. Things are going better this time.

Her daughter's bathroom door was solid wood, with a keyed lock. She jiggled the knob and knocked, calling, "Talk to me, Ruth, come out and talk to me. Just talk. That's all I ask."

No sound came from inside.

A Woman of Salt

She tried a more cheerful tone. "Debbie's pregnant again. I'm going to visit her next week. Anything you want me to tell her?"

She pressed her ear to the door, cupping both hands around it. Nothing.

"Your cousin Lavina's in two Bible study groups and she got pearled by Dan Spyckaboer last night. She'll probably get her diamond this Christmas."

She knocked again. She beat the heel of her hand against the door until it bruised.

Inside the bathroom a hair dryer turned on.

Ruth was stubborn, had been since the moment she was born. She could bang on that door all day, the way she had rattled the back door the day she and Clay arrived and steadily blown the car horn for an hour the next day, and still her daughter would not let her in.

"Why won't you talk to me?" she screamed at the door. "What have your father and I ever done to you to be treated this way? We gave you and Russell everything in this house. We paid for your wedding, all those pictures, champagne, Fuji mums, that foul-mouthed jazz band."

She joggled the handle hard, rumbled the door against the jamb, kicked the lower edge.

The dryer whirred steadily.

"'Honor your father and your mother,' the Bible says. You may be smart, but you're our daughter and we know what's best for you. My mother was hard on me, much harder than she was on my sisters. She had to be, for my sake. 'God loves the one He chastises.' But I still obeyed her. She tied my left hand to the chair when I ate, just like I did to you, so you would learn good table manners, and I never complained. When my mother was dying, *I* took care of her. Calvin wasn't even two and I was pregnant with you, but I spent half of every week at her house feeding her, bathing her, changing her bedpan—and even then I didn't get a kind word from her. All she could talk about was how wonderful Gert and Verna had been to her, but I took care of her just the same."

Helen scuffed down the gritty stairs to the kitchen, directly below the bedroom, and sat at the antique pine table she had given Ruth. The wood was eaten with wormholes, rubbed smooth by countless meals. She ran her hand over it and began to cry, quietly at first, then louder, convulsed by sobs.

She rested her elbows on the table, her face in her hands, too tired now to cry. The heavy cotton vest was soaked with sweat. It clung to her back and breasts. She unzipped it and fanned her face with her hand. The shard of glass had fallen from her hand, leaving a red hole. She let the blood drip on the table.

She pushed herself up from the table and wiped her hand hard across the vest.

In the hallway, at the bottom of the stairs, she called, "Sweetheart, sweetheart. There's something wrong with you, *liefje*. Someone's been influencing you. Your friends are making you do this. Those lesbians. You need help."

The hair dryer buzzed steadily.

She pulled "The Secret of Satisfaction" from her vest pocket and placed it in the center of the table, open to the page on which she had circled Dr. Farber's words: "You were born with a sin nature that you received from your spiritual father, the devil. Jesus said to the unsaved, 'Ye are of your father the devil, and the lusts of your father ye will do' (John 8:44)."

"The second you came into this world you hated me," Helen bawled to the ceiling. "You tried everything to make trouble for me. You've caused every problem this family ever had. If I didn't have my faith, I couldn't bear it. The Bible says 'Forgive seventy times seven. All those times you lied to me, went out with those Catholic boys behind my back and did God knows what, insulted me in front of your friends, dressed like a whore to work in that bar, stole, brought dope into my house, lived in sin with that artist, Lennie, shamed me before the dominee and elders and in front of my sisters, and I forgave you, forgave you, forgave you. My mother never forgave me, not once, not even when she was dying and I begged her, but I forgave you *every time*. And now you're an *adulterer*."

Helen felt the whine of the hair dryer in her cheekbones and jaw.

"Your father and I only want to help you."

A Woman of Salt

She gripped the banister to steady herself.

"Why are you doing this to me?" she screamed. "Why? Tell me. *Tell me what I did. I didn't do anything.*"

Back in the kitchen she found the pad by the phone and wrote a message in her flowing Palmer script. She drew a pocket New Testament from her vest pocket and, making sure that the edges of the paper protruded, placed the note inside to mark Matthew 5:31. As slowly as she could, without causing a creak, she climbed the stairs to her daughter's bedroom. She was exhausted and her shoeless foot started to cramp. The cuts in her hands and abdomen stung. But she would not give up.

At the top of the stairs she rested. The door to the bathroom was shut tight. Behind it the hair dryer droned on.

Quickly she tiptoed into her daughter's bedroom. The shades were drawn, the closet door closed. Newspapers, files, manuscripts, and books—English and foreign, open and closed—littered the unmade bed and the floor on either side. Careful not to slip on a pile of loose papers, she lifted Ruth's pillow, placed the pocket Bible and note under it, and crept downstairs.

She scraped a kitchen chair across the floor as if pushing it back to the table, then walked noisily through the front hall, opened the door, and let it bang shut behind her. She retrieved her shoe and hobbled across the front lawn, jamming the hat and vest into the plastic bag and hiding her dirtied and bloodied hands with the bag. She could wash her hands and throw the bag in the trash at the shopping center. By the time she got back to the Holiday Inn her daughter would have found the note. Maybe Ruth had already discovered it. Maybe her heart was even now relenting as she read:

Dear Ruth,
I'll go to my grave justified.
Where will you be?
> Your mother

Helen headed resolutely toward the road. Why look back? She had done her best. Surely no one could fault her for not doing her duty. Not even her sisters.

MARY POTTER ENGEL

At the mailbox she swung around, hoping to catch a glimpse of her daughter. Maybe Ruth was standing in the upstairs window, bent in sorrow and regret as she watched her limp away heartsick, excluded from her love.

Helen shielded her eyes with her hand and squinted. She cupped her other hand over the first to get a better view. But the sun was hitting the glass all wrong. All she could see was empty glare.

Dizzy from the light, Helen turned back to the road and slumped away, leaving her daughter curled up on the floor of her bedroom closet, fast asleep.

A Woman of Salt

She Beheld the Shekhinah

This midrash continues:

> The wife of Lot could not control herself. Her mother love made
> her look behind to see if her married daughters were following.
> She beheld the Shekhinah. . . .

In the silence of this text of the wife of Lot, a narrative of dis-
tanced judgment and destruction, the rabbis hear the Shekhinah,
God's presence dwelling among his beloved people. If this rabbinic
imagining into truth can be trusted, when the wife of Lot, T'shukah,
looked back to see her daughters in the furnace of Sodom, she did
not see the seven depths of hell descending before her, Sheol, Abad-
don, Beer Shachat, Tit ha-Yawen, Sha'arei Maweth, Sha'arei Zal-
maweth, Gehenna, swallowing the wicked into darker and darker
forgetfulness; she saw the presence of God. When she turned toward
her beloved daughters caught in the incinerator of God's justice and
looked upon God's mothering love holding them—

T'shukah saw the presence of God, the rabbis say. What this honor
of seeing the Shekhinah meant for the wife of Lot, they do not take
the trouble to reveal in this midrash. Yet we know that for the rabbis
(as for the church fathers and the authors of the Bible) to *see* the
presence of God is an honor not granted to many. Moses himself was
allowed to see only the back side of God's glory as it passed by him in
the wilderness by the burning bush. When Elijah fled to the wilderness and hid in a cave, God called him out and made him watch as a
great and mighty wind, the power of the Lord, swept by. God made
him stand there and witness an earthquake that shook the founda-

tions of creation. God forced him to look upon a world-devouring conflagration. Elijah saw the glorious power of God and trembled in the cleft of the rock. But Elijah did not see *God*. God was not in the wind or the earthquake or the fire. After they passed, a great silence covered the face of the earth, and in that silence born of tumult, Elijah heard a soft, murmuring sound. The moment he heard it, he drew his mantle over his face. His eyes blinded, looking into the darkness, he heard the voice of God, a still, susurrating voice, asking, "Why are you here, Elijah?"

Far more terrifying than *seeing* the presence of God is *being seen* by God, standing in the harrowing gaze that searches one's folds, pursues one's fears, unburies one's heart and exposes it to a deathly light.

Intolerable to be seen by God.

The rabbis and church fathers agree: No one can look upon the face of God and live.

But this is also true: No one can be seen by God and not perish.

When T'shukah turned round, longing for her daughters, she saw God gazing at her in judgment. In the silence born of Sodom's destruction she felt the gaze of God calling her into question, murmuring, Where have you been, T'shukah? Where are you going, T'shukah? T'shukah, why are you here?

She saw the presence of God and she was petrified. (The rabbis do not mention this.) Standing in the presence of God, she could not bear her shame.

God did not punish the wife of Lot by turning her into a pillar of salt. God did not work her death upon her. T'shukah killed herself. She died to save herself from the gaze of God, hardening into crystals that would not absorb the disturbing light of her questioner but reflect it back to its damning source.

In the middle of our journey we lost our way.

DANTE, *The Inferno*

Carousel

t was dark by the time Ruth arrived at the headquarters of Women Against Violence Against Women. Sweat tickled the back of her ears, stuck her T-shirt to her skin. Her heart beat fast. She was eager to begin the tour of Times Square, a new adventure to recount at work. She enjoyed watching the faces of her colleagues and students as she revealed that she had worked as a hotpants-outfitted nightclub waitress, hitchhiked across the country, lived in a battered-women's shelter (as an observer), spent time in jail (less than twenty-four hours) for possession of illegal drugs and an unregistered weapon.

She pulled open the unmarked steel door and stepped inside.

The room was spare and dimly lit. Several women clustered around a card table strewn with pamphlets. A few others sat on folding chairs arranged in front of a movie screen. Near the back a sturdy woman in high-top sneakers, cutoffs, and a T-shirt was bent over a projector, fitting a slide carousel into position.

Ruth walked over to her. "Need any help?" she asked.

MARY POTTER ENGEL

"Got it, thanks," the woman said, locking the carousel into place. She thrust her hand to Ruth. "Joan."

Joan looked about the age of Ruth's students, but she exhibited none of their maddening self-doubt.

"I'm Dr. VanderZicht," Ruth said.

"You're the one who wanted a bibliography?"

"Yeah."

When Ruth called to sign up for the WAVAW tour, she asked how to prepare for it. "Just send in your donation and show up," the volunteer said. Ruth spent the rest of April researching articles on pornography. In May she read Laura Mulvey's essays on the industrialization of the female body, intrigued both by Mulvey's theory of man as "bearer of the look" and woman as image connoting "to-be-looked-at-ness" and by her argument for women's "mask of visibility." Before the semester ended she showed "Killing Us Softly" at the Women's Center and facilitated a discussion on culturally constructed images of women in advertising. The evening went so well that she reserved the documentary for the first week of her fall seminar. It was essential, she believed, for students to shed their romantic views of a gender-blind world if they were to see how women were forced everywhere to perform for the voyeur's gaze.

"Sign in," Joan told Ruth, "and take a seat with the others. We're ready to start."

They began with introductions. "I'm here doing research for my new seminar, Eros and Violence," Ruth told the group. "I'm considering making this tour one of the class requirements."

"Married?" Joan asked. "Single?"

It didn't occur to Ruth to say she was married. Since Dirk never accompanied her anywhere (her colleagues called him "The Phantom"), in public she thought of herself as single. "Beyond the means of a free-clinic physician," Dirk said of the films and plays she invited him to. He couldn't attend faculty dinners and other free events because he had so little time off. He liked to spend his evenings and weekends poring over the thick, fine-print manuals of his World War II board-game collection and playing the elaborate games against himself while he smoked joints and sipped Rémy-Martin. The games required immense concentration. To avoid interruption, he turned on the answering machine whenever he played, instructing Ruth not to pick up the phone when it rang.

Ruth was proud of their relationship. Their respect for each other as independent individuals was uncompromising—something she and her first husband, Russell, had never achieved. And their partnership was based, as Dirk liked to say, "on life, liberty, and the mutual pursuit of happiness." This was a concept of marriage Ruth's mother would never have understood. "No one expects to be happy in marriage" was Helen's response to all reports of marital differences—her daughter Debbie's, her nieces', her sisters', Debbie Fisher's, Liz Taylor's. "You want too much. You made your bed, now lie in it."

"Lesbian? Bi?" Joan asked Ruth. She stood by the blank screen, her purple WOMEN AGAINST VIOLENCE AGAINST WOMEN T-shirt almost covering her cut-offs. "It's okay to say it."

"Married," Ruth said, "but I kept my name."

Most of the other women were social workers and counselors. The youngest, Mandy, was a college sophomore who had just started volunteering at the Ramapo Rape Crisis Center. She reminded Ruth of the naïve woman in her spring feminism seminar. The student had seen a ski-masked man approaching her on a jogging path and instead of immediately running away, she ran right toward him! If she had been less trusting and more alert (a ski mask in May?), she wouldn't have ended up knifed in the breast.

The older woman in the front row, wide everywhere, with heavy glasses and blackened hair, said her goal was to bring people to The Light, including her alcoholic husband, whose bed she hadn't shared for eighteen years.

"We can follow The Light," Bea said, extending her right hand and turning to face it, "or stay drunk in the darkness of illusion." She stretched out her left hand and turned to it. Smiling, she folded her hands in her lap. "Last year I journeyed to The Light, and it was offered to me to be released from the wheel of reincarnation. But I chose to come back. I chose to stay until every grain of sand is in The Light."

"Like a Bodhisattva," Mandy said softly, almost to herself.

MARY POTTER ENGEL

"A what?" a woman in the back asked.

"According to Buddhist philosophy," Ruth explained, "a Bodhi-sattva is a person who has reached enlightenment, but who, instead of entering nirvana, chooses to remain in the world of illusion to help others. It's the supreme act of compassi—"

"These women don't need pity," Joan said sharply. "And they don't need to be saved." She leaned toward Bea's puffy, heart-shaped face. "Rule number one: Don't talk to the sex workers. They have a right to make a living. *Leave them alone.* Understand?"

"I do," Bea said quietly.

"That goes for everybody," Joan said to the group, scanning for nods of agreement. "Okay, then. On with the briefing."

Ruth was impressed by Joan's handling of Bea. Needy women often showed up in women's groups, sapping everyone's energy. The "tyranny of powerlessness" Ruth called it. Once, an older student like Bea, un-aware she was trapped in an impossible marriage, had registered for Ruth's Women and Mysticism course. During the first class the woman announced that she had been happily married for twenty-eight years and wasn't a lesbian, that she was against abortion, and that she had decided to take Ruth's class instead of going to a shrink. When she dropped out the next day, Ruth was relieved. She didn't want to field the woman's bizarre comments week after week, see the pathetic woolies peeking out from under her skirt.

Joan handed out copies of WAVAW's Mission Statement—"to com-bat the covert and pandemic war against women"—and began the slide show. All the examples had been taken from popular culture: an article from a teen humor magazine article promoting rape of "retarded girls" because their testimony was not credible; fashion-magazine photos of women in submissive positions and as the targets of guns; newspaper ads displaying little girls in poses echoing standard pornographic ones; record jackets depicting other classic porn poses—a naked woman with her head shaved and hands shackled, a women with her head in a toi-let, a woman's fishnetted, stiletto-heeled legs protruding from a meat grinder.

As the images on the screen changed, the other women in the group shifted nervously or blew out their breath. Ruth grew impatient. Having just researched the topic in the library, attended several soft porn flicks with Dirk, and read *Penthouse* and *Playboy* for years (at Dirk's request, with him pointing out his favorite pictures, making her try things detailed in the letters), she was not shocked by the slides. Before that, she had had years of practice distancing herself from the life of the flesh, taking refuge in the mind. To her the body was like a foreign country, worthy of respectful observation. And nothing Joan said was new to her; much of it was an oversimplification of complex theories, calculated to incite protest by magnifying women's vulnerability. Ruth was anxious for the tour to start. She wanted to draw her own conclusions.

The tour began in the Best Sex Shop on Forty-second Street. The women entered with their assigned buddies, Joan first with Bea, Ruth and Mandy last. Inside, squinting against the lights, they searched racks of videos for the titles of snuff films Joan had mentioned. They perused the S & M section for examples of eroticized violence, flipped through the shiny pages of fantasy magazines looking for the "Black Bitch," the "Asian Kitten," and other examples of racism Joan had stressed. Ruth concentrated on kiddie porn magazines, searching for poses inspiring the ads Joan had shown them. Joan's weakest claim during her presentation was that pornographic conventions lay behind the classic Coppertone billboard of the girl with her underpants being pulled down by a dog, as well as behind recent Macy's newspaper ads for girls' underwear. Ruth suspected Joan had overinterpreted these ads to make them fit her ideology.

She paged gingerly through several magazines. There were shots of girls looking over their shoulders at the viewer, a look of mischief of their faces. And in some photos the girl's hands-on-hips pose vaguely resembled that of the Macy's models. But Ruth found no evidence to support Joan's claim of influence. What disturbed Ruth was the fleshiness of the girls in the magazine. At nine and ten these girls were soft and rounded. Ruth had never been like that; even now she was angular. Boyish was how her friends described her and how she liked thinking of herself. "You're Bauhaus, not Rubens," Dirk said whenever she (following his stage directions to the letter) modeled the lingerie he bought her.

She closed the magazine over the girls, stacked it with the others, and headed for the back of the store. Joan had said that if they were up to it, they should have a look at one of the movies playing "Five Minutes Per Quarter" in the jack-off stalls lining the wall.

As she passed Mandy, Ruth pointed to let her know where she was going. Mandy put down her magazine and followed.

"Get out, bitches." A stocky, gray-haired man with a head too large for his body bustled toward the two women inspecting the video display.

"Get out," he hollered. "Move it." He dropped two fingers in the pocket of his short-sleeved shirt and pressed out his red plastic MANAGER pin. "Manager, see?"

The pair maneuvered toward the door, nervously looking for Joan. The manager followed a few steps behind, flapping his arms at their backs and yelling, "Out, out. Back where you belong."

Ruth, with Mandy close behind her, quickly joined the women he was pushing out. Bea approached from the opposite side. In one movement Bea hooked her arm in Mandy's and swung her around. As she led her toward the back of the store, she called over her shoulder, "Come awn, Bitch, Ah mean to find me a souvenir to take home to mah honey in Geowgia."

The rest of the women laughed, Ruth joining them after a moment.

"I said *leave*," the manager shouted. *"Now."*

"Goddamn dykes," a customer nearby muttered.

Joan squeezed between the women and the manager. "Mr. Lamas, this—"

"*La*-mas."

"This is a public place and we have a right, like anybody else, to browse—"

"Not if you're not buying!"

"How do you know we won't?" Joan asked.

Bea rushed past Joan to the checkout near the exit and laid three magazines on the counter. "I'll take these," she said.

A Woman of Salt

The cashier glanced at the manager, who signaled him to take the sale. He rang up the items, folded his arms across his chest, and stood behind the counter glaring at Bea.

"How much do I owe you?" Bea asked.

He jabbed his middle finger toward the figure on the register.

Bea searched her slouchy purse for her wallet. "It's hiding from me," she said as she felt among the contents. "Patience, patience, here it is!" She removed two twenty-dollar bills and, with a grandmotherly smile, handed them to the cashier.

He slapped the change on her purchase.

"Thank you, sir." Bea fitted the bills and change into her wallet, each denomination into its own compartment, then rolled the magazines into her purse.

Joan nodded to the manager and headed for the long display case on the other side of the exit, motioning the others to follow.

Mandy stuck close to Ruth, almost touching her, giving off a smell of Noxzema and sweat.

Mandy's timorousness reminded Ruth of her sister. Debbie had been born cautious, afraid to stray from home, whereas Ruth thrived on new experiences. Like her brother Calvin, Ruth had felt no fear staring into the guts of sharks slit open on the pier, rescuing confused hatchling turtles from a busy highway, swimming through underwater tunnels.

Ruth increased her pace. Surely Joan's buddy system didn't obligate her to be a Siamese twin. At the display case she wedged herself between the two women nearest the end, leaving Mandy to find a spot of her own.

Each item inside the red-velvet-lined case was accompanied by a hand-printed price card. There were dildos of all sizes, colors, and textures; love pearls, Spanish fly, French ticklers, packages containing life-sized inflatable dolls; blindfolds, handcuffs, chains, whips; and more knives than Ruth had ever seen—belt knives, city knives, slip-joint jackknives, hunting knives, bowie knives, combat knives; butterfly knives, lockback knives, one-hand knives; knives with thin- and thick-edged blades, straight and curved blades, serrated and smooth-edged blades; knives with drop-point blades, skinner blades, Tanto blades,

Damascus blades, knives with blades intricately etched with acid, knives with blades as big as mirrors; there were knives with ebony handles, Chinese quince handles, mother-of-pearl handles, India stag handles, coffin-shaped handles, handles carved with Indians hunting buffalo and inlaid with turquoise; knives with handles curved so perfectly they invited Ruth to hold them, feel her fingers curl around their smoothed power and drive them to the hilt.

Ruth stepped back from the case, heart racing, hands itching with last night's desire. In the middle of the night she had sat up tensed and alert, listening for an intruder. Though her hearing seemed preternatural, she could detect no unfamiliar sound outside or inside the apartment. After what seemed hours, she lay down to sleep. But as she lay in the dark, eyes wide open, she heard a voice. Distinct, insistent, the voice spoke within her. *Go to the kitchen,* it commanded. *Open the drawer. Pick up the chef's knife. Bring it into the bedroom. Close your fingers around it. Hold it fast and hack away the filaments joining Dirk's body and yours.*

Pinching her arms and breathing deeply in the darkness, Ruth had recited forgotten phrases from her kindergarten alphabet: *And God saw that it was good, Be ye kind one to another, Create in me a clean heart, O God.*

But the voice would not be stilled. The desire for the knife had prickled in her hands. She grasped the mattress edge to numb her fingers, but she could think only of walking to the kitchen, opening the drawer.

Terrified, she shook Dirk. She called him, scratched her nails across his chest. But she couldn't rouse him. The extra joint he smoked before bed every night made him a deep sleeper. He lay sprawled beside her, tight blond curls flattened against the pillow, mouth open, his pale, lax flesh stolid. Ruth hunched on the edge of the bed, gripping the mattress and staring at the window until dawn.

The next morning Dirk laughed about Ruth's dream. They joked about it over café au lait the way they had teased about his accident the year before, when he stumbled during an argument and broke the glass over their wedding photograph. Commitmentophobia, idol-smashing, his rebellion against Calvinist reverence for duty and order, they

A Woman of Salt

had said then; pre–Times Square tour anxiety, Freudian tremors, her horror of desire, her Genevan dread of dancing and other forms of pleasure, they said this time.

"Game's up!" the Best Sex Shop manager yelled. He huffed toward the display case, dangling an enormous ring of keys in front of him. "We're closing. Everybody out. Move it."

The women retreated before him. He rushed past them, held the door open, and barked, "Closing time. Out. *Out.*"

Joan nodded to the group to follow her out. As the last of them scuttled through the door, one of the customers called out, "Big-butt women!" Ruth instinctively glanced over her shoulder. Her butt was small, high, and firm. He must have been looking at Bea, she thought.

It was 10:30 when the WAVAW group reached Show World, the largest establishment of its kind in the country according to Joan, more lucrative than some Fortune 500 companies, and more than likely under Mafia control. Show World's wide glass doors were littered with messages: Girls! Girls! Girls! Live Sex Show! Fantasy Dates! Best Variety in Town! Everything YOU Want! While the women waited on the sidewalk watching the automatic doors slide open and shut with customer traffic, Joan reminded them to fan out toward their assignments as soon as they entered the arcade. One pair was to observe the video booths on the right, another the phone theaters on the left, another the bar with the striptease farther down. Bea would go with Joan to the Live Sex Show, halfway down the arcade. Ruth and Mandy would continue to the door at the far end of the corridor, the Carousel. At 11:15 P.M. everyone would meet outside and walk back to WAVAW to debrief.

The doors slid open and a tall man in a khaki suit emerged. Scowling, he shouldered his way through the women to a waiting cab. Joan stepped through the doors into the main corridor with the group bunched behind her, Mandy tripping on Ruth's heels.

Inside, cacophony engulfed them. A scuttering crowd choked the hallway. The garish lighting dissolved all color, leaving everything ashen.

As the women advanced, men pressed them on all sides. Heavy feet, insistent shoulders, sharp knees, tensed limbs, and damp-shirted chests herded them down the hall. The air, thick with clamoring and the bitter odor of desire, tightened around Ruth and she felt the arcade closing in on her, as if she were falling down a funnel. She stood on her toes and looked ahead to make sure the corridor wasn't narrowing. But the glut of bodies made it impossible to see.

An opening in the tumult appeared and Ruth broke away from the other women to head for her assignment. Mandy followed, her thumb and forefinger gripping the edge of Ruth's T-shirt. Ruth turned to her, frowning, and shook her head. Mandy let go of her.

The farther down the corridor Ruth traveled, the more slowly the horde crushed forward. As they passed each exhibit, the men craned their necks, stood on tiptoes, pushed against one another harder. Near the entrance to the Live Sex Show, the progress slowed almost to a stop. Outside the open doorway a group had swollen. Stretching around the cologne-drenched man beside her, Ruth saw three bodies entangled on a small platform stage. A black woman, a white woman, and a white man locked in a gymnastic embrace were moving in slow motion, changing positions in a carefully arranged sequence—"Stunning choreography!" Dirk would have said—while the people crowding near them yelled encouragement and directions.

A man with a baseball cap nudged ahead of Ruth, blocking her view. Straining for a new vantage point, she caught sight of Joan pushing through the crowd toward the Live Sex Show entrance. Bea was beside Joan, waving a twenty-dollar bill overhead and calling, "Paying customer, make way, make way, paying customer," her irritating, high-pitched voice rising above the din.

The press in the corridor carried Ruth past the Live Sex Show and she began edging ahead, squeezing around and between the men surrounding her. In the confusion, she no longer felt Mandy close to her. The girl had probably fallen behind deliberately, realizing she wasn't ready for Show World. If so, Ruth hoped she'd have enough sense to make her way out and wait for the rest of the group on the sidewalk. Without looking back for her, Ruth headed toward the end of the corridor.

A Woman of Salt

The crowd jostled ahead, closing tighter around her.

"This way, baby, this way" a ponytailed man next to her cooed. "I'll show you the way in!"

"Umm-umm," another called out, a man in his seventies with a tidy moustache and kind eyes.

"You're a nice tall, thin one. Got a long, tight cunt to match?"

"Where's your costume, honey?"

"Ten dollars to watch you change. Twenty? Thirty?"

A fifty-dollar bill waved in front of Ruth. She hit it away and kept on.

A man with flaccid white arms and tight blond curls caught hold of her sleeve. She pulled free and slipped between two men ahead of her. Someone goosed her. She surged forward. When she saw the black door with CAROUSEL stenciled in red, she glanced over her shoulder. The curly-haired blond was heading straight for her, brandishing the fifty-dollar bill. Ruth lunged for the door.

Without waiting for her eyes to adjust to the darkness, she stumbled into the room. Driving music blasted from the ceiling, but the cavernous space seemed to swallow the sound. A semicircular wall lined with narrow doors curved toward her. She tried the nearest door, but it was locked. The next one, too. She yanked at several others. When one gave way she rushed in, pulled the hollow door tight, and with shaking fingers slipped the latch in place.

The booth was smaller than she had expected—hardly enough room to turn around. She had never thought of herself as petite, but her body took up far less space than the average man's, and she wondered how they managed their bulk inside this cramped place, what they did with their coats in winter. Everything inside was gray-green, including the metal chair. Black scuff marks streaked in all directions, and gouges pocked the lower walls. The No Smoking sign on the left wall was so defaced it was hardly legible. The smell of sour sweat and semen leaked through a fresh coat of Lysol, reminding Ruth of the back of the van she and Dirk used to camp in before they were married, when they were still crazy about each other. Before the fights. Before the abortion. Before the requests to try threesomes and the constant demands for anal sex—"Like *Last Tango in Paris,*" Dirk said. "A nice tight fit for me, you buttered up to make it painless, more fun for all."

Ruth pulled her T-shirt over her face and sank her nose into the warm cave. She closed her eyes and breathed deeply. The smell of olive oil soap mingling with the sweat of her breasts calmed her. Opening her eyes she was surprised by the deepness of the cleft. Not quite fried eggs, Dirk called her breasts. He preferred over-endowed women, like his best friend Raymond's lover, Amey. "Thanks for the mammaries," he would sing whenever Raymond stopped over to smoke a joint and talk about Amey's latest enthusiasm—crotchless pantyhose, smoking hash and licking chocolate off each other, straddling Raymond while he sat on a small exercise trampoline.

A bass guitar drove its repetitions through the thin cotton of Ruth's T-shirt. Straining to recognize a tune, Ruth heard heels clicking across a floor, scraping noises, moans. A loud thump startled her. Probably a dancer jumping onto the wooden floor of the Carousel, she thought.

Joan had told them how the Carousel worked. A ring of private booths curved three-quarters of the way around a revolving circular stage. As the stage turned, it carried the dancers past the stationary booths, each of which was equipped with a twelve-by-twelve window facing the stage. The window was blocked by a screen, which customers raised by dropping quarters into a slot. When a dancer saw a screen slide up, she stepped from the Carousel onto a narrow, fixed platform between the turning stage and the booths, grabbed the front wall of the booth with the raised screen, and hung there by her hands, displaying her vulva in the window. If she saw a ten or twenty dollar bill waving over the open top of the booth, she dropped to the fixed platform in front of the booth, pushed a button to open the window, took the money, and gave the customer a hand job or blow job. If not, she moved on to the next open window and hung there. It all took incredible upper-body strength.

Ruth pulled her head out of her T-shirt and sat facing her blacked-out window. Overhead a woman's voice bawled what sounded like a popular song, but the volume was so loud it distorted the words and melody beyond recognition. Ruth looked up, as if locating the speakers would help her identify the tune. Ductwork snaked across the ceil-

A Woman of Salt

ing. She pulled four quarters out of her jeans and as she stacked them on the shelf under her window, an electronic buzzing began in the booth to the right. Her neighbor's screen was sliding up for viewing.

A body thudded against the front wall of the neighbor's booth. Ruth leaned forward, propped her hands against the walls and raised herself carefully off the chair, angling her head so she could peer over the separating wall without being seen. At the top corner of the next booth a small hand edged over the front wall. Ruth ducked down, her heart surging.

Though tiny, the dancer's fingers gripped the wall like talons. The nails were hot pink—some perfectly tipped, others broken. Ruth wondered if the polish was part of the uniform, or if the dancer enjoyed wearing it, like Debbie. Her sister never left the house without fingers and toes blazing, her personal revolt against a Calvinist childhood. Ruth painted her nails only when Dirk begged, wanting to see those drops of blood stippling the sheets, parting her labia.

"Come on, come on," a voice grunted inside the booth.

The electronic buzzing began again. Either the man's quarters had run out, forcing the screen closed, or he had paid the dancer to open his window.

"You a foreigner or something?" the man next door said. "I said blow me."

"It ain't enough," the dancer said.

"Goddammit. They told me—"

His window buzzed down.

"No, wait." He pounded on the window. "Here it is. I got it. See?"

The window hummed open. The man's chair fell, knocking against Ruth's wall.

Ruth checked her watch. Five minutes to eleven. She dropped two quarters in the slot and watched the screen roll up.

In the center of the revolving circular stage a dancer in a peacock-colored G-string was swaying slowly. Behind her, just beyond the turning Carousel, there was a conventional stage framed by partially closed, heavy maroon curtains. A lean black woman sat on a high stool near the left curtain. White patent-leather boots rose to her smoothly crossed thighs. Her arms, elongated and brilliantly white in her leotard, crossed near the wrists and rested on her knee. She was following the movements of the dancers, watching the ones working the windows as well as the G-stringed one dancing in the center of the Carousel. Impassively the woman scanned the wall of booths rimming the stage. When she reached Ruth's window, instead of shifting methodically to the next customer, her eyes lingered. Fighting the urge to crouch, Ruth held still before the staring mask. The music screaming over the speakers vibrated in her teeth. Barely breathing, afraid to blink, she tried to keep her eyes on the supervisor's. When her body began quivering from the strain, the watchful eyes moved on.

Ruth closed her eyes, blew out a long breath.

A dancer slammed against her wall, spilling Ruth's stack of quarters on the shelf.

Ruth started, opened her eyes. Her screen was still up, but the Carousel had disappeared. Filling the window were swatches of pale skin, whorls of darker goose-bumped flesh, the purple flaps of a split-crotch panty, tufts of mud-colored hair, salmon-brown vulva—all brushing jerkily against the smeared glass, out of rhythm with the blaring music. The wall shook as the dancer jerked her bottom close to the window, away, close, away.

Ruth's screen began buzzing down. As if to stop it, she looked up. Tiny hands, clenched white and bordered with hot-pink nails, clung to the wall. Over them a head appeared, its face turned to the side.

"Tell her after this round it's my break or I'm done," the face said to a dancer working another booth.

A tortoiseshell clip held the dancer's dull brown hair off her cheek, exposing a small pearl in her earlobe. A makeup-slathered cold sore bulged on one nostril.

"Tell her I mean it this time. I'll go to Girl Review. She can't make me stay, the fucking bitch."

She called out the last words loudly over the music and, as if to check who else was listening, the dancer looked down into Ruth's booth.

Her fine-boned face was set for the next transaction. But when she saw Ruth looking back at her, every muscle gave way. The blue-shadowed eyes widened, the sullen mouth went slack.

A choked cry escaped the girl and she let go of the wall.

A Woman of Salt

Behind her blacked-out window Ruth heard the dancer fall hard on the Carousel floor and scramble to her feet several windows down.

Ruth rushed to insert another quarter. Her screen crawled up.

The frightened dancer was scrambling away from the ring of windows. She was skinny but pretty, her body, like an adolescent's, somehow promising more. She flew past the G-stringed woman dancing in the center of the Carousel, jumped onto the stationary stage, and disappeared behind the curtain.

The supervisor leaped from her stool and strode to the other side of the stage. She stopped at the edge of the curtain, one white-booted leg stretched before her, the backs of her hands resting on her hips. She spoke to someone behind the curtain, listened a moment, and then threw back her head in laughter. She looked like a glorious giant laughing at the foolishness of mortals. The supervisor's dark face settled into its indifferent mask once again, and with marvelous grace she bent down, reached behind the curtain, and dragged the runaway dancer into view.

The girl was sitting on the floor, her body limp, her legs fully extended. Grasping the girl's tiny wrists, the supervisor pulled her toward the front of the stage.

Two of the other dancers working the booths ran off the Carousel and joined the relief dancers that had clustered around the supervisor and the girl.

Tightening her grip on the girl, the supervisor raised her chin to the idling dancers and jabbed it toward the Carousel.

They hesitated a moment, sought each other's eyes, then scurried back to work.

Ruth's screen began buzzing down. Quickly she fed in her last quarter.

The girl was on her feet now, the supervisor tugging her by one arm. The runaway dancer shook her head no, flailed her arm, her whole body, trying to wrench herself free, but the supervisor dragged her toward the Carousel as steadily and as patiently as if she were a mother leading a willful child. As they neared the hem of the revolving stage, the girl lunged forward, grabbed the titan's arm and bit it.

The supervisor stopped. Without letting go of her charge, she

MARY POTTER ENGEL

turned around. She glanced at her arm, then smiled at the dancer, a smile neither malicious nor forgiving. Then with remarkable efficiency she twisted the dancer's arm behind her back and forced her onto the Carousel. Without hurrying, she marched the girl across the stage toward Ruth.

Hands shaking, her breath coming fast, Ruth searched for a button to close her screen.

The supervisor drove her past the G-stringed worker swaying in the center of the Carousel. As they neared Ruth's booth, the runaway dancer's shoulders and head bowed lower to the spinning floor. She shook in terror, knowing that on the other side of the window she would see not the familiar stranger's face, a face easily played to, but a face like her own—and she would not be able to run from it. Unbearably horrified and shamed, the girl was collapsing inside herself, falling into a consuming darkness, a solitary hell in which she became an infinite point of grief.

Ruth's heart wrenched itself round inside her.

She was the terrorized, not the terrorizer; the one afraid of being seen, not the one seeing. Seeing this girl hiding from her in grievous fear was a sorrow she had never imagined.

Ruth sprang to her feet, knocking over the chair, and swung around. She fumbled with the latch and bolted from the booth toward the red and white EXIT sign. Yanking open the door leading to the arcade, she rushed into the corridor. As she shoved herself against the swelling crowd, voices called out to her. *Fucking bitch, Dyke, Stupid cunt, Wait! Dr. VanderZicht! Make way! Make way!*

But Ruth didn't hear them. She was running too fast, her world spinning, shades crawling up all around her, faces in the windows watching her, the face of a woman staring back at her everywhere, from every direction gazing into the wound, the seer and the seen.

A Woman of Salt

She Beheld the Shekhinah II

Try again.

The wife of Lot beheld the Shekhinah. . . .

The Shekhinah, God's dwelling presence. The Shekhinah, God's presence dwelling with her estranged beloved in exile.

In other midrashim the rabbis imagine the Shekhinah accompanying Adam and Eve out of the garden of Eden as the angel with the flaming sword chases them into exile. They see the Shekhinah living among the Israelites in their bondage in Egypt, journeying with them out of captivity to freedom, rejoicing with them in song after crossing the sea, wandering with them in the wilderness. They see her abiding with God's estranged beloved in Persia, Babylonia, Syria, Rome, weeping with them in their loss and longing, comforting them. They feel her coming to God's estranged beloved each Sabbath at sundown, her wings brushing their cheeks with lovingkindness, to dwell with them for a day's eternity in joy.

Bereft of God, God's daughters and sons are never without God. Exiled by God, they are never alone. God has absented himself in power and righteousness, plunging his wayward people into exile wherever they may go; and, overwhelmed by longing, God remains present with her people as the Shekhinah, dwelling with them in goodness wherever they go, "rejoicing with them that rejoice, weeping with them that weep."

God the Estranged Beloved and God's estranged beloved—joined by a bridge of longing.

Could it be that in looking back in longing to see her daughters once more, T'shukah saw God overcome by longing for her estranged beloved? That in that moment the wife of Lot and God met on a bridge of longing?

To save their own lives, Lot and his two angels set their faces toward Zoar, a little place of pinched hearts, and turned their backs on the dying sinners. The Shekhinah did not accompany Lot as he fled God's destruction of the cities of the plain. She remained in the midst of burning flesh and unrighteousness, in that infinite point of grief. God was present there among the suffering in Sodom and Gomorrah, bearing witness to their end, washing over them in a balm of silence. Whatever they had done or failed to do, whoever they had been or were or would become, God was present with them, bearing their pain with them—because she could not overcome her longing and remain removed from them.

T'shukah turned around in longing to see her daughters and saw God present with them, embracing them in silence.

Twelve thousand angels hid the face of God in Sodom and Gomorrah as the cities were destroyed. They were not angels of destruction, the executors of God's just plan, the rabbis say, but angels of mercy. They hid the face of God, torn with grief at the failure of love. Sodom and Gomorrah were dying and God could not save them.

T'shukah turned around longing to see her daughters and saw ring upon ring of angels surrounding God, each one beating its wings to dry God's tears, waves of wings rushing against the air, breathing in, "Love blesses," breathing out, "Love is not enough."

When T'shukah looked on the Shekhinah in the midst of the fires of power and righteousness, God's presence surrounded by twelve thousand angels of mercy beating their wings in a song of goodness, she covered her face with her arm. And in the dark silence she heard God weeping. And in God's weeping the wife of Lot saw her own obdurate self. Terrified at the long hardening of her heart, the flinty depths, the emptiness erasing more of her each year, T'shukah stopped breathing.

All that remained of her was stone.

A dead body revenges not injuries.
WILLIAM BLAKE, "Proverbs of Hell"

Plastic Natures

In the middle of writing her first book, a comprehensive study of the Cambridge Platonists' theories of the homunculus, Ruth was overcome by an irresistible urge to make a doll for her sister Debbie's third child, due in three weeks.

It struck her the third Tuesday of her leave of absence. As usual, she biked to the university library and spent four uninterrupted hours in her cubicle. At exactly twelve o'clock she gathered her books and notecards, organized them in her backpack, and pushed through the electronic arm blocking the exit. Her habit on Indian summer days was to eat her peanut-butter sandwich and apple in the main courtyard, the best location for observing undergraduate courting rituals. But on her way to buy a coffee at the Rivers Avenue snack wagon, Ruth found herself stuck on a side street peering into a fabric store. Soon she was inside, searching the heavy catalogs for a Raggedy Ann pattern, and before she knew it she was hurrying home with the pattern and materials to produce a twenty-inch doll.

Once home she worked feverishly, cutting out muslin body parts,

MARY POTTER ENGEL

striped denim legs, black feet. She embroidered black eyes ringed by lashes and brows, a red triangle nose, and a mouth stretched to a thin smile. Embroidering the heart over the breast that announced "I LOVE YOU" took longer than she had expected, as did stuffing the trunk and narrow limbs with the linty polyester fiberfill. By midnight she had not attached the body parts, and because it was difficult for her to leave anything uncompleted, she decided to stay home the next morning to finish the project. A break would be good for her writing, she told herself. Work on the book, designed to win her promotion and tenure, had not been going well for some months. Allowing herself time for indirect and unstructured reflection might help the troublesome points come clear.

In the morning Ruth woke at six to complete the Raggedy Ann, charged with more energy than she had felt since moving to Ann Arbor five years ago to start her teaching career. Because she was getting up earlier than usual, Ruth took greater care than normal not to wake her husband, a night owl who always waited until the last minute to rise. She had met Dirk within days of arriving in Ann Arbor and been attracted to his nocturnal energy, as well as to his intensity and sense of humor. "You don't look like a professor," he had said, eyeing her jeans and T-shirt.

"What am I supposed to look like?" she countered in friendly aggression.

"Unkempt beard, brown tweed coat, tattered trouser cuffs." He slapped his trim abdomen with his hands. "Flabby gut."

She broke from his piercing green eyes. His carefully rolled white cuffs exposed strong, tawny-haired forearms and delicate hands with nails cleaner than hers would ever be.

"No doctor ever neglected his appearance for the sake of ideas?" she asked. "Pasteur? Jonas Salk?"

"Not even Schweitzer," he said, grinning.

"They teach you this stuff in medical school?"

"Who better than a physician to appreciate that marvel otherwise known as the body?" he asked.

"You can have the body. I'm more interested in people's minds."

Ruth closed the bedroom door gently, threw on an old pair of Dirk's

A Woman of Salt

scrubs hanging in the bathroom, and set to work at once on the unfinished doll. She stitched limbs and trunk together, sewed in two hundred strips of red nylon hair with her heaviest needle, cut out a red calico dress and white apron and bloomers, machine-sewed the clothes, finished the snaps and hem by hand. By four-thirty that afternoon she was gingerly pulling the clothes on the soft body. Holding the dressed doll at arm's length to inspect her work, she felt its open face questioning her, its round eyes searching her. It was as if the doll expected something from her, was prompting her to remember or do something. Not knowing what the doll wanted from her disturbed Ruth. She stroked its brow repeatedly, as if to pacify it. *"Popkop,"* Dollhead, she said to it, surprised to find herself using Oma Reka's favorite name for her. "There's nothing wrong with you, *Popkop,"* Oma Reka would say. "Your mother loves you, *Popkop, natuurlijk."*

Hearing her childhood name unsettled Ruth more than the doll's insistent yet obscure desire. She shook out the doll's dress and apron, tousled hair over its wide black eyes, and set it on Dirk's West Virginia Medical University rocker in the living room. Then, not comfortable being idle, she closed herself in her small sunporch-study to pore over Cudworth's *True Intellectual System of the Universe* until her husband came home, hoping that a previously overlooked elucidating phrase or connection would emerge from the familiar pages.

When Dirk walked in the door that evening, pale and depleted as usual from his work at the free clinic, Ruth held her creation before him proudly.

"I thought you hated dolls," he said, removing his stethoscope and laying it on top of the refrigerator. "'Cultural encoding,' 'the tyranny of gendering,' the whole *schmeer."*

"It's for Debbie," Ruth said.

"She's about to have a new living doll of her own to fuss over, isn't she?"

Her sister had always loved dolls. When she was a toddler, everywhere she went she carried floppy dolls that sucked bottles and forever needed changing. When she was five, Debbie was desperate to get her hands on the Madame Alexander doll the aunts had given Ruth after Oma Reka died, to comfort her. Debbie would sneak to Ruth's bed and gaze at the doll's Shirley Temple curls, rosy china face, and brown-black eyes under moving eyelids, stroke her sky-blue satin dress with the white rosettes at the waist. Ruth would gladly have handed the doll over to her. She hated the way it lay on the bed, inert and perfect, as if daring her to touch it, to mar it; the way its polished eyes followed her everywhere, waiting, like her mother, like God, for her to reveal the flaw in her and reproach her for her sins.

But when her mother found the Madame Alexander in Debbie's bunk, she was furious. Her sisters had worked hard, she said, to find a doll whose eyes matched Ruth's exactly. And they had paid a lot of money for it, too, way too much for a seven-year-old girl who was acting like a baby, crying all the time. Ruth *had* to keep the doll or the aunts would be offended. "And besides," her mother added, looking through Ruth with her gray-green eyes, "it's *you* who needs practice being loving to others, not Debbie."

The doll returned to Ruth's bed. She smothered it with pillows, covered it with books, but she could still feel its eyes following her everywhere. She pretended it saw only the shell of her, her flesh and its postures, but when she closed her eyes at night she knew it penetrated her thoughts and fears. Two weeks later the doll was lying in the basement crawlspace, jumbled with broken lamps and mildewed boots, one glass eye shattered, the other still watching.

The following morning, after kissing Dirk good-bye, Ruth headed for her spot in the library to sink back into her work. She felt eager to resume writing, sure that the sewing break had cleared her mind. She had completed the introductory chapter well over a year ago, during the summer. It had been relatively easy to situate the homunculus in the philosophical tradition. An agent relating mind and body, the homunculus was analogous to Plato's World Soul, an organic principle mediating between pure spirit and base matter. The second chapter had fallen into place over the fall semester, a straightforward explanation of the fact that for Ralph Cudworth and his fellow Platonists Henry More and Benjamin Whichcote, as well as Culverwel, Rust, and Stillingfleet, this mediating agent in "man" (she insisted on the quotation marks), the homunculus, was not a metaphor. Without exception these seventeenth-century intellectuals believed that a miniature

A Woman of Salt

human being, responsible for controlling all bodily action, actually existed inside each person's brain. Ruth planned to include in the published book the more fanciful of their illustrations of a tiny man floating in a human head.

The third chapter had moved more slowly. Classes and meetings that winter had stolen more time than usual. And it had proved harder than she had anticipated to clarify her argument concerning Cudworth's influential theory of "plastic natures." That Cudworth believed mechanical principles alone were not sufficient to explain nature, and that he considered it necessary therefore to posit that between the spiritual and material orders there were organic natures relating the two, was obvious. What took her months to outline was the specific way in which Cudworth connected his plastic natures to the tradition of the homunculus. It was late spring before she was able to start researching the crucial fourth chapter, and by the time her leave began in September she had not begun writing it. In spite of frantic rereading of the texts, she could not detail how, according to the Cambridge Platonists, plastic natures or homunculi in human beings related the otherwise divided mind and body. Until she figured out their theory *precisely*, she would not be able to resume writing, no matter how many hours she held her pencil over the lined yellow page.

In the cubicle she opened her books and spread out her notes, determined to discover by day's end how the homunculus transferred the mind's commands to the body. But again during her lunch break she found herself in the shop on the side street running fabric through her fingers, feeling its sheen and softness. And again, instead of returning to the library, she went straight home with yards of thick muslin, white shirting material, calico, rickrack, and yarn. By three-thirty the next morning she had produced a second twenty-inch Raggedy Ann, this one wearing a yellow dress and sprouting black hair. She set the new doll beside the first, more traditional one, thinking it not unpractical to have a gift in store for Debbie's next child—which would surely follow this one quickly, since Debbie had always wanted nothing more than to be a mother of many children. When Ruth returned to her demanding teaching schedule—two sections of Introduction to Philosophy, a seminar on Neoplatonism, and a new course on feminism and logic—she would not have time for handmade gifts.

She fell asleep on the couch, where she rested fitfully. The next morning she was waiting outside the fabric shop when it opened. Without worrying about price or ease of fabric care, she heaped supplies on the counter: textured whites for aprons and bloomers, wildly striped denim for the legs, imported batiks and handwoven silks for dresses, natural wool yarns, and rickrack in all widths and colors. Over the weekend she completed two more dolls, each with a different set of clothes that gave it a distinctive look—personality, Ruth might have said, had someone asked her.

The following week Ruth worked on three new dolls, one with tan skin, one reddish-yellow, and one dark brown. For each she designed a one-of-a-kind outfit, dresses of satin, silk velvet, or brocade, aprons and bloomers of tea-dyed dimity and hand-crocheted lace, adorned with tatting, gold braid, pieces of old jewelry, antique buttons and beads.

Dirk came home each night to find the living room covered with snips of fabric, loose threads, white fluff, bits of yarn, the dining table and chairs hidden under piles of material and pattern pieces.

"Shouldn't you be writing?" he asked Friday night. "I thought you took time off to earn a raise." Keeping time by clapping, he chanted, "Homunculus, homunculi, cute little devils, here's mud in your eye." At "eye" he broke off clapping to point his finger at her.

"These sell for twenty-five dollars in that fancy children's shop downtown," she said, looking up from her machine. "With painted-on faces and cheap materials. I could sell mine for a lot more, maybe thirty-five."

"Cause-effect, Ruth. You don't finish the book, you don't get tenure."

"It's not that simple," she said quietly.

He picked up the one designer doll she had finished, examined the nineteenth-century beaded flowers edging the apron, rubbed the silk velvet skirt between his fingers. "Looks like these gewgaws are costing us about twice that to produce, not including labor." He held the doll

A Woman of Salt

by its neck in front of his face, making it dance and talk in a high, silly voice: "We could have given all that money to the Southern Poverty Law Center. Or to the Children's Defense Fund!"

A fiscal conservative with a bent toward abstemiousness, Dirk insisted on donating 20 percent of their income (hers, mainly, since his salary fluctuated with the availability of grant funding and the number of people on staff) to progressive and humanitarian causes. In the first years of their marriage, because of his goal of living within the Federal Government's figures for a low-income family of two and Ruth's penchant for collecting books and combing salvage stores for small indulgences, they had had their disagreements over money. By contrast, in their differences over sex Dirk was the bold experimenter while Ruth held back. "Sex is play," he often coaxed when introducing something new. "Hey, Professor, turn off your brain and let yourself have a little fun" was what he said the second night of their honeymoon, when he opened his *Joy of Sex* to the heading "Sauces and Spices" and showed her a line drawing of a woman fastened to a four-poster bed, her head thrown back and her body arched in pleasure. He kissed her hand and said, "You deserve it. All those years of school. All those late nights finishing your dissertation." Though feeling silly about refusing the man who adored her and who had supported her as she struggled to complete her Ph. D. while teaching full-time, Ruth balked, explaining that she couldn't stand to wear chokers, turtlenecks, high collars, anything binding. Dirk promised to release her the second she felt uncomfortable. When she continued to demur, he tickled her belly and ribs, saying, "Take a chance. Don't be a prude, like your mother."

It was that taunt that led Ruth to agree to being bound, wrists and ankles, to a gleaming brass bed in an Upper Peninsula resort.

The first time she asked him to untie her, he said, staring between her spread legs, "Not yet. Do you know how beautiful you are? All salmon and shell pink. Forget the beach. I'll do my diving right here." The second time, licking spirals around her nipples, he said, "You're not giving it a fair chance." The third time, with her thrashing under him, screaming hysterically, he said nothing.

Afterward, he brought two tumblers of Johnny Walker Black to the couch, where she sat reading Plotinus. When their glasses were half empty he began entreating her in his rich, lulling voice, like a stream purling over stones—"carried away by my love for you, no intention of harm, insufficient communication, unfortunate mistake on both sides." Reaching for her hand, he joked, "In sickness and in health, with error on both parts." He brought her hand to his lips and kissed it, his eyes pleading for forgiveness. Ruth leaned her forehead against his and sighed. He squeezed her hand, put his arm around her and let her nestle against him, her head pressed against his shirt, a tired smile pushing her lips against each other. How could she argue? She was unsure what had happened. Dirk, less emotional and more good-natured than she, was probably right: an unfortunate *malentendu*. Anxious to move on to the comforting predictabilities and eloquent silences of married life, she decided to put the incident behind her. When Dirk produced a legal pad minutes later and suggested that they take a rational approach and draw up a contract to avoid further misunderstanding, she accepted.

They both promised to listen harder to each other's needs and desires. In exchange for two promises from Dirk—to stop making her justify every purchase over five dollars and to quit pressuring her to participate in a threesome—Ruth consented to providing oral sex on demand. She also agreed to let him continue taking nude Polaroids of her, especially when his parents visited. The minute they retired for the night, Dirk and Ruth would go to their bedroom and Ruth would undress, following Dirk's commands to the letter—"Let the straps fall slowly, Hook your finger in your panties and lower them one inch, Walk away from me while draping your shirt over your ass." Naked, she would pose for one roll of film, standing in front of the floor-length mirror, sitting cross-legged on the edge of the bed, lying down with her arms stretched over her head, on hands and knees before him—however he directed her. In return for these photos, which he kept in a manila envelope on his nightstand, Dirk promised to quit buying porn magazines. He made it clear, though, that this concession didn't prevent him from pressing her from time to time to account for how she, longtime ACLU member and staunch defender of freedom of speech

A Woman of Salt

just as he was, could object to such freedom of expression. She countered by asking that he not argue with her until she was reduced to tears or other illogical outbursts.

Finally, Ruth agreed to anal sex, but only after Dirk had promised never to call her a prude again *and* he had assured her, several times over, that he would not request it more than once or twice a month and that he would take care to be exceedingly gentle.

From the beginning of their relationship Ruth had argued that though she enjoyed nothing more than intellectual theories and she considered the mind the refuge of the spirit, she was not ashamed of the body. "To me the body is an indifferent thing," she explained once, "a country with its own customs and celebrations. *Laissez-faire,* that's my policy." Since that argument had failed to persuade Dirk, she hoped that by agreeing to the terms of their new contract and adhering faithfully to them, proving herself irreproachable, she would convince him and herself once and for all that she was not, as he teased, a "crypto-Puritan."

Dirk jiggled the Raggedy Ann in front of his face again. "What'll it be, Ruth?" he asked in the doll's voice. "Me or the Children's Defense Fund?"

Ruth took the doll from Dirk, placed it in the rocking chair with the others, and resumed her sewing. Arguing for the relative good of an antique-jeweled, silk-velveted Raggedy Ann over against worthy causes was not a challenge she was willing to take up: she was tired and there was too much work left to do.

Though on Fridays Ruth and Dirk usually made dinner together and sat up late drinking Rémy Martin—it was easier for her to play with him when she was tipsy—that evening Ruth worked right through dinner. Late that night, when Dirk washed his brandy glass in the kitchen, turned off the TV, and blew her a kiss on his way to bed, she was still sewing, puncturing a thick muslin head with her long carpet needle, pulling the yarn through, knotting it tightly in the scalp.

Intent on finishing the other two designer dolls, Ruth sewed every minute that weekend, racing from one task to the next, stopping only to devour a cup of peach yogurt or fistful of pretzels, or to sip the cappuccino Dirk surprised her with from time to time—made just the

MARY POTTER ENGEL

way she liked it, with a half teaspoon of sugar and a dusting of bitter chocolate shavings. Saturday night she sent Dirk off to the Roxy to see *The Story of O* with Raymond, his closest friend at the clinic, and Raymond's girlfriend Amey, whom Dirk idolized, not for her enormous breasts or waist-skimming chestnut hair, but for what she had done for Raymond. "She shows up at the clinic sometimes with nothing on under her long down coat," he told Ruth one night, shaking his head in disbelief. "She drizzles him with chocolate and licks it off, keeps him awake all night. She's a magician. She's boosted Raymond's confidence so much he'll probably be the next head doc when Harrison leaves."

Sunday Dirk went river-canoeing with friends who lived on a communal farm two hours away. He didn't return home until midnight. Long after he had gone to bed, Ruth cleared the table, hauled the sewing machine to the corner, stacked the sewing basket and usable remnants in an old trunk. The seven finished dolls she propped into a sitting position on the couch, some with their legs crossed, some with their arms around their neighbors. They looked like schoolgirls hamming for the camera, sure of their friendship, themselves, and their dreams of being loved.

She went to bed planning to return to the library the next morning for a fresh start. She would comb Henry More's *Divine Dialogues* and *Enchiridion Metaphysicum,* looking for clues in his notion of spissitude, spirit's ability to set matter in motion, for help with her Cudworth chapter. Or maybe More's speculations about fairies having an artificial way of making a homunculus in the brain would suggest a way to understand concretely how the Cambridge Platonists thought a body and mind could be united.

Over their morning café au lait, her backpack packed and waiting by the door, Ruth showed Dirk her fashionable clique.

"What if your sister has a boy?" he asked.

At the bank an hour later, Ruth withdrew a hundred dollars from their savings and bought muslin for six Raggedy Andy dolls, the highest quality denim for overalls, 100 percent cotton gingham and mother of pearl buttons for shirts, imported white piqué, navy kettle cloth, and tiny brass anchors for sailor caps.

Instead of completing one doll at a time, she went to work on all of them at once, cutting out six bodies, twelve arms, twelve legs, twelve feet, six overalls, six shirts, six caps; embroidering six mouths, six noses, six hearts, twelve eyes; assembling twelve arms and legs, six bodies; stuffing six bodies; sewing in six heads of hair; making six overalls with shirts, six caps; dressing six soft boys.

Every night that week Dirk came home to find her surrounded by stacks of ironed faces, piles of yarn strips, partially stuffed arms or legs. He would kiss her hello, change into his jeans, mix a scotch and soda, and lie on the bed watching old war movies or reading Albert Speer while she worked, occasionally calling out information and questions: "God, that Rommel was a genius," "Did you know Speer pitched the concept of *ruin value* to Hitler, the aesthetics of the way buildings would look when they crumbled?" Once he came out stomping and singing an American marching song in his deepest voice,

> *Goering has only got one ball.*
> *Hitler has two but very small.*
> *Himmler is very similar,*
> *And Goebbels has no balls at all.*

Ruth almost ran the machine needle through her finger she laughed so hard.

Late Thursday night, as she hunched over her work, Dirk stood behind her, massaging her neck and pressing his warmth against her.

"I'll come to bed as soon as I finish this part." She bent her neck backward, raising her face for a good-night kiss.

"And you think *I'm* a fanatic?" he asked, looking down at her.

His green eyes—their piercing brilliance always a shock—looked steadily at her, but she couldn't tell whether they shone more with humor, anger, disappointed desire, sorrow, or something else she couldn't name, and the confusion she felt settled in her stomach, leaving her queasy.

"I promise," she said.

"Good night, Doll," he said, giving her shoulders a final squeeze before walking away.

Though Dirk had never met Ruth's parents (they hadn't been invited to the wedding), Ruth had told him stories when they first met

MARY POTTER ENGEL

of her father calling her mother Doll— *Come on, Doll, take a walk with me. Got a clean shirt for me, Doll? Any more of those good cookies, Doll?*— instead of speaking her name. Soon after they were married, to celebrate their freedom from the patriarchal assumptions of inequality, they began playing the Helen and Clay game. Dirk would call Ruth "Doll" and she would answer "Yes, Clay" or "Right away, Clay" and they would laugh, happy to have escaped the world of "duty, decency, and diminishment," as Dirk referred to it. Ruth wished that this time, too, she had answered "Good night, Clay," to make sure of the joke.

It was late Friday afternoon when Ruth placed the last cap on the last Raggedy Andy, setting it at a rakish angle. She laid the six on the dining table to examine for omissions or errors. Sure that each was perfect, she placed them, one by one, on the couch with the others. Next to each Ann, she set an Andy. *Two-by-two they went into the ark,* she thought as she placed their hands in each other's. Stepping back to admire the six pairs and the single Annie in the rocker, she decided that she would mail one of the couples to Debbie, the most traditional one. Whether Debbie had a girl or a boy, she would be pleased for her child, and surprised at her artless, ivory-tower sister's handiwork.

With the thirteen dolls looking on, Ruth cleaned the apartment. She shoved the sewing machine in the bedroom closet, the leftover fabric under the bed, the extra stuffing behind the couch. On hands and knees she picked up straight pins and snaps, vacuumed threads and clouds of fiberfill that clung to everything. She wiped the table and set two candlesticks on it. As she fitted tapers into the sockets, she paused for a moment to admire her creations. The profusion of colors, designs, textures, and styles amazed her, as did the professional, flawless crafting of each detail. The thirteen dolls sat up pertly, smiling broadly at her, as if pleased with themselves and with *her,* and she was surprised to find herself grinning back at them with pleasure.

Dirk came in when she was preparing the *nasi goreng* and *gado-gado,* their favorite celebration meal. Raymond was with him. He sniffed at her pots admiringly, then followed Dirk into the living room to smoke a joint.

Ruth closed the kitchen door so she wouldn't smell them, hear them laughing, and returned to her vegetables. As she worked, driving her

A Woman of Salt

wide chef's blade through a skinned Bermuda onion, halving it, noisily chopping both halves to pieces, Tom Lehrer's voice filled the living room with his witty lyrics. Halfway through the album Ruth opened the door to tell Dirk she was ready for him to fry the egg pancake and *krupuk,* his *specialité de maison.* Seeing Dirk and Raymond sitting cross-legged on the floor below the crowded couch, engrossed in a game of chess, she announced she was going to take a bath and they would eat as soon as she was through.

Raymond completed his move, then turned to her. "Nice dolls," he said, raising his eyebrows and shaking his head approvingly.

Ruth glanced at the couch then down at her breasts, which seemed to protrude impertinently from her gray T-shirt. She crossed her arms over them, not sure whether he was mocking her, teasing her, or just high.

"I'll be out in a half an hour," she said.

As she turned to leave, she felt the dolls lean toward her, follow her with their expectant eyes, but she did not answer them.

She locked the door and ran a bath with lavender oil, planning to soak away for a few moments all thoughts of transcendence and corporeality, plastic natures, homunculi, minds directing bodies, bodies divided from minds, needing to be united.

In the living room Dirk played favorite cuts from his collection of Lehrer albums for Raymond. When he got to his favorite satire, a papal rag, he pushed up the volume until the bathroom door shuddered with the music. He played the chorus, "Get on your knees and genuflect, genuflect," over and over, both men bawling along with the record.

Ruth unstopped the drain, dried off, and began to dress. As she tucked her violet sweater into her best jeans, the music stopped. She let out her breath, grateful for the quiet. "Dinner in five," she called through the door.

The living room was empty when she entered. They had left the chessboard on the floor. The album cover was propped against a stack of books nearby. She knelt to read the note taped to it. *Gone for Heineken's and Amey. Back in a flash.* Maybe Amey would help her finish peeling the cucumbers and assembling the platters, Ruth thought. She could try explaining the problem of plastic natures and homunculi to

MARY POTTER ENGEL

her, mind over body, body without mind, the need for a mediating agent to unify the self, see if she had anything to say about the way it might work.

Rising, Ruth noticed that the Annies and Andies had been jumbled together on the couch. Angry at Raymond and Dirk for the mess, she bent to straighten the dolls. Only then, pulling the first two, the traditional pair, out of their tangle, did she see Annie's legs spread wide, her bloomers bunched around one ankle, and Andy's head shoved under her skirt. She let go of them. Flopped at her feet, clothes a mess, limbs askew, they went on grinning.

Debbie's baby can't touch them now, she thought.

Her heart pounding with the strain of anger and fear competing within her, she turned to the next pair. Annie was lying face down, her dress hiked up and lace bloomers shoved down, Andy mounting her from behind. Struggling for breath, a gaping in her stomach, as if everything inside, the numbness and confusion, had emptied out of her, scraping her raw, Ruth surveyed the remaining pairs of Dirk's *Kama Sutra:* sixty-nine, a blow job, missionary position.

The last couple had been joined by the single Annie, all of them stripped, their clothes heaped on the floor. One Raggedy Ann sat on Andy's crotch, the other Annie's legs were spread over his mouth. Both were smiling, their embroidered hearts blazing "I LOVE YOU." Under his navy brim and red fringe of hair, Andy's stitched blue-black circles stared back at her, open wide in surprise and glossy with delight.

She found the ten-inch Fiskars buried in her basket in the closet and hurried to the Andy who'd had his head under Annie's skirt. Gouging the eyes was easy. She had only to jab the point of the lower blade into the muslin under the eyebrow and slit a clean circle back to the beginning. The doll looked back at her with frothy white holes.

The next cut was more difficult. She had stuffed the bodies so hard that the doll's neck resisted the closing blades. She had to punch a hole in the neck with the closed tips of the scissors, then dig the blade deep inside and jag it toward the edges, tearing the muslin, before she could hack through the filling. Severing the rest of the body went more smoothly. Less polyester was bunched near the joinings and her scissors cut through the stitching and fabric without too much pressure.

A Woman of Salt

Anal Andy, Sixty-Nine Andy, and Fellatio Andy she dismembered the same way, eyes first, next head, hands, arms, then feet and, finally, legs. As she cut, eyes, heads, limbs, extremities, and trunks, all leaking cloudy webs of fiberfill, dropped to the floor, scattering around her.

Missionary Andy she did not cut. She took him, whole, to the bathroom, where she jammed his head down the toilet, his gaily striped legs flopping over the white bowl. Returning to the living room, she grabbed Ménage à Trois Andy and dragged him to the kitchen. It was hard work to stuff his wide head down the garbage disposal, but she managed to pinch it all in. She flipped the switch and the disposal whined on, catching Andy tighter, sucking him down a few inches and throwing his legs into a spin before jamming. She switched it off and hurried to the bedroom for the Polaroid on Dirk's nightstand. As thoroughly as a police investigator at a crime scene, she snapped photo after photo. When she had used up the last film cartridge in his nightstand drawer, she placed the camera on the bed, near her pillow. She stacked the photographs as neatly as Dirk would have, all corners matching exactly, then secured them with a piece of yarn and deposited them in her backpack with her books and manuscript. The load secured on her back, she hurried to the sunporch to stuff papers, notecards, and books into her briefcase. In the living room she swept all seven Annies into her free arm and strode to the front door. She pushed the latch open with her briefcase, letting the door bang closed behind her as she raced for the bus shelter.

Pressing herself into the corner behind the other riders, she waited for the crosstown. Blood pulsed in her ankles, her stomach, her groin, and at once she became aware of the difference it made in her, this fall from willed innocence, knowing now that sex could lead to a child, knowing that her sexuality wasn't separate from who she was, a hireling she employed for this purpose or that, but a creative force bringing together body and mind, joining life to life. Without Dirk's drama of dolls she might never have seen it. At last she understood the mystery of plastic natures, how the homunculus spurred the body to action. Cudworth and his crew were right: The process by which mediating agents joined bodies to minds was *not* analogous to mechanistic causation. The mind was not a billiard ball hitting a plastic nature, which

MARY POTTER ENGEL

in turn hit the distant body, setting it in motion. Nor could the coupling process be explained organically, the body's chemicals and rhythms flowering into thought. Spissitude and fairies aside, the Cambridge Platonists had seen rightly that mind and body, each a walled city, could meet only by creative force: They collided in the seismic theater of the imagination.

Her bus pulled to the curb. The doors wheezed open and Ruth maneuvered her belongings to the back, the Annies clutched to her side. The library closed at midnight on Fridays. As soon as she arrived she would hide herself in the stacks and begin writing.

Pillar of Salt

The wife of Lot became salt, a different midrash says, because she betrayed her husband and the angels for a handful of salt. As these rabbis imagine it, Lot the devoted husband divided his dwelling in two parts, one for himself and his guests, the other for his wife, so that, if aught happened, his wife would be spared. Nevertheless it was she who betrayed him. She went to a neighbor and borrowed some salt, and to the question, whether she should not have supplied herself with salt during daylight hours, she replied, "We had enough salt, until some guests came to us; for them we needed more." In this way was the presence of the strangers bruited about in the city.

One advantage of this interpretation is that it does away neatly with the need for theodicy, the effort to justify God's ways to the human mind; for it implies that it is not God who is responsible for the destruction of Sodom and Gomorrah.

This is how the logic works. If the neighbors had not discovered Lot's two guests, they would have kept their evil desires under control. If they had kept their violent lust under control, they would not have tried to assault the two messengers of God. If they had not clamored to rape God's messengers, Lot would not have been tempted to betray his two virgin daughters into the hands of the rapists. And if God's messengers had not been threatened and Lot had not been forced to offer his daughters to protect them, Sodom and Gomorrah, in spite of their wickedness, might still have been spared punishment, since it was this outrage that brought the final punishment upon the inhabitants of the cities of the plain.

The rabbis' unspoken yet unavoidable conclusion is this: It is not God who is responsible for the destruction of Sodom and Gomorrah; nor is it the angels, those mediating agents between God and humankind who spur human beings to action; neither is it Lot with his heinous paternal crime. It is the wife of Lot alone who must be held accountable for bringing her two virgin daughters to the brink of ruin and for bringing about the destruction of the cities of the plain.

A clever bit of blame.

Just as revealing as the rabbis' assignment of causality for God's punishment of the world is the way they account for the wife of Lot's fatal error: it was her craving for salt, her trivialness, her thoughtlessness, her loose tongue—the legacy of Eve—that caused the world's destruction. How like a woman, they imply, to risk the death of all because she could not control her own selfish, base desires.

These rabbis never imagined that it was precisely T'shukah's craving for salt that led to her redemption. For her craving for salt was nothing else than the desire for God alive in her flesh. She wanted with all of her being to flee God the destroyer and to hide in the cave of her mind and hollowed heart; yet as she fled, her body in its mineral craving pulled her round to God, longing with all her being to witness God restoring bodies to life, to be present at the joining of body and mind, flesh and spirit.

Nor could these rabbis imagine—dangerous even to whisper it as her possible sin—that the "slip" of T'shukah's tongue was intentional: her revenge for Lot's eagerness to sacrifice his vulnerable daughters for two strange men of God more than able to defend themselves. She and her daughters had been defiled by Lot for the sake of God and men. Revealing the angels' presence to her bruiting neighbors invited the just punishment of Lot and his friends.

There is yet another midrash on Genesis 19 to consider, one that leads away from blame and revenge. This imagining into truth says that the city became sulphur, or brimstone, and the people salt. Rebecca Goldstein comments on this midrash in Buchmann and Speigel's *Out of the Garden,* saying that when the wife of Lot saw that her daughters had become pillars of salt, she wanted to be with them.

In such a moment of grief one knows only one desire: to follow after one's child, to experience what she's experienced, to be one with her in every aspect of suffering. Only to be one with her. . . .

T'shukah looked back, longing to see her daughters one last time before she lost herself in exile. But when she saw Dini and Chesed running toward the city gate, in terror and afflicted, crying out for her, their breath burning within them, their flesh growing heavy with agony, whitening, stiffening midflight, every cell in her body rushed toward them to join with them in a mineral love.

No longer running away, she was running toward, her whole being running after—*shuk*, to run after or desire, *T'shukah*, longing, desire.

"And it was for this desire," Goldstein writes in her unsettling conclusion, "that Irit was turned into a pillar of salt. She was turned into salt either because God couldn't forgive her this desire . . . or because he could."

> The fox condemns the trap, not himself.
>
> William Blake, "Proverbs of Hell"

I Know Why You're Here

s soon as Cathe finished her post-lumpectomy radiation treatments and started chemotherapy, Ruth suggested she have nude photographs taken of herself.

"It's the perfect time," she said.

"Yeah," Cathe said, "perfect."

"You're not sick from the poison yet, your hair hasn't started falling out, and your face hasn't begun ballooning from the prednisone."

"Makes sense," Cathe said. "Document the scars. That way they can identify me if I'm decapitated and my body is found in the woods."

"Wouldn't it be great," Ruth said, "when your hair's grown back—maybe straight and black the way you always wanted it—to have pictures of the way you were before, so you won't lose that part of yourself?"

"I already lost a chunk of my breast and half my lymph nodes."

"But once it's over, you won't be able to remember who you were before."

"I'll remember," Cathe said.

A Woman of Salt

Ruth didn't give up. She bought a book of black-and-white self-portraits by a photographer, a chronicle of her mastectomy, and left it on Cathe's kitchen table after work with a note: *C—Saw this today and thought you might be interested. I think the composition of the pieces is wonderful, as is the play of light in the mirror shots. See what you think. See you tomorrow. Much love, R.*

"What'd you think of the book?" Ruth asked the next day.

"Rita hates it," Cathe said.

"Rita's in denial. She's too busy to take you to the doctor but she's out every night playing softball with her team."

"I'll look at it when I'm ready," Cathe said.

The night the first clumps of hair pulled loose, Cathe agreed to have photos taken of herself. Ruth suggested they try Amey, a freelance photographer with a studio in her home. She knew Amey through her soon-to-be-ex-husband, Dirk. Amey and Dirk's friend Raymond had been lovers until Raymond dumped her to marry his grade-school sweetheart.

After spending hours questioning Amey on the phone and reviewing her portfolio, Cathe agreed she was well suited to the job. Her fee, though, she thought too high for an amateur's work. Ruth talked Cathe back into the deal by recounting Amey's struggle to support her nine-year-old daughter. Amey had worked her way off welfare by organizing Lunch 'n' Lingerie shows in a downtown bar, but quit two years ago because she needed more flexible hours, fewer calls from men, and a better environment for her daughter. She supported herself by freelance photography and, when she had to, selling small bags of dope to her boyfriends and their friends. Cathe, a corporate manager who served on the board of a program for women in crisis, agreed to Amey's fee, and they made an appointment with her for next Sunday afternoon.

"Who's first?" Amey asked Cathe and Ruth when she opened the door.

"It's just me," Cathe said.

Amey turned to Ruth. "You changed your mind?"

Ruth shook her head no.

"What gives?" Cathe asked.

"I don't know," Ruth said, looking out the front window. "I thought I might . . . I thought maybe I'd have a few pictures taken, too, if there was time after your session."

"And you didn't say anything?" Cathe said.

"I wasn't sure."

"But why would *you* do it?" Cathe asked. "You're sick, too?"

"I guess I thought it would be a way to reclaim myself, after Dirk— I don't know." She glanced at Amey, then stared at her sandals. "He used to make me pose for Polaroid shots for him. Other stuff, too."

"Why didn't you tell me?" Cathe said.

Ruth shook her head to clear it. "Forget it. We're here for you. It was a bad idea. I get crazy sometimes." Raising stiffened claw-hands over her head and distorting her face, she growled at Cathe.

"Jesus, Ruth."

Ruth knew Cathe hated surprises. That was why she got along so well with Rita. Cathe also disapproved of people who weren't direct. Once, when the two of them argued about a friend who seemed stuck in her life, Cathe said, "Nobody's *confused.* Everybody knows what they want. They're just too scared to ask for it."

Cathe removed a blank white envelope from her bag. "Here's my deposit," she said to Amey. "Cash. I'll pay the next third when I see the proofs and the remainder when you deliver the prints. Let's get started. I have to be somewhere at three-thirty."

"You can wait in my daughter's room down the hall," Amey told Ruth. "She won't mind. You," she said to Cathe, "can change in my bedroom over there. Did you bring any hats or shawls with you?"

"I thought nude was nude," Cathe said.

"Most people don't know how to be naked. They get uneasy. All they can think of is *being seen* and they start folding their bodies away from the viewer or, worse, playing to the viewer. Doesn't matter if the viewer is there in front of them or is present only in their imagination. It flattens the shots. I like shots that get beyond that public body, get underneath that *being seen* to the person *being.* It's hard to explain. I've found that if you give people a chance to play with objects first, they have an easier time forgetting their body as an object to themselves and others and just start being in it."

A Woman of Salt

"My body won't let me forget I'm in it," Cathe said. "It's the one taking *me* for a ride."

Ruth slipped her arm around Cathe, squeezed her to her and kissed her cheek. "Come on, Dearheart. It's an adventure."

Cathe shook free of her. "Yeah. Death, the Great Adventure."

"Trust me," Amey said to Cathe, "and you'll get your money's worth. If not, I can't promise anything. And if you're not happy with the photographs, I'll give you your money back."

"Fair enough," Cathe said, shaking Amey's hand.

Ruth knocked on the door to the daughter's room.

"Entrez," a voice called.

The girl was sprawled on the floor at the far end of the room watching TV.

"Hi," Ruth said, closing the door.

The girl didn't turn around. Tight caramel curls massed about her head.

"I'm Ruth."

The girl kept her eyes on the screen. Her spindly legs folded at the knee, she bounced her feet up and down over her rear.

Ruth tried, "Watching anything good?" and "Okay if I sit on your bed?" but the girl kept staring at the screen and swinging her feet in the same hypnotic rhythm.

Ruth sat on the floor with her back against the bed. She double-checked her wallet to make sure she had enough cash. She cleaned out her purse, stuffing all the trash into a used plastic sandwich bag. She folded her arms across her chest and lay her head back on the mattress, staring at the ceiling. Water stains curved through one another like foam-topped waves.

The girl snapped off the TV and jumped on the end of the bed. Folding her legs under her in a cross-legged position worthy of a yogi, she leaned her elbows on her knees, rested her chin in her hands, and looked at Ruth.

Ruth sat up straight, resting her bent legs to the side and her elbow on the bed. She smiled shyly at the girl.

MARY POTTER ENGEL

The girl eyed Ruth calmly.

"I know why you're here," she said matter-of-factly.

Ruth stiffened. She imagined the girl watching photographs develop in the darkness, posing for her mother.

"It's okay," the girl said with a shrug. "I won't tell anybody."

She jumped to the floor, threw herself down in the same spot she had been before, and flicked on the TV. A class of barking dogs and their owners was learning how to sit.

Amey stuck her head in the door. "Ready?" she asked Ruth.

"Hey, Sweetie," she said to her daughter. "Be done soon. We'll pick basil and make pesto for supper, okay?"

The girl grinned at her mother and went back to her show.

Ruth followed Amey to the studio. Cathe's scent—like the juice of a cut iris stem—lingered in the room, but there was no other sign of her.

"Cathe left," Amey said. "I'll drive you home if you want."

"Maybe it's too late," Ruth said. "For the light."

"It's perfect. Go change."

In Amey's bedroom Ruth pulled off her jeans and T-shirt, bra and panties. Without anything around her she felt her scrawniness. Her body seemed empty, emptying. Even her bones seemed hollow, like a bird's.

All her life Ruth had been in search of weightlessness. She had swum through underwater tunnels to find it. She had starved herself to achieve it. She had bled herself to feel it. She lost herself in the vaporous possibilities of fictional worlds. She tried drowning herself in God, in the manifest glory of a spirit-ridden world. She climbed to dizzying altitudes to forget the pull of the body. She locked herself in a labyrinth of the mind.

And still she was dragged down by the burden of her flesh.

Still she remained her dyscarnate self.

But now, without warning, without any effort save the shedding of her clothes, standing naked by herself in the house of an unfamiliar woman and her strange daughter, Ruth had become weightless. The

A Woman of Salt

soles of her feet barely touched the floorboards. She seemed to be hovering over the surface of the world, thousands of wings beating inside her, filling her with air, lifting her.

Frightened, she put the heels of her palms over her glasses, pressing the glass against her cheekbones. Weightless, suspended, she clung to the weight of her glasses, willing herself toward the ground. She was glad she had not let Cathe talk her into trading her Coke-bottle glasses for contacts. If she weren't wearing them now, she would drift away.

"Ready?" Amey called from the other side of the door.

Amey's dark, grainy voice pulled Ruth back. She dropped her hands and made her way to the door.

"You all right?" Amey asked, laying her hand firmly on Ruth's upper arm.

"Sure."

"Everybody's nervous at first. You'll get used to it in a few minutes."

Ruth followed Amey into the studio. The floor and walls were bare. An umbrella light stood against one wall. Columns of dust filled the room, shimmering in the sunlight.

"Okay," Amey said. "I don't talk when I'm shooting, so I'm going to tell you what to do now. Lie down on your back in the middle of the floor and close your eyes. Just lie there and breathe. When you're ready, get up and move around the room however you want. I'll follow your lead and take the shots that come up."

"What about props?"

"Your glasses can be your prop." She pointed her thumb to the back of the house. "I'll go check on Ivy a minute while you get settled."

Ruth lay down, her hands resting on her stomach. The floor felt gritty against her heels, tailbone, elbows, and angel bones. She closed her eyes, surprised to find herself warm. She began counting her breaths, watching the air push her stomach up and letting it fall, rising and falling.

She woke up with Amey kneeling beside her, removing her glasses. The metal temples tickled her skin.

Ruth raised her head and squinted, to see where she was putting them, but Amey was already out of her range of vision. Without her

MARY POTTER ENGEL

glasses Ruth couldn't recognize her own feet. Squinting only made the world blurrier. She hugged her knees to her chest and laid her cheek against them. She could not feel the edges of herself; her body had disappeared.

With her mother, and later with Dirk, when he pulled out his sex books and insisted she prove she was not a prude, Ruth used to play a game: she would take off her glasses and become invisible. She didn't have to pretend; it was real: without her lenses her body dissolved into the world completely so that no one could find her. No matter what happened in the room, she was not there.

She had learned early that becoming invisible was safer than hiding or running away. The summer she was five, she had wandered into the dunes along Lake Michigan. Alone, she was free to explore, hear the wind singing in the beach grasses and trees, listen to the water talking. A flat-speaking man found her at sunset and took her to her aunts' cottage. When her mother saw her at the door with a stranger, she shook her, crying out, "*Duiveltje!* I can't trust you for a second. Don't you ever, ever do that again. Do you understand?" That night in bed, listening to the foghorn, Ruth understood: If you hid, they found you; if you ran away, someone returned you home; but if you became invisible, no one would even know you were gone.

Ruth was invisible now, lying on Amey's floor. She had dissolved into nothingness. Nothing separated her from the world. There was no boundary marking her and not-her.

She rose slowly, her eyes open. The world was blurred and calm, no shape battling another for the eye's attention, everything coming to her through a great silence. And she to it. She moved through the space as if she were floating underwater, carried along by invisible currents. She moved, the world moved. The world moved, she moved. There was no resistance. Her cumbrous female body, the body of death, had fallen away. She had escaped its bondage. There was no flesh to betray her, to be accused or desired. She was spirit. In the world but not of it.

She was pure happiness.

A Woman of Salt

All week Ruth called Cathe to apologize. She left messages on the answering machine. If Rita picked up the phone and told her Cathe was out, she said she'd call back and hung up quickly. Thursday she mailed a letter to Cathe.

Cathe, Dearheart,
Please forgive me for not being clearer about having photographs taken of myself. I really did go to Amey's for you— because I love you.

I know it's a hard time for you and you need to stay focused. And I know you love clarity and that I'm always complicating things and that sometimes I hide in ambiguity. But *please believe me* I didn't know until we got to Amey's house what I would do. Amey called me the night before and suggested I take advantage of the opportunity, too. All I told her was I'd think about it. When we got there, it just seemed right. The session was a total surprise to me. It was wonderful. I felt freer than I ever have. It was like I had shed my body at last. Can you be happy for me even though I didn't do everything completely right?

Can't wait to hear how your session went, and to see your proofs. Call me as soon as you get them. Maybe we can help each other choose the ones we want developed?
Much love,
            Ruth
P.S. I made you some *banket*. I'll bring it when we review the photos.

Ruth's photos arrived in the mail on Saturday. She slit open the envelope eagerly. Amey had attached a note instructing her to review the contact sheets, the five-by-sevens, and the one-and-a-half-by-threes she had enclosed and to mark the ones she wanted her to print, keeping in mind that she could print them darker or lighter, crop them, resize them, and so on. At the bottom she had written, "The two five-by-sevens I checked on the back are fabulous shots. Will you give me permission to include them in my portfolio? Your face doesn't show in either one, so there's no problem with privacy. They're really great photographs, form- and composition-wise. Hope you're as thrilled with them as I am."

Ruth tore off the letter and peered at the contact sheet on top of the pile.

The woman in the first frame was a stranger. Like her, she was tall, with never-ending legs, and her hair was dark and wavy. But it was someone else, not her. The same stranger stared back at her from the next few frames, too. Ruth was confused. She set the proofs down. Then, realizing that the smallness of the image was distorting her perception, she rummaged in her desk for a magnifying glass. Amused at herself for being so foolish, she picked up the contact sheet again and placed the glass over the first frames. Slowly she moved it over each frame, one by one, studying the face, the limbs, the feet. She was right. It was a stranger, not her. The body was all wrong. It was fleshed and rounded. Sitting, lying, standing, stretching, its curves created a daedal pattern against the empty background.

Ruth laid down the contact sheets to check the five-by-sevens. The first shot had been taken from behind, the face not visible. The woman was lying on the floor, head rolled to one shoulder, arms stretched like wings to the side, legs resting high above her on the wall. Ruth buried the picture on the bottom of the stack and looked at the next five-by-seven. In this one the woman was curled in a fetal position in a corner, arms wrapped around her legs, head tucked to her knees. The corner seam of the walls rose straight up from her shoulder, making her look like a Henry Moore sculpture suspended from a wire. Ruth could feel the weight of the woman's body, a luscious weightedness that pulled the viewer toward it.

The woman in the pictures was nothing like her. This woman's body, weighted and belonging, was unmistakably present, to herself and the viewer. Ruth's body was a stranger, a country with its own customs and rhythms, an affliction and torment that had been miraculously lifted from her in the silence of Amey's studio. Ruth was sure that Amey had captured that: her flight from her body. That's what she had been so eager to see: how Amey's camera had witnessed her escape into invisibility. There was no point in looking at the other proofs. They would all be the same mistake.

A Woman of Salt

Ruth returned the photos to the envelope and clasped it shut.

She felt queasy, as if she had spied on someone and seen something she would rather not have seen, a disturbing image which would pursue her, block her path the way the vision of the angel frightened Balaam's ass.

She called Amey right away. "You sent me the wrong proofs," she said. "When can I drop them off and pick up mine?"

"What do you mean?"

"It's not me in the proofs."

Amey laughed. "Everybody says that when they see pictures of themselves, especially art shots. It's like hearing your voice recorded on tape."

"It's really not me. It's somebody else in the pictures."

"Impossible. Cathe just called to tell me she loves hers—have you seen hers yet? They're more angular than yours, but nice. I thought yours came out great, dark and fleshy, with an edgy mystery, like the portraits I imagine hanging in a Spanish gallery. But if you're not happy with them, we can do the session over. No extra charge."

"I don't want another session."

"I'm sorry you don't like the photos. It's my best work."

"Look, I'll send you the rest of the money I owe you and let's forget the whole thing."

"But what do I do with the pictures?"

"Do what you like with them. They have nothing to do with me."

As soon as she hung up, Ruth stuffed the photographs back into the manila envelope. She threw them in the wastebasket under her desk and opened Plato's *Phaedrus* to find a reference she needed for her book on the homunculus. But she couldn't keep her mind on the text. Her knee kept bumping the hard edge of the manila envelope, tempting her to open it and look at the photographs again—just to make sure. Unwillingness to consider oneself wrong was a trait she abhorred. How could one ever be absolutely sure about anything, the world or oneself? There was always the possibility of being mistaken, always another possibility you hadn't thought of. Shouldn't she take another look? What if Amey was right? What if the photographs *were* her?

She closed the book and drew the packet out of the wastebasket.

The flap hadn't been closed properly and under the top edge of the envelope she could see black and white emerging, white toes resting on a dark floor, the instep curving up into the envelope.

She grabbed a newspaper from her desk and wrapped it around the envelope, stuck it under her arm, and raced out to her car. She drove through Meadville to Hurley and back again, the images of the stranger's incarnate self staring at her from the back seat. In Lynndale, at the far end of the Highway 7 commercial strip, she pulled into a McDonald's. The newspaper bundle under her arm, she bought a Coke and walked out. She leaned against the driver's door, sipping the Coke and watching the cars pull in and out, their lights too bright. When it was quiet, she walked to the Dumpster set against the hedge, lifted the lid, and threw the Coke and the envelope inside.

Walking back to the car, she stopped, plagued by doubt, and turned around. The Dumpster hulked before her, smelling of rancid grease. A car pulled in the lot and a mother with two kids got out and headed for the restaurant, too busy with themselves to notice her. Ruth went to the Dumpster, reached in, and pulled out the packet. In the car, her hands grainy with the salt that clung to the envelope, she sifted through the photographs again, recognizing in the dim light the woman she thought she never wanted to be, a woman of flesh, and longing now to be her.

A Woman of Salt

This Pillar Exists Unto This Day

The wife of Lot could not control herself. Her mother love made her look behind to see if her married daughters were following. She beheld the Shekhinah, and she became a pillar of salt. This pillar exists unto this day.

"I have seen this pillar," Josephus assures his readers in the *Antiquities* (200), "which remains to this day."

The poet Jacob Glatstein wonders, "Who will flee You over a bridge of longing / only to return again?"

Dyscarnate, we flee the body, longing to become discarnate. Yet each time we bury it, the body calls us back to unearth it and open ourselves to it in lovingkindness. Each time we let it drop from us like the scab of a wound, it forces us round in love to look back at it once more and gaze upon it in mercy.

If, in your wandering, you come to the edge of the plain between Sodom and Gomorrah and Zoar, the little place, you will find T'shukah, Longing. A daedal sculpture, she stands there caught in the moment of turning, right side to her married daughters, left to her unmarried daughters, turning forever world without end, her face gazing into the righteous face of God hidden by twelve thousand angels of mercy and shining with the light of the Shekhinah.

Arrested in the fullness of future *and* past, lovingkindness *and* truth, mercy *and* judgment, self *and* other, mind *and* body, she trembles with life. Captured in the moment of turning from fear to love, her rent self crystallizing into wholeness, eternally turning, she glistens in the sun, a woman of spirit, a woman of salt.

No one who looks on her will lose the way home.

> Truth can never be told so as to be understood,
> and not be believ'd.
>
> WILLIAM BLAKE, "Proverbs of Hell"

Lady Sarah

I never read the notice in the newspaper, but I know it by heart:

> Anyone witnessing the accident on eastbound Grace Memorial Bridge into Charleston last Thursday, January 6, at approximately 10:15 A.M. is requested to contact the police (538-6241) or *The Observer* (737-5889). A man riding a bicycle was hit by a white BMW sedan and is in serious condition in University Hospital. Your help will be greatly appreciated.

I drive a white BMW sedan. I have driven over that bridge in the morning. I know the story.

A woman no longer young is traveling from the country to the city on a clouded January morning. For miles her car is surrounded by dense clumps of pines and cottonwoods. Occasionally a bare sycamore lifts a globe of mistletoe to the sky, like a skeleton offering up the green roundness of life, and she remembers she has left something behind,

MARY POTTER ENGEL

though she cannot recall what it is. Ahead, turkey vultures pick at the carcass of a possum. Only at the last second, when she can see the blood staining their beaks, when her fender is almost touching their feathers, do they fly away, scattering. She hurtles forward, over the body but not touching it. In her mirror the birds return to their meal.

You're wandering down a dangerous road. Turn back.

I don't know where to turn.

Miles slip under the woman's wheels without notice, minutes without her presence. When she looks through the windshield again, the trees have become sparser, the shrubs scrawnier. The ditches, brimming with trash moments before, have shrunk into shallow troughs. Suddenly the sky widens before her, and she is in the open, on a road that is all bridge, a layer of asphalt poured over pilings sunk in water and sand. No room for a shoulder; spartina grass swamps the road on both sides, swallowing it. Though the gray surface is dry, a sign announces SALT WATER ON ROAD. One sneeze, one ill-timed turn of her attention to the children in the back and she will be sinking in pluff mud, brine seeping into the car, pulling her under.

That low road through the marsh is not Grace Memorial Bridge. You are blurring what should not be blurred.

This is the part of the story I know—falling through emptiness.

If she had no passengers, the woman thinks, she would turn off at Garden's Corner, head for Hunting Island. There, striding the beach, she would find a way out—distinct beginnings and endings, a reassuring boundary proclaiming, Here is land, there water. In the marsh, houses and docks leap out of watery grasses and where is their foundation? Who can see where land ends and water begins? In the marsh, everything blurs into everything else. On the brightest of days the marsh is deceptive, a landscape of lies in which one loses the way.

A Woman of Salt

It is you who are confusing everything, falling into fear.

Once, passing through the marsh, just after I moved south, a shrimp boat surprised me in the shallows. It was resting in the grass, so close to the road I almost reached out to feel the ragged letters on its bow, LADY SARAH. Sure it was my imagination, I blinked hard several times as I approached, hoping to erase it. But the boat remained. I looked for a hidden channel of deep water running from the boat to the ocean, searched the drab grasses for a green-gold swath signaling the presence of a tidal creek, but there was nothing. Sunk in the marsh, its enormous metal wings raised over its head, thick black netting suspended from them, the boat looked like a bird arrested in midflight, ensnared, as if on its way to a kingdom of joy it had accidentally grazed the tall grasses and, enchanted by their touch, fallen into a deep sleep.

The January morning darkens over the road through the marsh and the woman removes her sunglasses. Sometimes the colored lenses play tricks on her, revealing what is hidden, obscuring things present.

You must try to be clear. You must find a new vision, composition of the whole. Let the forms of things guide you. Begin again. Begin with what you know.

I know less and less, understand nothing. I have forgotten my name. I came to a time when I had to leave behind everything I knew, feel it bleed out of me.

The woman drives on, following the black ribbon into nothingness. Beside her, her sister-in-law Ellen chatters endlessly about Matisse, form and representation, the clarity of objects when touched, her latest sculptures showing at a Chicago gallery. The woman's nieces, Brittany and Amanda, giggle wildly in the backseat, blazing with joy. In her rearview mirror the woman watches them bounce shoulders against each other in rhythm with their chanting. She drives faster, as if by pressing her foot down harder she could escape the expanse of choking grasses, leave behind the car hurtling through emptiness, the

MARY POTTER ENGEL

girls in the back, her self with all its turnings; as if by leaning forward she could propel herself out, lift herself into crisper air, fly back from where she came, the city up north, a city with neatly mapped streets, engraved monuments, spires splitting the world into Above and Below, Here and There, Now and Then.

As they near the city, traffic thickens. A wide old pickup, burdened with tree limbs, bush-axes, a rusted wheelbarrow, pulls ahead of her. She drags behind it. After what seems hours, Grace Memorial Bridge appears in the distance. Over the river an osprey flies high, preparing for a dive. The road, buckled from repeated flooding, ripples under the woman's wheels. The slope toward the drawbridge begins. Preparing for the car's vibration when it hits the mesh insert, she grips the wheel harder. Ellen patters on, her hands carving the space in front of her, vivid and sure—the way she is about everything, her marriage, her mother, her girls. In the back the girls shout and slam against each other, rocking the car. Glancing in the mirror to scold them, the woman driving hears a thud at the right rear of the car.

Not like the squash of a chameleon caught in a door joint, the thump of a sparrow against the windshield, the crush of a turtle's shell under a wheel, a tiny heart stopping; not like those and yet exactly them, carrying in a moment's thud all that terror bleeding into past and future.

What's more likely, that you hit him or someone else? You don't live anywhere near the city. You drive miles to avoid bridges, especially Grace Memorial Bridge, with its scandalously low Department of Engineering rating. And how many white BMW sedans do you think roam the Lowcountry? There's a dealer on Highway 21 near the bridge. Be sensible. Go and see for yourself. Go and look at your car. Touch it.

I must try to remember it clearly. Everything depends on it. The moment the tires crossed the seam in the bridge and began buzzing across the metal insert, Ellen stiffened and said, "Someone fell back there."

I slowed down, but the car, my jaw, my eyes continued to vibrate as we skimmed across the steel mesh, the surface shifting beneath me.

A Woman of Salt

Ellen swung around to look, her strawberry-blond hair flying. "That cyclist," she said. "Don't stop. He looks okay." When she turned to me again, she had lost all her brightness. "Listen, Ruth," she said, aiming her words at my face, which was fixed on the windshield, "we weren't anywhere near him. He probably got scared by a truck and lost his balance. It's simple: he lost his balance and fell. You know it's impossible to maneuver a bike onto one of those narrow ledges without falling."

We crossed over the seam on the other side and felt the grip of the pavement again. "Keep going," Ellen commanded. "Did you hear what I said? Don't make it harder than it has to be. Forget about it. It's over. Whatever happened, it's not your fault. Everything is not your fault." She said the last words as if each stood alone, as if they were not related to one another.

In the car the woman's body seizes up, breath arrested, blood clotting, skin like ice. Only her stomach moves, heaving green and black.

Memory is demonstrably unreliable. Any judge will tell you that. Evidence is what you need. Go and look. Look at the car. Touch it.

Maybe Ellen said it wasn't my fault to help me, or because she sees everything so definitely—facts, sharp edges, everything in its place— or because she didn't want her vacation inconvenienced by accident reports, or because she is giddy and crafty and cold, as my mother never misses a chance to tell me. Or maybe she didn't say it at all. Maybe I needed to hear her say it—that I wasn't anywhere near him when he fell, that we passed by—safely, unharmed—and *then* he fell, *after* we happened by—so I could go on without trembling, her decisive words piercing the spell binding me. I don't know. I can't make it come clear, no matter how hard I try. Everything runs into everything when I think about those months.

That was a lost time, those first months after moving out of Dirk's city, his state. Everywhere I looked—the grocery store, the library, sidewalks—I saw nightmares: impatient mothers pushing children's heads into water fountains; desiccated women wandering the streets; gnarled fetuses grown old in the womb. There was no skin separating me from

MARY POTTER ENGEL

the world: I was the bones and hearts that ached, the hands that inflicted suffering, the minds and mouths justifying it, the absence of God. As fall turned to winter, I stopped leaving my house. I would lock myself in the bathroom and sit on the floor staring into the dark, willing someone to cut away—at whatever cost—the hallucinatory caul grown thick and tight around me, a viscous shroud.

Ellen probably insisted on visiting me that January because she and my brother Mark were worried. Around Christmas and New Year's she called every day, sometimes twice, asking, How often did I cry, drink, take pills? How many days of work had I missed? Could I get out of bed in the morning? Was I pregnant when I left Dirk? Had I had an abortion, was that it? Did I daydream about suicide, have a preferred method? "Dirk wasn't that handsome," she said one night. "Not enough to die for. Or was the sex that good? Have you been holding out on me?" When I didn't laugh, she said, "Stop being so hard on yourself. Lots of people get divorced. Why do you think they call it 'no fault'?"

The woman never crossed that bridge that morning. She started for the city with her sister-in-law and nieces, but five miles from her house they hit a pothole. "What's that hissing?" Ellen asked. As she turned around, her handmade monkey earrings brushed against the collar of her red jean jacket, their tails curving into smiles. "I don't hear anything," I said. "Open the windows," she ordered, *"quick."* Air escaped noisily from the right rear tire. Before I could slow down, the wheel rim began knocking against the road, throwing the car up and down. I pulled onto the shoulder. We waited an hour before a man stopped to help. He made us follow him to a mechanic friend of his who wouldn't cheat us. While waiting, we walked downtown to have a vanilla Coke in the drugstore, play in the hat shop. Three hours later the hole was patched, the front end realigned. By that time it was too late.

Liar. You were born a liar, just like your father. Like him, you know how to tell just enough of the truth. Yes, you had a blowout, but within an hour it had been fixed and you were back on your way toward that bridge. Your father lies about everything, too, important things like the size of his bonus,

A Woman of Salt

but things that don't matter, too. If I ask where he's having lunch, he'll say, At my desk. But I'll wait outside his office and follow him to a restaurant in town, watch him meet other men, eat a sandwich, and leave, then ask when he comes home what he had for lunch. Some kind of a sandwich, he'll say, meatball, my secretary ordered it from the deli. Liar! I'll shout. You were at the Blackstone Grill. Why do you lie to me? What difference can it make if you ate there or at your desk? Why not tell me the truth? I saw you with my own eyes. Why not just say it was you who did it, you who hit him? Wouldn't it be better to confess, be out with it, and escape this labyrinth of lies? Remember the summer you visited us in France? how much better you felt after finally confessing you had smuggled a bag of marijuana into the country between your breasts? I knew from the beginning you had done it, that you intended it as a slap in my face, a way to corrupt your brothers away from me. You were lucky you didn't get caught. Things go easy for you, too easy; your life has always been charmed, everybody thinks you're wonderful. But I'm your mother. I know the truth about you. It's simple: you ruined Dirk with your whoring after strange men. I predicted you would, remember? When you called to say you were marrying him. I told you if you hurt that boy like you hurt Russell I would disown you. Dirk was lost after you left him for that Lebanese painter, broken. He said he pleaded with you to try again, but you told him you didn't need him, even to forgive you, because you had forgiven yourself. Forgiven yourself? What pride! The Devil's trick! God alone can forgive and you know it. You think nothing of killing whatever stands in the way of your pleasure, don't you? I bet you had abortions, too. You did, didn't you? Dirk told me, rocking and sobbing next to me on the couch, like a wounded child, that he had always wanted children, begged you for them, but that you were too busy with work, worried about money, rigid in your habits, selfish. I said you had always been that way, from the beginning.

Listen to *me*. It was *Dirk* who didn't want children, "hostages to fate"; insisted you live on the welfare office's food budget for a family of two; made you sign a contract to pay his rent the first year after he left; forced you into court demanding maintenance payments; argued for a lump sum compensation for pain and suffering, lost months at work, lost heirs; blamed you for his slashed tires. And after he called that night about the tires, accusing you of malice aforethought and threatening to sue for harassment, you lay awake until morning worrying, wondering if you *had* done what he said—the way you wondered when you heard him, a week later, swear before the judge that you had aborted a child without consulting him because you feared the results of an adulterous encounter. You *knew* it was a lie—that there was no lover, not then, that it was Dirk who wanted you to have the abortion, Dirk who drove you across the state border, Dirk who plied you with French fries and Two Thousand Year Old Man jokes on the way home—and yet you believed his story, believed you had flown with your lover to New York to scrape away the evidence. You went home from that hearing and charted the days, weeks, months, to sort everything out, so there could be no question. And still when you finished, you thought, What if he is right? What if I have shifted the truth so many times inside myself I can no longer see what is true and what is not, what happened and what did not, what I am capable of, who I am?

The last semester of college, I moved into Ned's tiny apartment across from the Acapulco Bar. Every day, winter or summer, Ned wore blue jeans torn at the knees and a long-sleeved khaki Army surplus shirt—neatly pressed—under a frayed jean jacket. Every day he ate oyster crackers and tomato soup made with milk for breakfast, a can of peanuts in the late afternoon with glass after glass of draft beer, each mixed with tomato juice—to replenish the vitamins the alcohol stole—and at night dry popcorn with bottles of Budweiser. Every day he got up at two, walked to the Acapulco to check the sports pages and place his bets. After supper he cruised the bars for pool games. When the bars closed down he traveled from house to house, gambling until dawn. Ned carried a stillness about him that soothed me, a clarity about his life that quieted me. I loved him.

Once, after the bars had closed, before we started our poker rounds, we drove his growling Buick to the park overlooking downtown. We rolled down the windows to let in the fragrant June air and sat watching the city lights.

"I want to tell you something," Ned said after a few minutes. "It's bad." He took two quick swallows of his beer. "Real bad." He tapped

A Woman of Salt

the long neck of the bottle lightly against the steering wheel, paused, then hit it hard in the same place. "So bad you can't tell anyone. You'd get in trouble if you did."

I pulled my head off his shoulder and tried to meet his eyes, which were fixed on his beer.

Staring into the hole at the top of the bottle, he said, "I was with Juan Corona in Texas."

A mosquito flew from the dashboard and began bumping itself against the windshield, trying to get out. It threw itself against the glass, beating its wings furiously. Each time it hit, there was an almost imperceptible thud.

Ned sucked down everything left in the bottle. He laid the empty on the floor next to my feet, then sat up straight, looking into the dash, both hands stiff on the wheel.

"Years ago. Before he was on the front page of all the papers. I know you read about it. The one who hacked up all those people. They said it was a hatchet, but it was a small machete, about this long." He stretched his index fingers a foot and a half apart.

I tried not to breathe.

He gripped the wheel again. "I was with him when he started, before he jumped the state line."

He dragged his thumbs across the top of the black wheel, starting in the center, pushing hard to the outside, as if rubbing away a thick layer of grease or paint covering the words he wanted to say. Over and over his fingers met, slid away from each other, lifted, and met again, squeaking dully each time they pressed over the plastic.

"I didn't kill anyone myself, not directly, but I was with him." He paused, everything still, then knocked his thumbs against the wheel. "That's it."

He started the engine and I jumped, kicking my foot against the empty bottle on the floor. The glass felt cold and hard against my skin.

Backing the car up, he said, "Don't say anything about this, ever. If they find out, they'll come after you, shut you up."

We went on with our night as usual, drinking, playing cards until daylight. He never mentioned it again, never hinted at it, and I began

MARY POTTER ENGEL

to think I had imagined the words, made up a story to fit my fear of him. I never dared to ask him if he had really told me that or not.

After a while I began to think maybe he had told me, but that it was just a story: that he hadn't been with Corona; he just wanted to think out loud, for one moment, before another person, that he had done something horrible so his outside would match his insides and he wouldn't feel torn apart all the time. Later I thought he couldn't have done it, because of the quietness inside him. And then I was sure that I must have heard the words wrong because I wasn't listening, or because I was scared by something else, some shadow with me in the car, some darkness inside me; or that I had imagined it—everything: the car, the lights, the mosquito, the conversation, because it happened during a time when I needed to be always close to a threat I could feel and touch outside myself, to keep me from falling into the terror inside. That's what had drawn me to Ned—fistfights at pool tables, knives in parking lots, gunshots over money lost, prostitutes breaking beer bottles on tables and wielding the sharp points. Still, when I moved out of his apartment, I told friends not to give him my number or address when he called, not to tell him which state I had flown to. I thought by leaving him I had become dangerous, that he would hunt me down, silence me.

The woman sees the cyclist a long way off and makes a note to stay clear. "Hasn't anyone heard of bicycle lanes down here?" Ellen asks as they approach him. "Look at those buns pumping! Wouldn't I like to sketch *him!*" The man is lean and well muscled, black shorts stretched across his thighs, black nylon jacket splashed red with VERO! billowing behind him. As the car draws level with him, he cycles harder, hunched over the bar, head thrust down and forward, curly blond hair fringing his purple helmet. Though he is young, the sun has left crevices around his blue eyes, the kind of blue that doesn't reflect light, that draws one into them, eyes belonging to a man who would charm a woman as he poisoned her, gradually, so there would be no trace, and then stand over her corpse and kick it, again and again, calling it whore, liar, murderer, with a smile; the kind of man who can be silenced, bumped off

A Woman of Salt

his trickery, knocked down only with violent force, like the force of announcing one's adultery to an unsuspecting husband, like the force of a speeding car.

If you won't go and look, feel the paint and the metal, what then? Trade in your BMW for a beat-up red station wagon? Donate it to the shelter for battered women and children and move back north?

Move away, run away, as far as you please. You won't escape. You think I don't know it was you who ruined your father's new Buick that Christmas break? You claimed you found it damaged when you left the A & P—no one around, no note on the windshield. But the hole in the door, the scraping around it, could not have been made to a parked vehicle. You denied running into anything and he believed you. But I knew.

Don't listen to her. You are making up that VERO! cyclist. The man struck down that morning was more likely an older black man on his way to find work in an exclusive neighborhood on the peninsula, traveling slowly, his front wheel wobbling. How could you have seen all that detail? You are seeing what is not there to be seen. You still believe you saw Dirk crouching in the backseat of your car that night, his blond curls and fine-boned face hidden under his navy balaclava, a knife in his hand, ready to spring? It couldn't have been Dirk—by then he had moved to another state—yet you slammed the door on his leg, the blue intensity of his eyes, and ran into your office and locked yourself in, heart thudding, to wait for a colleague to drive you home.

You believe her? Giddy and crafty and cold as she is? All artists twist the truth into unrecognizable shapes, hide it in a litter of possibilities. They're selfish and vain, afraid to look straight at the world, to see themselves as they are: not perfect, without any beauty; too proud to admit they can't save themselves from their own evil natures and need to be washed in the blood of Jesus Christ.

Driving to my office in the morning, I see a three-year-old girl, slight and dark and mischievous, like I used to be, but as curly-headed as Dirk. She watches me through the rear window of the car ahead, waves to me as I pass. In the night I wake dreaming, anxious and afraid. Three times now I have opened my eyes to see a phone number written on the ceiling—each time the same, 556-7921, but each time larger, heavier. A voice repeats the number slowly—over and over, louder each time—so I can memorize it before it disappears; and when it does, I have to use all my power to keep myself from reaching for the phone and dialing.

Because of the pickup lumbering ahead of her, the woman sees the cyclist too late. She veers, but—

You know that was Dirk's number, the number of the apartment he rented after you asked for a trial separation, "to sort things out." You remember, that efficiency in the high-rise where the police broke down his door and found him starved, catatonic, living like an animal, all because of you, and the hospital room the ambulance brought him to, where he stayed so long and where you refused to visit him, to call him even. Heartless.

The clinic where Dirk drove me, not speaking for hours, refusing to discuss it. Mothers-to-be in the waiting room. Evergreen disinfectant inside. Cold vinyl sheets to catch the blood. The doctor asking whether I was old enough to remember the time before *Roe v. Wade,* when it was a crime. Signing my name to the forms—human life, complications, consent.

She sees the cyclist ahead, refusing to slow down, riding the line, daring the cars not to make way for him. As she passes, he veers away, loses his balance.

Why bother being clever when I know, as I have always known, the truth about you, in spite of your constant attempts to alter it, shift the pieces, like the Devil, hoping I won't notice? It's useless. You may as well do what that

A Woman of Salt

twenty-six-year-old motorcyclist did last week when he hit that six-year-old girl playing in the street: fall on your knees in the road, shout "Forgive me, forgive me," and shoot yourself.

I was reading in the cramped cabin of a Chris-Craft anchored in a frigid Canadian lake. My brother Mark was in the head. Dad had gone above to start the engine. My mother was lying in the bunk across from me, pretending to sleep. She hated wilderness, water, boats, being trapped in small places, my freedom. She and my dad had been fighting all weekend. She opened her eyes, propped herself on her elbow, and stared at me.

"Stand up," she said after a few moments.

"Why?"

"Just stand up I said."

I stood up, shielding myself with Pascal's *Pensées*.

"You whore," she said, clenching her jaw. "You wore that to tempt your father. You've always been jealous of our relationship."

I looked at my muslin nightgown. It was opaque and hung loose to the floor, the neck rising higher than any on the negligées she wore.

"I bought it on sale," I said. "It's all cotton, no dyes."

She swung her legs to the floor and stood up, facing me. "Put that book down. See? You can see right through it and you know it. Look at yourself. Those big brown nipples, like a cow's. And no panties. Disgusting."

I looked down but I couldn't see what she saw.

Pinching my shoulder with one hand, with the other she pulled the cloth tight against my breasts. "There. See it now? Proud of yourself, aren't you?"

I bit my lip, squeezed my eyes shut, shook my head side to side.

"You think if you cry your father will feel sorry for you, don't you? I know your tricks. You think you can do whatever you want because you're smart, going away to college, but you'll find out, just wait."

When we returned home, I asked Mark if I should have worn a robe on the boat, if I dressed provocatively; but he was neutral as always. I studied myself in the mirror for hours, pulling the muslin tighter and tighter against my body until I could see what she saw. Then I threw

MARY POTTER ENGEL

away the nightgown, all my jeans, and the peasant tops that clung to my breasts. I started wearing thick materials, dark colors, large sizes, more and more layers—to cover my offending body, to hide the urging inside me that was so potent and so clever I had never before— before she uncovered it—seen it crouching, lying in wait.

She never saw him, not before entering the bridge, not crossing, not after, crumpled in her mirror, bleeding. And she never heard a thud against her car, a crash of thin metal falling on pavement, brakes whistling and squealing behind her. If she had, she would have stopped just over the bridge, at the marina, walked back to find him, waited with him until the police and the ambulance came.

She hadn't wanted to drive into town. It was Ellen who had insisted. Why miss an opportunity to scope out the galleries, ride a carriage past pre-Revolutionary houses, eat shrimp fresh off the boats? They drove in, toured the town, drove out, returned home exhausted.

She was driving alone that morning and turned off at Garden's Corner to walk the beach at Hunting Island. She never crossed Grace Memorial Bridge that day.

She hadn't moved south yet, hadn't crossed Grace Memorial Bridge, hadn't heard of the Ashley River with its abandoned rice fields and tidal creeks. She moved shortly after the accident occurred, bought the BMW at Mama's Used Cars months later, after the final settlement arrived—which took much longer and left her poorer than she had imagined.

You should be locked up. That's what that Christian psychiatrist we sent you to in high school told me. When I showed him your diaries and your letters to me, explained to him what you were up to and how you kept changing your story, how you defied me one moment and repented in tears the next, he advised me to commit you, for your own good. "Psychotic," he said. "Not to be trusted."

A Woman of Salt

Stop! If you refuse to go and feel what is there, rub your fingers over the car, let *it* tell you, then go back to when you first read the story in the newspaper, for that is where this began.

I don't recall reading his letter—don't get the paper anymore, too disturbing—but I can quote it word for word.

> Dear Editor:
>
> Is there an epidemic of moral callousness in America today? We let murderers out of jail, kill unborn babies, stand by while people get knocked down. In January I was the victim of a hit-and-run on Grace Memorial Bridge and the driver of the white BMW sedan has not come forward. I spent two months in the hospital. It will take years to pay the bills. The doctors say I'm lucky to be alive, but I'm twenty-two and I'll never use my right arm freely again, my neck will always be stiff, and I may not be able to return to law school, while the driver is off playing golf or shopping aimlessly. How do rich people get away with their crimes? Are the rest of us ants they crunch without noticing as they rush to their yacht clubs for another drink? The person who injured me knows who he is. I hope he can't sleep. I hope he has no rest until he stands up and faces me.
>
> Sincerely,
> John Steedley (556-7921)

I am rich. I shop aimlessly at times, bloated with guilt. I drink. I drive a white luxury sedan. I know how easy it is not to be seen, how quickly one is thrown between the wheels of a car. Riding my bike home one afternoon, I was struck down in the middle of the street. By the time the car stopped, all but my shoulders and head lay under the front end. The driver helped me under a ginkgo tree and drove off. The police found me there, a junior-high girl in a yellow canvas skirt and red voile top, bleeding and staring, and brought me to the emergency room, called my parents. In hours I was released. My bike had to be junked. They never found the man. I never think about him. I feel gravel pressing under skin; hot metal soothing me; tires, marvelously close, em-

bracing me, happy to have been struck down at last, the incontrovertible evidence of my wrongfulness in my flesh.

Pathetic, like the time you told all those people I pushed—

—Just one, and I said I wasn't sure, couldn't be sure because—

*—I pushed you down the basement stairs because you had broken my green
lamp with the hand-painted roses, the only thing of my mother my sisters
didn't get. How could I have pushed you? I was down doing laundry. You
were alone at the top. You raced down to get to the Easter chicks by the furnace and slipped. Whose fault is that? You didn't break any limbs in that
fall, did you? You weren't hurt. You always had a vivid imagination. You
can't be sure that you fell at all, can you? that you didn't almost slip and
become so frightened that you might fall, that you could have fallen, that
it seemed to you ever after you had and, searching for someone to blame,
you chose me because you would never blame your father? Why are you
punishing me? What have I ever done to you?*

What then? Fall on my knees and cry out, "O Lord, if my hands bear
the guilt of wrongdoing, let my enemy pursue and overtake me?"

You don't fool me. The Devil can quote scripture, too.

Go to the car, Ruth. Feel if anything is broken, marred, awry. Touch
the right rear bumper and all around the wheel. Rub your fingers over
the paint and metal, all the surfaces, inside and out. Any break in the
smoothness—a dent, a scratch, a nick—would remain, a sign for you.

A body is not a car. Bodies heal without trace of rupture.
  Every seven years all cells are replaced, all of their lives, all their
memories.
  Years after I left Ned, a letter with his scrawny handwriting arrived
at Dirk's and my apartment. I didn't open it for weeks. When I did, I
was shaking. He asked if I had heard about the shooting, while he was

A Woman of Salt

driving a cab, making a better life for himself, a robbery, a .38 in the back of his head, up through the brain and out, and he couldn't talk anymore but he could still read and write and he wanted to say that I was a good woman, that I was better off without him but that he missed me, loved me, always would, no matter what. I burned the letter, because by then I was respectable and a teacher and I knew many things other people didn't and wanted to; and I was afraid that if I didn't destroy the letter, that that time of not knowing would return and I would slip back into a time where everything keeps turning into something else, my insides into what is outside, and what is outside into my insides, and I would keep losing my way because there is no way, no Yes and No, no This and That, True and False, Life and Death, Here and There, Thus Far and No Farther Shall You Go. Who can live in an uncertainty in which there is no boundary between one's body and the world, actions and suffering? no respite from doubt? no refuge? And what would I trust in if everything is moving, wobbling, shifting back and forth without warning, without pattern, like the sand in the desert, like that man on the bicycle, no sky and no land, no rock to cling to?

What if nothing can be separated, unraveled? What if there is no golden thread leading out of the labyrinth of falsehood to the light of truth? dividing dream from reality? what might have been from what is? what is inside from what is outside? daughter from mother? mother from child? victim from executioner? No path—not through denial, alteration, confession, expiation, acknowledgment of error, exoneration, blame, regret, imagination—no way leading from the restlessness of uncertainty to surety and peace? No pillar to guide the way from the unknown to the known? What if there is nothing to find, nothing to touch and be touched by, except the terror of the unknown, the unknowable?

Touch the car. Let yourself feel it.

But if, once I'm there, feeling for signs, there is nothing? Only emptiness? If I reach out my hand and nothing meets me, nothing? Should I seek out in that darkness an answering voice? Call him? Should I call him?

MARY POTTER ENGEL

What, if he answered, would you say? I don't know you, never did, never will, but meet me tomorrow at 10:15 A.M. and I'll give you a thousand dollars—two thousand, five, two hundred a month for the next seven years, for the rest of my life, for your trouble, and mine, for Ned's, Dirk's, our baby's, the world's, born and unborn?

I don't know what I'd say. "Answer me, O Lord, when I call"?

Say to yourself, If, once I'm there, I see nothing, if there is nothing to feel—

—if, under my fingers, the metal and paint are smooth everywhere—

—here and there, above and below, inside and out—

—if they reflect me back to myself, there and here, then and now, inside and out, whole, without break, without rent—

—believe them—

—believe that I—

—that the world is whole—no all or nothing, victim or executioner, Eden or Hell; no choice between purity and danger, rupture between innocence and evil; no Fall, but falling, always, with no escape from freedom into blamelessness or fault, falling, off a map with certain coordinates, into the knowledge of good and evil, falling, now, into the mess of the world—

—falling not through emptiness—

—but into life—

—a woman not emptied but living—

—not divided but whole—

A Woman of Salt

—feeling her body in the darkness—

—the body that swelled with nausea and fear, the body that rode to the clinic with Dirk not speaking, the body that signed the papers, cramped up, gave way, bled life on cold vinyl sheets, staggered out to heave green and black, live in terror of the possibilities within her—

—feeling in that darkness my rounded body, heavy with life, and saying, I want to tell you something: you are not my first child.

MARY POTTER ENGEL

The Cattle Lick It Away

The wife of Lot could not control herself. Her mother love made her look behind to see if her married daughters were following. She beheld the Shekhinah, and she became a pillar of salt. This pillar exists unto this day. The cattle lick it all day long, and in the evening it seems to have disappeared. . . .

If you go to the edge of the plain and visit T'shukah, longing, you will see the cattle gathered round her. Patiently they drag their tongues over her feet, her legs, her stomach, her buttocks and back, arms, breasts, shoulders and neck and head, her face, absorbing her life-giving minerals.

All day their rough tongues stroke her and all day she diminishes, disappearing into their blood, her hardened self shrinking until she is a smooth column, a small rock, a handful of crystals crumbled into the earth.

And when evening comes, T'shukah seems to be gone.

The cattle lie down to rest.

The night air cools and all falls still.

But in the dark silence you can hear her mineral self. It pulses in the blood of the sleeping cattle, strengthening their flesh and sweetening their milk. T'shukah, woman of spirit, woman of salt, fills their bodies with longing.

And in the morning when they rise, their tongues will seek her again, their bodies longing to be made whole.

When you visit T'shukah and see the cattle gathered round her, you must go to her and lick her, too, so your flesh will be strong, your milk sweet, your wounds healed with the salt of longing, a woman of spirit, a woman of salt.

> You never know what is enough unless you know
> what is more than enough.
>
> WILLIAM BLAKE, "Proverbs of Hell"

Tissue

I can't remember the exact moment—water on the brain these seven months—I severed my head from my body; but for decades my brain, relieved of its burden, has pumped itself forward, lighting up the darkness, dazzling all around me, flashing a way through confusion and securing me a place in reason's fortress, my father's world, where he reigned uncontested and my mother was an exile.

It was glorious.

But now, *prima gravida,* bellyful of invasion, my body—cunning traitor—has swollen against me, raising a tumor for all to see, a condemning witness crying, "Look at her, at *her,* the *mother*"; and the cut that freed my head to fly from the reach of my mother, the long-ago cut I so carefully cauterized, bound up, and tended, has begun to bleed.

The first twelve weeks, before the growth began to show, the cut oozed and I dabbed at the pink froth round my neck with a cold, damp cloth. Soon—sixteen weeks, twenty, another's heart beating, tissue advancing—my neck began to trickle, first on the right side, then on

MARY POTTER ENGEL

the left, too, leaving sticky trails of reddish brown wherever I went, though I splashed it with a styptic, smeared it with ointment, trussed it with gauze. At twenty-four weeks—the lump encroaching, pushing aside organs, bones, nerves—in spite of recauterization and winding the bandages tighter, tighter, the cut started gushing. Blood tumbled out like a waterfall, burbling behind me as I walked, filling up room after room, whole wards, hospitals, states, countries, worlds. A deluge of blood. Waking or dreaming, I lay drowning in its slick heaviness.

I tried to swim in that viscous sea but could not. Buffeted by breakers, gripped by an undertow, my eyes washed red, I sank deeper. My head—that shining gibbous, my personal savior—was sinking and I saw that it would not rescue me. It had never saved me. Though it had built me an ark of reeds and pitch, it had never attracted any doves, any olive branches to me. Though it had kept me alive, not once, with its torches and blazes, had it seduced the right man, the right powers, the right circumstances; nor, with its furies, its fierce and frigid reasoning, had it turned one aggressor—even my mother—into stone. I saw, too, that through all those years of exultant flight, my body had been dragging behind me. Like a slave dogging its master—never too close or too far—it pursued me. Like the chains of a fugitive, it called out to me as I fled, chanting the shape of me, the mark of my sex. And though I closed my ears against it, running ever faster from its husky pleas, it would not let me go.

And now it has caught me, pregnant and afraid, consumed by fatigue, to submerge me in its distractions. And my head, old friend and comforter, can not save me.

Unsure where to go, where I am, I reach behind me in the slippery turbulence until I feel a shoulder, an arm. I grab hold and draw my importunate body close. I pull it, my body, bloated, buoyant with death, back to myself; and, hauling myself up, high atop the distended belly, I begin to float upon it.

Bobbing on the waves, woozy with relief, I drift, dozing in the darkness of dawn, waking from dreams again and again to survey the body ferrying me over a sea of blood.

A Woman of Salt

The feet I am proud of, the feet of a prodigal—yellowed with calluses, itching with fungus, flattened and splayed from much wandering. They will never fit the slim, high-heeled cast-offs my mother used to send me—writing in her Palmer script on the package, *Ruth, These will improve your arches, your image, and your possibilities, WEAR THEM!!!*— and that I threw unworn into the Dumpster.

These feet, fast and tireless, are my father's. A demon walker, he hurtles forward, always the immigrant, escaping horror and pursuing hope. Only I can keep up with him. Whenever he visits—always on business—the two of us race wordless until I am glowing and he has quelled what possesses him. The skin on my feet, like his, roughens, peels, bleeds when I tear at it: the feet of a leper no matter how much vitamin B I ingest, sweet almond oil I rub in. My feet will never be hers, white, bird-boned, soft and smooth under my fingers as I rubbed and tickled them for her while she lay on the couch. Alive to the slightest stroke, her feet would stretch and flex in my lap, wiggle and twist, sometimes jerk in my hands, twinned creatures lost in pleasure.

Let her have the feet and their pleasures.

There are no veins cracking purple and blue by these ankles and knees, swollen with blood like my mother's—not yet.

The legs, ankles to upper thighs, are slender and shapely, admired by strangers, even now, untouched by the fetus's incursions. "Your best feature," all my lovers have said, "just like your mother's."

Until the growth, gravid and obdurate, began bearing down on this body, there was no sciatic nerve or sore rib here. *Oh, my sciatica,* my mother would moan from her darkened bedroom, *Oh, my floating rib. Bring me the Bufferin, Ruth, and a Coke with a glass of ice.*

Buttocks high and firm, nicely rounded, refusing to spread even under my growing weight and indolence. My mother has no buttocks. A flatness there, as if something had been cut away.

MARY POTTER ENGEL

The heart a machine pumping blood, efficient and terse, disdaining the wild rhythms of fear and love. No matter if she claims it, snatches its secrets from diaries, confides to the dominee and elders, *My sixteen-year-old is stone inside, hardened like Pharaoh, so strange for a daughter, How can I break her spirit?*

The breasts belong to her. That's easy: they were hers before they appeared. Whenever I went out she would scrape her knuckle down my back as she cooed *bye-bye have fun be home on time I'll be waiting for you,* feeling to make sure I was wearing a bra to cover what wasn't there, to see if I was offering them, naked, unsolicited, to boys from our church, tempting them beyond their powers of restraint. She anticipated that sin and others by years, planting seeds of flowers not yet imagined.

I have always been flat-chested. Even now, hormones unbalanced, my breasts do not alter the shape of a dress, split open the front of blouses, capture others' eyes the way hers do. They do not bounce when I run, float in the tub, dangle in the shower, swell periodically into stinging points of pain that swallow the world and then shrink away. I don't need them and their vagaries. My friend Brenda manages fine without hers, is proud of refusing reconstructive surgery, not being fitted for a fake bra. Better off without them disrupting serious conversations, making it impossible to walk unnoticed. Let my mother worry about my breasts, their striations and puckers, swellings and darkenings, the sweat gathering under and between them. The rest of the flesh will be mine to control.

For years I searched for a way to counter the drag of my flesh, slip away into lightness. I ran until I fainted, swam through underwater tunnels until my lungs were on fire, flew from a rope into a quarry. When I was fourteen I succeeded. My dad came home one Friday night, set his papers on the counter, and slapped my butt playfully, saying, "You're getting a little heinie!" That night, after I had fallen asleep, she came to my bed, sat beside me for hours, saying, *I know what you're up to, you little whore, don't think I'm blind, God'll teach you a lesson you won't forget.* The next day my dad stopped flicking me with a towel at the beach and in the kitchen, hugging me good-bye, sitting next to me on the sofa. I stopped eating. For nine months I allowed myself a quarter of a cup of skim-milk cottage cheese, one dill pickle, two leaves of iceberg lettuce, and one small apple a day—sometimes less. Every morning at five I weighed myself, pleased with the plunging numbers and the roominess of my clothes. One afternoon my mother took me into her room and made me sit on the bed, where she had laid out her wedding dress, white satin with a long, fitted bodice. "Try it on," she said. I turned over the dress and held it up. Scores of satin-covered buttons lined one side of the back opening, matching loops the other. I stepped into it carefully, relieved that I could pull it on though I was three inches taller and broader-shouldered than my mother. My mother began fastening the back below my waist, her fingers nimbly slipping the buttons through the tiny loops. "I was so skinny in high school," she said, "the doctor made me drink a milkshake every day, sometimes a beer with a raw egg in it, but I couldn't gain an ounce." The dress tightened across my hips. She pulled the sides together at my waist, but they wouldn't meet. She began buttoning from the high neck down, but near my angel bones the buttons and loops gaped again. This time when she tugged on them the two sides didn't come near one another. "I didn't think it would fit," she said. "I weighed ninety-seven pounds when I got married." I ate less. More flesh dropped away. I loved the way I was disappearing, how easy it was to slip between tight spaces, the freedom from breasts and cramps and rusty-smelling blood. I gloried most in my lightness, a fierce lightness that made me whirl like a demon, without stopping, without sleeping, without fatigue. I crammed a lifetime's achievements into those days. I had become pure energy, unburdened by mass, not constrained by time. I didn't labor, I surged. I never walked anywhere, I flew. I glowed with the elemental power of the universe. I was omnipotent, invincible.

I still mourn the passing of that time.

It ended as it began, without warning. I woke one night with a terrible ache, longing for weight, weightedness, the heaviness of blood, the pull of the earth inside me. I went downstairs and ate a banana and two crackers in the dark, letting their odors fill me. "It's about time you made her eat, Helen," my aunts said at Sunday dinner. "She looks like a prisoner of war." When I had filled out, my mother took me shopping. My first two-piece suit, pink with white polka-dots. When we got home, she made me try it on for him, walk around him as he lay on the den floor reading the paper, hiding. As I circled and circled, she said to me, *Don't stop! If you got it, flaunt it!* and asked him, *Doesn't she have a cute little shape? Doesn't she? Answer me.*

The flesh is a liar, untrustworthy—now swelling, now contracting, now child, now woman, now borning, now withering and being eaten away, shape-shifting always—nothing to depend on. She can have the flesh, however she wants it. She knows how she wants it.

The anus she has to share; she wouldn't like that, if she knew. She was checking for worms. That's what she announced every Saturday as she stretched my cheeks wide, her seated on the toilet, me thrown over her lap, butt high, feet and head on the floor. She fingered and probed the soft tissue until I was sore, until I was too big to lay across her lap, to slap when I balked; but she never made me bleed the way Dirk did when he rammed me to teach his old girlfriend a lesson, me not to be a prude.

Arms, long and thin—*You look like a skeleton,* she would say every summer, *Wear long sleeves*—not long or wide enough to cover my shame before them. I was twelve. I loved swimming. I hoisted myself out of the water happy and went into the bathroom off the pool to change. She sent my cousin Peter and my brother Calvin in after me. They each grabbed an arm and pulled me, naked, crouching to hide my nakedness, to the threshold. I screamed, held back, kicking and biting them. They laughed, tightened their grip. "Don't be too rough," my mother called, laughing, from the lounge chair where she sat knitting with my aunt. One got a hold of my wrists, the other my ankles, and they dragged me between them, writhing, shrieking for help, onto the patio. The sun was so bright it made me shiver. On the edge of the pool they began swinging me. "Watch her head, boys," my mother warned. Calvin and Peter began counting. Three times I flew high and away, then toward the boys again, between them, exposed, my stomach heaving. With a shout of "Three!" they threw me in. I pulled myself into a

A Woman of Salt

ball and held myself together at the bottom. Then I swam, underwater, to the stairs and crouched alongside them, keeping myself hidden while I looked for my escape. Debbie and the other younger kids were in the middle of the pool hanging on to the edge and not making a sound, staring at me like dumb animals. Peter and Calvin were watching from where they had swung me, grinning sheepishly. As I ran past my aunt and my mother, stretching my arms and twisting them around me to cover myself, I heard her laughing, saying *It's good for her, She's too proud.*

The hollows under my arms and between my legs where I rubbed Lysol, believing—foolish child of eleven—it would disinfect me, wash me whiter than snow, blot out my iniquities, burn away my impurity. . . .

Skin. Experts claim the skin is the largest organ, specializing in respiration, elasticity. . . .

She would pay me nickels when I was five, quarters when I grew wiser at seven, to tickle her, her sprawled across the bed in underpants and bra, me beside her, running my fingertips over her—*slower, do it slower*—until my arms grew heavy and numb. It's been years now and still, everywhere I touch—the peel of an apple, bread dough, lovers, the naked bottoms of my nieces on the changing table, my belly, myself—I feel only her skin, the stretch of it across her shoulder blades, her slack upper arms, rumpled stomach, dimpled backs of thighs and knees, the way all her cells tensed with pleasure, tingling, vibrating into my hands, alive and sentient.

The scarred tissue is mine: half-moon on the left wrist, clumped starburst in the palm. The summer I was eight I broke a milk jug against concrete steps and my fist closed hard around the piece caught in my hand, pressing into the sharpness—pure, clarifying, happy pain. When I pulled the edges free, blood splurted out, filling my hand, spilling over, each drop a ruby shining. The red pool at my feet glistened with the sun and I saw my face there, gleaming red. She's pretty, I thought. A dragonfly flew close to my head, impossible colors reflected in its enormous wings, big enough to enfold me, carry me away. I heard the dragonfly's heart pulsing, its mind thrumming, telling me it had

MARY POTTER ENGEL

been sent to me for a blessing and suddenly the green beauty of the dragonfly flying mingled with the red beauty of the blood pool where my face lay floating and I felt myself rising, hovering outside my body, without my body, at home in the world.

Ruth, where are you? my mother's voice called from far away. Then closer, screaming, *What have you done now?* Holding my arm high, she ran me two blocks to the doctor, saying, *I told you not to carry both gallons at once, Now you'll learn to listen, to obey me.*

Afraid that if the doctor closed the wounds, I wouldn't be able to cross over into that lightness again, I struggled against his stitching. They sedated me. When I woke, I had been sewn tightly shut.

I have relied on my stomach for all the wisdom I have ever required. Its burning, cramping, dry heavings—rejecting what did not belong— have counseled me to stop dropping acid and popping white crosses, leave my first husbands, remove my Dalkon Shield, concede I was pregnant. I still count on it, infallible barometer, to signal impending dangers. This is why I refuse to take tranquilizers, though specialists in Chicago, Ann Arbor, New York, have recommended them.

I have lived with its griping since I was six. Just as my dad arrived home one evening, my stomach seized up. My distended, hardened belly seemed all of me. The faintest touch was intolerable and I ripped off my loose blouse and jumper for relief. Naked, I lay on the hard wood, writhing. My mother ran from the kitchen. *What's wrong now?* I howled at the thought of her coming near that boundless hurting. *Put your clothes on and go upstairs!* My dad appeared, carried me to my bed. That night I heard her say, *You favor her, love her more than me.*

Every day that winter, at six-fifteen, the spasm returned. It was always the same: tearing off clothes and thrashing until taken away. I told the doctor, Two giants fight in my stomach. Their swords slash the walls and blood runs everywhere, stinging in the cuts, and my belly stiffens like a rock, a rock that is bleeding. Nerves, he told my mother. Give her one of your little white pills every afternoon at four. It'll pass.

Certainly by now these fingernails belong to me. The white streaks marring the pink have been gone for ages, scrubbed away with bleach, silenced. Before I started kindergarten, she began examining my nails each evening, saying, *Each spot is a lie you have told. You may think you are clever, you may escape for a time, but you cannot blot out your iniquities. There will always be marks where I will read the truth. You cannot hide from me.* They're decorations, snowdrops, I would answer, pulling my hands out of hers, curling them into fists and slinking them under my arms. Yet later, alone in my room, I saw only ten rosy-faced traitors staring at me, white mouths stretched open, crying out my sins.

If I, this moment, held them close to me, questioning them, would those voices still chant against me a rasping litany: the sins of deceit and the sins of pride, the sins of anger and the sins of fear, the sins against others and the sins against God, the sins hidden from her and the sins hidden from myself, the sins of the body and the sins of the mind?

Bones endure; long after flesh and blood, keratin and cartilage have been eaten away, bones remain, immaculate witnesses. Mine are my dad's, sturdy, capable of bearing great weight, knitted together perfectly, no sign of the break where I fell down the basement stairs at three, running from her metal spatula, her at the top screaming at me. . . .

My nose is mine alone. Otherwise she would not have pinched its sides when I was newborn—How many times has she told me this, always so pleased with herself? *You have me to thank for your good looks*—to narrow it, improve my looks, my chances. If it were not mine, she would not have rubbed it raw that first year, trying like a potter, like God with His clay, to have her own way, to mold the soft, spreading tissue into a shape that flattered her.

I take credit for her failure; I consider my nose, puggish and lumpy, my first successful rebellion. I refuse to powder it, let a surgeon sculpt it. Still, occasionally it betrays me. Like now, when it detects, doglike, barbecued ribs across town, malt scotch on a salesman: that is like her. Nothing—neighbors' candy on my breath, firecracker powder on my fingers, boyfriends' cologne on my neck, desire leaking from my

MARY POTTER ENGEL

pores—escaped her nose. When quite small I learned to anoint myself with the White Shoulders on her dresser. Later, it was dimestore gardenia, Je Reviens, patchouli oil—all to cover my tracks, to mask the odor of my misdeeds, the smell of me she found so hateful.

My voice is my pleasure, the sound I, only I, make when breathing out my song to the world—*Whenever you breathe I am there*—or when, in silence, I withhold myself, safe with my ponderings, minding my own rhythms of exile and return—*Whether you speak or keep silence, stand up or sit down, I know it, I am familiar with all your ways, for my blood is yours, yours mine, I will always know your secrets, who you are, even when you do not, for are you not my daughter, did I not carry you in my womb nine months?*

There are so many parts left that do matter, that she has nothing to do with, surely—hair, for instance. My hair belongs to me because she hates it. I have wedged mine and layered it, smoothed and frizzed it, stripped and dyed it, hidden it under hats and dangled it over me like a mask, twisted it out at the roots, leaving bloody pinpricks on bare patches—and still she says, *You could have such beautiful hair if only you would love me.* I no longer know what I hate and what I love. She loves what is dead. Let her have my hair, then—dead tissue, and if I run to what is dead, she is there; if I dive to the pulsing center, she waits for me there, too. If I fly to extremities, surfaces, empty spaces, she holds me fast. If I say, "Surely my bones and my organs, my dark interiors, will conceal me," she finds me out, for their hiddenness is no secret to her, their darkness as light as day. I suffer her terrors wherever I turn, for she is everywhere, outside and in, inside and out, inside turning out and outside in, like Möbius's strip, no lines parting them to show which side we're on, who we are and where can I escape you? Where can I flee your presence? Oh, to be outside this tissue of lies, outside of her, out of the body, *out.* This has been my unquenchable desire, my constant ambition: to be out of the body *by any means*—if not by constricting myself into the realm of logic, then by obliterating the mind; if not by blacking out all thoughts, then by emptying my

A Woman of Salt

heart; if not by deadening feeling, then by moving so fast my body cannot take root in the world; and if not by frenetic activity, then by slitting a hole in this chamber of horror and watching as it exhales all life and collapses upon itself, leaving me free.

High atop my distended belly, rocked by the waves, I float on a red sea. The sun is up now, scarlet, its heat already drying to a paste the blood covering me. On the horizon an oil tanker appears, two ships hauling cargo, and I float past bell buoys and lobster pots, through a flock of ring-billed gulls, under a bridge where a man and his son stand fishing, waving as I pass by, past my mother on the other side, her floating, too: on a pallet, prone, legs paralyzed from the birth of her fifth child; on a wooden raft, playing the piano after her mother died, not Handel or Bach, but the unchurched Brahms; on a hospital bed, curled into a ball, bald, eaten away by cancer in her flesh, her bones, her body collapsing like a shepherd's tent, too light to leave an impression in the mattress, crossing over, whispering my name, calling for me, her recalcitrant daughter pregnant at last, begging me to come and see her after all these years of absence, before she dies. And as I drift toward land, carried along by my body's fat stench, inhaling its decay and feeling its smooth, stretched skin beneath me, I wonder what to do: whether to stitch the cut at my neck back together, body to head, head to body—with stitches learned from her, "chain" and "overcast" for strength, "blanket" to hold fast the edges, "feather" for beauty—or to bear my severed head back to her, lay it at her feet the way Hindu pilgrims place the fragrant, flowered head of a goat at the feet of Kali, after pouring over her—in appeasement, propitiation, hope—the blood of the sacrifice.

MARY POTTER ENGEL

When Morning Comes

The wife of Lot could not control herself. Her mother love made her look behind to see if her married daughters were following. She beheld the Shekhinah, and she became a pillar of salt. This pillar exists unto this day. The cattle lick it all day long, and in the evening it seems to have disappeared, but when morning comes it stands there as large as before.

Why can't T'shukah, longing, be like Daphne, forever a laurel once she had changed? Why must she harden and soften, shrink and return, over and over again?

Why must her body return? Wasn't it a relief for her, after all those years, to finally have done with the body, its treacheries and deceits? To have it licked away from her so she could be herself at last, not the wife of Lot, the daughter of Aicha, the mother of Emet, Rachamim, Dini, and Chesed? To be not a woman but a spirit?

And you, God, why embrangle the spirit in flesh? Why create us mind and body, spirit and flesh, making of us an unstable union so confusing, so misleading, so easily torn apart?

Can it be, as Blake's proverb of hell declares, that "Eternity is in love with the productions of time"?

T'shukah's body embraces her spirit again and again. She can never escape it. Purging the flesh cankers the spirit; spirit grows from the scarified seed of the body.

Each day this miraculous joining of what has been torn, spirit from flesh, comes undone in her and each day it must be renewed again, spirit enfleshed. By nightfall every day a woman of salt is licked to nothingness and each morning she returns whole, shining again.

Each morning T'shukah's body returns to her spirit and she rises in fear. Each day she runs from the city of destruction in fury. Each day she must turn again in terror and longing, look into the hidden face of God, be held fast in the wholeness of mercy and truth, self and other, body and mind, be sculpted in the eternal moment of turning from fear to love, be born again as flesh enlivening spirit and spirit embracing flesh, a woman of salt.

An everyday miracle.

Who will flee You, over a bridge of longing / only to return again?

T'shukah arising anew on the plain each day, a testament to the permanent transformation of the self.

Go to the edge of the plain between Sodom and Zoar at sunrise and watch T'shukah rise again into her body. Watch her turning from fear to love, held fast in the splendor of God, becoming whole, a woman of salt.

What then is the God I worship?

Augustine, *Confessions*

Learning to Swim

usk. Light rain. The traffic in Boca Raton frenetic. Gray heads with nowhere to go race against one another, push to the head of the line. I've been on the road too long without stopping. I'm tired of fighting. I want to rest. Instead I keep driving.

WAYS I AM LIKE MY MOTHER: excellent driver.

At the hospital I park the car in the ramp and follow the signs to the main lobby. In the restroom I brush my teeth and wash my face, dry it with acrid paper towels, rough against my skin.

WAYS I AM NOT LIKE MY MOTHER: never wear makeup.

I comb my hair and smooth out my comfort dress, the funky yellow one my friends handprinted for me. Helen will call it sloppy and tacky. To wake up my body after the long drive, I climb the stairs to the fourth floor.

WAYS I AM LIKE MY MOTHER: prodigiously energetic.

As I search the garishly lighted corridors for Room 409, the fetus rolls over and kicks. It senses danger, a pressure in the blood. Outside Helen's door I stop to catch my breath, wondering if my sister's husband is inside. If Jake starts witnessing to me or telling me "Reconcil-iation delayed is stiff-necked rejection of Christ," I'll walk out. I'll drive to exhaustion, grab a motel, and surprise Michael at his office tomorrow for lunch.

WAYS I AM NOT LIKE MY MOTHER: never religion's cully.

I crack open the door to Helen's room.

"'What is your only comfort in life and death?'" an unfamiliar voice intones. It's the first question of the Heidelberg Catechism, the one every kindergartner had to memorize. "'That I,'" the man continues, "'with body and soul, both in life and death, am not my own, but belong unto my faithful Savior Jesus Christ—'"

Peering through the crack, I see a tall, sandy-haired dominee stand-ing beside Helen's bed, his black-suited back to me. He's young, unsure of his vocation.

WAYS I AM LIKE MY MOTHER: uncannily perceptive.

"'—who with His precious blood,'" the dominee continues, "'has fully satisfied for all my sins, and delivered me from all the power of the devil; and so preserves me that without the will of my heavenly Father not a hair can fall from my head; yea, that all things must be subservient to my salvation, wherefore by His Holy Spirit He also assures me of eternal life.'"

The dominee shifts his weight, rustles the pages of his *Psalter Hym-nal.* Where, I wonder, did Debbie find a Dutch Calvinist minister? Helen has moved so much she's never had a regular dominee. And Debbie and Jake go to an independent church where no one has ever heard of the Heidelberg Catechism, the Canons of Dort, or that poi-sonous TULIP—Total depravity, Unconditional election, Limited atonement, Irresistible grace, and Perseverance of the saints.

"'What comfort does the resurrection of the body afford you?'" the dominee reads in the catechism.

I have never taken comfort in the belief that God frees us at death by joining pure spirit to pure body in the afterlife. I believe the body is a trap now and ever shall be. I believe freedom is won when we escape the snare of the body through reason, the life of the mind unencum-bered by flesh. To lose one's reason, as my father has, and be cursed to live on in a body that refuses to die—*that* is hell.

MARY POTTER ENGEL

"'That not only my soul,'" the dominee continues, "'after this life, shall immediately be taken up to Christ, its Head; but also that this my body, raised by the power of Christ, shall again be reunited with my soul and made like unto the glorious body of Christ.'"

Helen's body has swollen and contracted five times giving birth to new life that does not resemble her. It is not her body that wants a miracle, but her soul, pinched and vengeful.

I let the heavy door slide shut and turn my face to the wall, squeezing back tears, blotting them on my sleeves. If Jake saw me, he would gloat. "At last," he would grin, "the submission of the defiant spirit, the tears of the prodigal." Debbie would take my tears as a sign that she's been right all these years to play the dutiful daughter, to stay close to Mother, calling Mother twice a day, accepting Mother's bribes and criticism, watching Mother scald her family with God's words, letting Mother's whims trump her own and her family's needs.

I lumber to the stairwell and lower myself heavily to the top step.

WAYS I AM NOT LIKE MY MOTHER: avoid difficult encounters instead of pursuing them relentlessly.

Fourteen years ago, when I divorced Russell, my mother broke into my house so she could scream in my face I was a whore. I haven't seen her since then. Last year, when she found out I had married Michael, she said to Debbie, "At least he's not black." When Debbie told her I was pregnant, she called on my fortieth birthday to say, "Your children will go to hell if they're not washed in the blood of Jesus." My mother started beating on the gates of hell for me the second I was born. You'd think her fists would be bloodied by now or she would have lost her voice. But she only gains strength. My mother is blessed with perseverance, one of the signs of God's elect. My perseverance is the cussedness of desire: an unquenchable thirst burning in me to be held in God, to give myself to the World and its glorious possibilities. But I am afraid, and so I am torn, between longing for God and terror of God, between desire for the World and fear of losing myself in it, between drowning in my body or exiling myself in my mind. I don't know how to immerse myself—in God, in the World, in my body—without drowning and so I run away. I flee what I seek, seek what I flee. I cannot rest.

A Woman of Salt

I'd like to curl up on this landing and sleep for a week, at least until the dominee leaves Helen's room. No doubt Debbie has warned him about her wayward older sister who left the church and worked and traveled *op Zondag,* the Lord's Day; who shoplifted, did drugs, got arrested, lived in sin, divorced twice, campaigned for abortion and women in ecclesiastical office, married a Jew, and did not invite one family member to the wedding.

WAYS I AM NOT LIKE MY MOTHER: I burn bridges.

A few months after we watched the sea turtle give birth, my mother and I drove across the seven-mile bridge to Key West. We were on our way to sell antiques she had scrounged from thrift shops and strangers she befriended, hoping to get a better price from the dealers there than in Fort Lauderdale. The low-flung bridge hovered over the water. We could hear waves slapping against the concrete pilings, smell the sea's fecundity. The wind blew warm and moist through the windows, clothing us in a fine salt mist. The sun bleached the world so we could barely see. Peering ahead, my mother's eyes farsighted and mine myopic, we marveled at how the road disappeared in the distance, merging with the shining white-green of the water. We skimmed over the surface as if we were driving headlong into the ocean. I was sure that when we reached the point where the ocean swallowed up the road, we would slip beneath the surface to another world. Every cell in my body came alive with a terrible desire, pulling me forward and singing "Die, die, die and you shall live." I wanted to lose myself in the embrace of that dark, green world. I wanted more than anything to drown in my mother.

And over the sound of this conquering chorus of death, the voice in my head began shouting at me, urging me to leave my mother speeding across the bridge and run away to solid ground. "Jump out of the car!" it screamed. "Jump! Jump and run like hell!"

Surrender or escape. Submerge myself in her or be alone with myself. I wanted both. I was afraid of both. I had to choose one.

The decision tore at me and I felt myself splitting, my mind fleeing to exile on land, my body eager to drown in her.

MARY POTTER ENGEL

My only comfort was the motion of the car. I believed that as long as my mother and I kept moving, as long as we kept speeding over the bridge, as long as we remained suspended between land and water, exile and surrender, possibilities and losses, me and her, my body and mind would not be torn asunder and I would not die.

"I wish we could drive this bridge forever," I said to my mom.

Just because I drove twelve hours to get to the hospital doesn't mean I have to go in to see her. I can change my mind.

WAYS I AM LIKE MY MOTHER: not afraid to change my mind.

WAYS I AM NOT LIKE MY MOTHER: allow others to change their minds without punishing them for it.

It took me two hours longer than I expected to drive here from Charleston. I had to stop every hour to stretch my legs and let the intruder flip-flop. The midwife warned me against driving long distances in the seventh month, saying it might cut off circulation, make the edema worse. Michael was against it, too. He knew I'd been up all night wondering whether to go or not and he was afraid I'd fall asleep, get stranded with a flat. He considered taking a few days off to drive me, but couldn't manage it. "You never worried about my traveling alone before," I complained. "Why start now?"

The usurper kicks me hard. Michael hates it when I call it "the intruder" or "the usurper." "I don't see the humor," he says. The fetus kicks again, its heel bulging my skin. It's never quiet. During meetings, at my computer or desk, at the lectern or in bed, I feel it somersaulting, backflipping, punching. "She's training for the Olympics," Michael said when I placed his hand on it the first time.

"Fine," I said, "let it have its fun, but it makes me nervous. And I've never liked athletics—only swimming."

"That's what *our daughter* is doing in there," he said.

WAYS I AM NOT LIKE MY MOTHER: know how to swim.

Though my mother has always lived by water, she has never learned to swim. She thought it unnecessary when she could enjoy herself just as well sunning herself on the sand. She also thought it unnecessary to watch over her small children when they played in the ocean. She

A Woman of Salt

didn't worry when the five of us spent day after day at the beach without her. I suppose her faith in a providential God who lets not a hair fall from His loved ones' heads without His willing kept her from fear.

My mother trusts God and she trusts herself; she knows everyone else will eventually manifest the Original Sin hiding inside them—all she has to do is wait.

WAYS I AM NOT LIKE MY MOTHER: I do not trust God, I have never trusted myself.

I am always anxious—not for the baby's health, Michael worries enough for a minyan about that. I worry if I will be able to protect a child from danger. Each day the fetus grows, I grow more frightened. Will this child fall down the basement stairs while I am folding laundry? Will it cling to small ideas? Will it be in thrall to *things?* Will it refuse to wear anything but green, clamor for green blankets, green toys, green dresses?

WAYS I AM NOT LIKE MY MOTHER: can't stand the color green.

Will this child know whom not to trust? Will it live in terror of me as I lived in terror of her?

WAYS I AM LIKE MY MOTHER: I have given myself over to the desire to hurt someone I love, deliberately harmed that person, then thrilled at witnessing their hurting—confirmation of my power.

Will I take pleasure in hurting this child? Will my child be safe from *me?*

How can I be sure? Maternal instincts, good intentions, overprotectiveness, faith in the power of God to accomplish all things—none of these guarantees goodness against the furtive process of destruction. Who can understand the seeds of hatred, their source and originating power, their patient work underground, their exquisite flowering?

Will I hate my child as my mother hates me?

I have been too scared to tell anyone this, writing instead in my journal, keeping a list in two columns: WAYS I AM LIKE MY MOTHER on the left, WAYS I AM NOT LIKE MY MOTHER on the right. I am afraid to complete the inventory lest the final count go against me and the unborn child.

The light in the stairwell hurts. I rest my head on my knees and

MARY POTTER ENGEL

close my eyes. The sound of the road whizzing under the wheels fills my head and my body vibrates as if it is still speeding along in the car. I smell exhaust fumes. The pain in my head is crushing.

WAYS I AM LIKE MY MOTHER: Smells undetected by others make my head ache.

Why not take two Tylenol, leave a note at the nursing station, and drive home? Debbie will be able to make out my scratchings.

WAYS I AM NOT LIKE MY MOTHER: illegible handwriting.

Before I turned twelve my handwriting slanted evenly to the left. Then it lost its balance and pulled in every direction at once, dizzying the reader. After that my mother had to work harder to decipher my diary. She would pore over it while I was at school, seizing on a word here and there, "Catholics," "boys," "unforgiving," "Mother," "God," but unable to make out my meaning. How she must have raged: my secrets laid before her, incontrovertible proof of my wickedness, and she, preternaturally intuitive, unable to crack the code.

Debbie will read my note. She'll say, "Look, Mom, a letter from Ruth. She was here while you were sleeping and gave you a kiss. She says, 'Dear Mom, you were asleep when I arrived. I waited, but had to leave before you woke. I'm going over to Debbie's to rest now, but I'll be back soon. I love you. Ruth.'"

Debbie won't flinch when she invents the kiss and reads "Mom" for "Mother," or when she adds the two last sentences.

I sit up, rub slow circles into my hairline, temples, occipital ridge.

Another thing I get from her—migraines.

This my body—always dragging me down, betraying me. This my body, ever my enemy. And now invaded by another.

There is not room for me and my mother. How can there be room for me and any other? Exile *or* surrender—these are the only choices.

The dominee *must* have left Helen by now. Debbie will be back soon. She's probably been sleeping next to Mother's bed every night, sitting with her all day, running home for a few hours at suppertime.

No chance Dad will show up with Debbie. He's too confused to leave the nursing home. No longer able to look back, he is lost in an anxious present in which everyone is a stranger. He doesn't recognize

A Woman of Salt

Debbie some days. He hasn't seen me in so many years—Helen wouldn't hear of it—he's forgotten my name. "That girl," he calls me when Debbie gives him the progress report of his thirteenth grandchild, the one I am carrying. He no longer walks, Debbie says. He no longer reads. He sits in the same chair for hours, staring. I try to imagine him that way, but I can't. When I think of him now I see him in that second hurricane in Florida, struggling to close the wide steel door the winds had ripped open. He walked out into the furious dark and pulled with all his might on the door. He made no progress against the winds; they dragged him deeper into the roiling night. Calvin and I cried to him over the screaming storm to come back inside, but he couldn't hear us. He lost his hold on the door and crawled back to us. He looked like a man come back from drowning. "Here," he said, grabbing a rope and tying it around his waist, "hang on to this tight, both of you." Then he disappeared into the darkness, Calvin and I planting our feet against the wall and pulling against the chaos, holding him fast, praying not to lose him.

Above me in the stairwell, a door opens and closes, and footsteps echo toward me. Grabbing the metal stair railing, I haul myself up, determined—another way I am like her.

The muscles near my pelvis harden. I lay my hands on the sides of my belly. It's tight, a ball under too much pressure.

Why not breeze in, fulfill my obligation, and leave?

At breakfast, when I couldn't decide whether I wanted to go see her or not, Michael said, "It's a mitzvah, an obligatory good deed."

"For her or for me?" I asked.

"Both."

"Both" is a word I have never used with my mother. I have always had to choose, either her or me.

WAYS I AM LIKE MY MOTHER: I always choose.

WAYS I AM NOT LIKE MY MOTHER: The moment I choose, I long for what I have not chosen, and the choosing begins again, tearing me apart.

I walk down the corridor, place my hand on Helen's door.

I'm as stubborn as she is.

MARY POTTER ENGEL

I should have let Michael drive me down. Helen is kind to strangers—clerks, cashiers, chance traveling companions. With Michael present, she might put on her mask of charm, thank me for coming, squeeze my hand, and tell me she loves me.

WAYS I AM NOT LIKE MY MOTHER: can't stand lies.

I push open the door.

My mother is alone in the room, her head turned toward the dark window. Caught in a web of tubes, her rawboned arms stretch down the blanket. Above her the television drones, erupting perpetually into tinny laughter, and I think of the Jewish custom of never leaving a body unguarded between death and burial. Is this unblinking eye to be my mother's guardian?

"Mother," I say.

The television blares a commercial for allergy medicine.

"Mother, it's me, Ruth." I do not say "Mom." I do not say "your daughter."

A nurse whisks in.

"Are you family?" she asks, her braces flashing back the ceiling lights.

"Yes."

Checking the machines, she says, "If you have anything you want to say, say it." She looks over her shoulder at me, her fingers on the knob. "She almost didn't make it through the night. You know she's DNR?"

I nod yes.

She draws a small packet from her pocket and rips out a moist pad.

"Good. Last week a family fought like banshees over whether to put the father on a ventilator."

She pulls out the twin oxygen tubes entering my mother's nostrils, wipes away the dried blood under her nose, and reinserts the tubes.

My mother's face is gray, the color she always feared. "I can always tell when someone has cancer," she used to say, "even if they don't know it. They turn a yellowish-gray. I saw it in my mother and Oom Gerritt."

"Is she in much pain?" I ask stupidly, knowing the cancer has traveled to her bones.

A Woman of Salt

"We're keeping her as comfortable as possible with the morphine."

The nurse checks the IV bag, lifts my mother's hands one at a time to examine where the tubes disappear beneath the skin. My mother's hands are limp and pale, bruised. The antique emerald ring she never took off, even when stripping furniture or dyeing fabric for her quilts, is gone. Her fingers look naked without it.

"I'll be back in a bit," the nurse says. "Don't panic if one of the machines starts beeping. Someone will be here right away."

When the door closes I turn off the television. The room falls silent. I am anxious and afraid, the way I am whenever I am trapped alone with my mother in a car, a motel room, the cabin of a boat, my bedroom—shaking under her gaze, waiting for her to attack, my jealous and unforgiving god visiting my iniquities upon me, incinerating me in a fury of judgment until I fall into ashes at her feet.

WAYS I AM LIKE MY MOTHER: terrified of God.

I flee God everywhere and everywhere I long for God's presence. This impossible tearing within, rending body from mind, spirit from flesh, self from self.

What does my mother long for? Who is her God?

She was mine before the world began, when I swam inside her. She made herself mine when I was born, consuming all rivals and jealously guarding her place. She will be mine as long as I worship her image within me.

The fetus flutters inside me, disturbing my balance. I walk around the bed to the side Helen is facing, her head toward the dark window. Blue and purple and red veins weave across the pale green of her eyelids. The green of her eyes is leaking through the lids, watching me from behind a net veil.

"Helen?"

Her lids tremble, but do not open, and I am relieved that the severity of those metallic eyes remains muted.

"Mother?"

Bending close, I listen for her breath, watch the faint rise and fall of her chest. Her body's warmth spreads toward me and I back away. As she sleeps, wandering between worlds, I stand beside her, watching. The blanket lies flat, barely curving with the mass of her body, as if she

MARY POTTER ENGEL

had already folded up her tent and stolen away, leaving behind the scranny center pole. She is so small I do not know her.

On the mobile tray table, beside her sipping cup, there is a stack of handmade cards from the grandchildren. Beside it lies a Bible. Raising the cover with one finger, I see a tract stored inside, "The Book of Revelations Explained," distributed by Love Worth Finding Ministries.

Like a routed army, all my energy rushes from me. I let the Bible fall shut and lower myself into the vinyl recliner to rest, to wait. For what? The bossy nurse? Dutiful Daughter Debbie? Judgmental Jake? The final judgment? A miracle?

As I bend to remove my shoes, the fetus twists inside, jabs me, demanding I shift to make room for it.

I don't believe in the resurrection of Jesus on the third day or the resurrection of our bodies at the end of time. Even if it's true, at the final judgment, when the trumpet is sounded, I don't want to be transformed into "the glorious body of Christ." Though I ached for years to be freed from my woman-body and be made part of the spiritual body of Christ, "neither male nor female," that is not what I hope for now.

Nor do I want to go on hiding in my mind, living in exile in the land of the fathers, pretending the burden of my flesh does not exist.

What I want is to be changed. I want to put off this body of death from which my mind was forced into exile and put on a glorious body. Not the weightless body of the sexless risen Christ, but a glorious body weighted *with my own flesh*. Let me shed this treacherous enemy that tears against my mind, rending me, and be born again into a body that is friend—*that* is the miracle I want.

Bare feet against the cool hospital floor, I lean back against the vinyl chair and close my eyes against impossibility.

Just after Michael and I met, he took me to an uninhabited barrier island where he had seen bottlenose dolphins hurl themselves onto shore and roll in the sand. It made him tingle, he said, seeing those graceful bodies streamlined for water reveling in their heaviness and awkwardness on land.

When we pulled our kayaks onto the far side of the island, an older couple was wading in the inlet. Their runabout was anchored ten feet away. "Excuse me," Michael said, approaching them. "Would you mind standing out of the water? When the tide starts to ebb, the dolphins sometimes beach here."

"You mean *breach*," the man said.

"No. *Beach*. They come completely out of the water and lie on the sand. If you don't move, your presence may discourage them."

"Dolphins never come onto the beach," the man said, splashing to shore. "We've been coming here for eighteen years. We've walked every inch of this island and we've never seen anything like that." He looked at his wife, who had followed him out of the water. She nodded at him.

Michael turned toward the water. A hundred yards away, where the inlet joined a tidal creek, three dolphins were circling.

"See?" the man said. "Those two adults are teaching a young one how to herd fish."

The dolphins formed a large circle, trolling clockwise for food. After several rounds the three dolphins met at the top of the circle and torpedoed toward us, driving the fish ahead of them. They came whistling through the water and before we could step back, they heaved themselves onto the sand. They lay there within inches of us, twisting and writhing, scratching their smooth skin against the gritty sand; rolling against one another lustily, mouths laughing, white bellies flashing in the sun, their breathing loud and husky like gasps of pleasure.

Too soon the dolphins wriggled themselves, perfectly synchronized, flat tails first, back into the ocean. As they returned to their swimming, Michael and I smiled at each other and grabbed for each other's hand.

After a moment we saw the dolphins circling again.

"Did you know they fish cooperatively?" the man asked Michael. "They communicate with each other to drive the fish inside a circle and chase them into a shallow trap."

"Uh-huh," Michael said.

The dolphins sped toward the far shore of the inlet across from us and threw themselves on the beach again. After inching back to the water, they headed up the tidal creek. When they were almost out of view, the other couple raised their anchor and sped off.

The dolphin expert became Michael's and my joke. Whenever we encounter a person who has no imagination, who insists on a falsehood

MARY POTTER ENGEL

because he refuses to believe in anything outside his experience, we grin at each other and say, "We've been coming here for eighteen years."

The vinyl hospital chair is stiff and cold against my neck. The eyes in the back of my head, my twin horns of perception, begin to prickle, alerting me to run.

When I open my eyes, my mother is staring at me.

My hands spread over my belly to protect it from her. "Pregnant at your age?" she will say. "Disgusting." If I had the thick bundle of notes for my essay on the wife of Lot with me now or my books—*Out of the Garden,* Calvin's *Commentary on Genesis, Middlemarch*—I could shield myself with them.

I have spent my life hiding from my mother's eyes, covering myself up like Eve, disappearing into a lush garden of books—theology, philosophy, poetry, novel after novel.

WAYS I AM NOT LIKE MY MOTHER: read novels. Helen will not read fiction. Only the Bible and history, true stories, are worth her time. I need to lose myself in other worlds, drown in possibilities.

This time I am too tired to run away. I let my hands drop into the chair and look back at my mother. She lies inert, exposed to me. Her web of lies, in which I could not stop ensnaring myself, has fallen away from her; without it, she is helpless. Cradled in the pillow, her head looks like a doll's. Wisps of hair stand out from her skull like a luminous crown. Lacking eyebrows, her forehead is as endless as a baby's. It stretches thin and tight against her bones, permanently puckered in disapproval. Her eyes, barely green now, are dark pits. Lashless lids drag over them.

"Mother," I say, "can you see me?"

Her eyes squeeze together.

She is so small.

"It's me, Mother. Ruth."

At the sound of my name her eyes strain tighter until they are staring at me full, not vacant but sharpened, and I wonder if it is me she is seeing or herself.

The baby kicks, I flush hot and red, and I think that I will not be able to endure it another second, those eyes condemning me, that I

A Woman of Salt

must look away, haul my body up and walk out. No one can look upon the face of God and live. No one can be seen by God and not perish.

I turn away from her and stare through the window into the night. I don't have the courage of Lot's wife. I cannot look back to watch God destroy the world in judgment. I am afraid to die.

But my mother is there— *O God, Where can I flee You?*—in the darkened glass of the window. Almost hidden in the white folds of the bed, her face is turned toward me, her eyes keen with watching me.

I turn back to look at her.

My belly, my body, my face fall open to her eyes.

I am present to her gaze.

Can it be that the gaze of God does not destroy us? Can it be that when God looks upon us her eyes do not sear our hearts and tear our flesh from our bones?

In terror and longing the wife of Lot turned back to Sodom. She turned round to see God destroying the wicked in a rage of judgment.

But perhaps—though the Bible and the rabbis and the church fathers and the dominees and the television evangelists will protest, saying this is impossible, that no one can see the face of God and live, no one can be seen by the face of God without perishing—perhaps at the moment the wife of Lot looked back to Sodom, the angels covering the face of God dropped their wings.

In the midst of destruction T'shukah beheld what she feared and longed for most, the presence of God. She beheld the Shekhinah among the dying, God sorrowing even as Sodom perished by her own hand of judgment. Seeing both at once, in an eternal present, God destroying the world in righteous judgment *and* sorrowing in mercy, T'shukah died to her torn self.

And as she died, God turned her face toward T'shukah. Gazing upon her in truth *and* lovingkindness, wrapping her in an embrace beyond exile *or* surrender, sorrow *or* anger, victim *or* executioner, she held T'shukah into wholeness.

Tears of deliverance streamed down T'shukah's face, surrounding her self, whole, with the salt of redemption.

———

MARY POTTER ENGEL

At the final judgment, Saint Paul says, we will change, in the twinkling of an eye, shedding the body of death for a glorious one, both like and not like the one we knew. "Perverse men ridicule Moses," Calvin writes in his *Commentary on Genesis,* "saying [the wife of Lot's] metamorphosis has no more appearance of truth than those which Ovid has feigned. . . . How can they, who deem it inconsistent, that the body of a woman should be changed into a mass of salt, believe that the resurrection will restore to life a carcase reduced to putrefaction?"

A carcass reduced to putrefaction is restored to life.

Longing and terror, body and mind, are joined in the gaze of God. What was rent is made whole.

It is *my* body and *my* mind that want such a miracle.

Can it be that when we are held fast in the gaze of God we need not choose between death by escape or death by drowning? That there is no choosing—land or water, exile or surrender, mind or body, saved or damned, my self or my mother? That there is an end to the battle between terror and longing and the beginning of love?

A tear forms in the corner of my mother's eye, clings for a moment, and rolls down her sunken cheek.

When I was nine my mother and I stood side by side on the beach watching a loggerhead turtle dig a nest and lay her eggs. As the rubbery balls fell into the hole behind her, tears glistening with moonlight dropped from her eyes to the sand.

"She's crying," I whispered.

"Turtles don't cry," a man behind us said out loud. "It's a reflex, nothing more."

"Don't believe him," my mother commanded me. "She's suffering."

Turtles crawl onto land and suffer and cry giving birth.

Hatchling turtles find their way in the dark back to the ocean and paddle to safety to reach three hundred pounds swimming gracefully in deep seas.

Dolphins cast themselves whole onto land and rejoice in their weightedness.

A Woman of Salt

T'shukah, the torn wife of Lot, in exile from herself, is made whole and cries tears of deliverance to become a *woman* of salt.

God, present to the ineluctable failures of love, sorrows and rejoices over the world, flooding creation with tears that do not return to her unfulfilled, but soak the earth and make it bring forth vegetation, yielding seed for sowing and bread for eating.

What else, then, may be possible?

A place—God, *ha makom,* The Place—where truth and desire meet? Freedom and belonging, power and vulnerability, spirit and flesh?

My body and my mind joined in one self, flesh enlivening spirit, spirit embracing flesh, a woman made whole, a woman of salt?

My mother *and* my self? Both of us living?

A daughter, *my* daughter, swimming inside the salty sac of my self?

WAYS I AM LIKE MY MOTHER: in want of a miracle to become whole.

My mother closes her eyes. The lines combing her forehead relax. Her body's silence fills the room. I bend close, listening for the whistle of her lungs, feeling for the warmth of her breath, watching her face, sure I detect a fluttering here, a twitch there. But there is nothing. Nothing for ages. I grow numb with waiting.

WAYS I AM LIKE MY MOTHER: numb with waiting for God to justify me.

WAYS I AM LIKE MY MOTHER: ready to be born again.

My daughter wakes up, shifts position, bangs against the walls of my belly, and I press the buzzer on the bed for help. The nurse with the braces appears immediately, as if she had been waiting by the door. She stands by my mother's side, feeling for a pulse in her neck while checking the levels on the machines.

"The staff doctor's on another floor," she says. "Stay with her until he can get here to pronounce her."

She disconnects the machines, removes the tubes, and heads for the door, turning round before it shuts on her. "It'll take longer than you think, so don't come looking for the doctor or for us. There's nothing more we can do."

In the closed room I remain standing by my mother who is no longer my mother. The world touching me is as wide as a plain. I can feel silence against my skin.

MARY POTTER ENGEL

I have never seen my mother so still, her face softened, trusting, like a child's asleep. The beauty of her calmness surprises me. It is as if the evil spirit holding her captive, steeling her against the world, girding her for battle with hatred and suspicion, had finally loosened its grip.

When a Jew dies, the *chevra kadisha* comes at once to prepare the body for burial. After ritually washing their hands, the men or women say prayers and wash the naked body with water. When the body has been purified, they clothe it in white linen and ask forgiveness of the dead person. When they have finished, they ritually wash their hands to separate themselves from the world of death and reenter the world of the living.

My mother was not a Jew. I do not know the precise order of performing *taharah.* I have no prayers, no pure water, no linen, no other women by my side to lift and tilt the body heavy with death. I do not know how to ask forgiveness of her.

Yet I cannot leave her unprepared.

She is so small.

At the sink near the foot of her bed I wash my hands, pouring water from a paper cup three times over my right hand, three times over the left. I refill the cup with warm water and carry it to her side.

Already her face looks waxen, a doll's head.

I pour some of the water over her forehead. It streams over her scalp, soaking the feathery hairs, runs down her nose, her cheeks, pools in the corners of her eyes. Drops fall from her jaw and collect in the hollow of her neck.

Gently I slide my hand under hers and lift it, weightless, free of the crumpled linens. I pour water into the palm, watch it spill over the cracked bowl of flesh onto the bed, turning the white sheet a soft gray where it falls. I lay her hand down and slip mine, tremulous and wet, from under it.

I carry the cup to the opposite side, in the shadow of the machines, and set it on a silenced monitor. I raise my mother's bruised right hand and turn it over in mine, holding it a moment before reaching for the cup. I pour water on her palm, watch it run over the side, drip off the bed, stain the tops of my shoes, hit the bare skin of my insteps.

Turning, I tug the sheet free from the bottom of the bed and fold it

A Woman of Salt

back to expose her feet. Slender, high arches, soft and white. Graceful as always, in spite of her littlest toes being permanently squeezed out of place by narrow high heels. I lift her right foot and pour water over the toes. It cascades down her curves, splashes onto my wrist, the inside of my arm, and I feel in my own skin how it would tickle her, that water dribbling over the skin of her feet, how she would enjoy it if she were alive.

I lay the right foot down and lift the left, pour the last of the water over it. It flows down the sharp edge of her shin, over her shriveled calf.

When I am finished, I return my mother's foot to the bed, placing it close to the other one, and cover both with the sheet.

Returning to the sink, I fill the cup and wash my hands again, pouring three times on the right, three times on the left. I bend to throw the cup in the trash and, rising, face myself in the mirror over the sink. Though I have not slept in two days, my face looks rosy and childlike against the lemon color of my dress. My daughter tumbles inside me, unconscious with joy, and my hands fly to her. Fingers spread, they lay themselves on her, cup themselves around her. A verse from Psalm 71 rises in me, "While yet unborn I depended on you; in the womb of my mother you were my support," and I hope for the blessing of sea turtles, dolphins, women of salt, praying that my daughter, unlike my mother and my self, will learn how to swim in God while yet unborn and enter the world whole. Channah, I will call her, grace.

Turning round, I step to the foot of my mother's bed. My hands still embracing my daughter, I stand there, both of us staring ahead into the shining distance where the bridge becomes the ocean—the end of running to exile on land or drowning in possibilities, the beginning of learning to swim.

That's the way Debbie finds me, guarding Mom's body. She puts her arm around me and leans her head on my shoulder. I thread my arm around her waist, kiss her damp and fragrant hair, and rest my head on hers.

"I hope she's finally happy," Debbie says.

"I hope she's swimming," I say. "Swimming in God."